DILIGENCE IN LOVE

by Daisy Newman

DILIGENCE IN LOVE · NOW THAT APRIL'S THERE

DOUBLEDAY & COMPANY, INC., GARDEN CITY, N.Y., 1951

by Daisy Newman

Diligence in Love

TO ONE WHO WALKS CHEERFULLY OVER THE WORLD

Kendal is not quite an imaginary place, though one may cover the whole of Rhode Island without seeing it. Philip Ludlow and the others there are not quite imaginary people, though—unlike Vaughn who is wholly fictitious—one may not be able to take a train at Grand Central and find them. They live, not in the flesh, but in the aspiration of those who cherish a particular way of life.

The key to the Meetinghouse hangs on a nail in the south wall, above the syringa bush. Anyone may open the door.

D.N.

Hamden, Connecticut

He who metes, as we should mete,
Could we His insight use, shall most approve,
Not that which fills most space in earthly eyes,
But what—though Time scarce note it as he flies—
Fills, like this little daisy at my feet,
Its function best of diligence in love.

T. Burbidge, *Hours and Days*, 1851

Part 1

1. Her city eyes, always accustomed to being stopped by walls in the apartment and the office, even on the street, looked out with deepening pleasure as the train sped through meadows close to little inlets of the Sound. Vaughn never thought of herself as hungry for green fields or stretches of sky. She loved New York. The idea of having to spend the week end in the country had appalled her.

"I'll feel like a traveling salesman stuck in a small town," she'd told Denny, when he took her to Grand Central.

Yet now, as the train crossed the Connecticut and she glanced quickly upstream at the darkly wooded banks, then down toward the mouth of the river, where a little lighthouse stood outlined in brilliant sunshine, Vaughn felt the stir of a vague emotion that occasionally rippled up from the depth of her being and which, for some reason, she never cared to analyze.

It subsided immediately when the train, with sudden shift in mood, nosed its way into a grimy city and stood still.

Vaughn's thoughts returned to the assignment she was on her way to cover. The success of this trip to Kendal would mean so much to Denny and the children that, only thinking about it, she felt herself tauten with ambition. She was lying back against the reclining seat, but her body was tense.

Security, she told herself, as the train started to move again, the certain prospect of holding her job—they absolutely had to have this, so that if Denny's petered out they could go on living in the same apartment, Susan could have the right social things, they could send Neil away to prep school. He must get in with a crowd of boys and learn to hold his own. And if Denny really—— But Vaughn didn't want to think about that.

Her suit, she noticed, examining the crook of her arm, was inclined to wrinkle. She'd always supposed pure silk would keep its shape. Still, it looked smart. Black made her paleness interesting when she used enough lipstick.

She'd certainly had a break finding the hat—such a honey—at the

15

last minute. Given time to shop around, she might have landed a bargain, but chic like this—the luscious cherries and gooseberries and tiny little bananas crowning the imported white straw—such chic always cost money. It had an unmistakable mid-century look.

Coming back after the last smoke, Vaughn had caught a glimpse of herself in the coach mirror. Yes, she was definitely important.

That's what Denny had told her when she left, though he hadn't said so right off. She'd turned toward him in the taxi on the way to the train, smiling seductively through her new chickenwire veil, anticipating his surprise when he noticed the hat. But Denny, absorbed in his own thoughts, didn't even see her, so that finally, unable to bear it any longer, she'd prodded him.

"Like my hat?"

At last his eyes had taken her in, yet the surprise she'd expected to see break over his face wasn't there.

"I always liked that hat," he answered absently.

"Why, Denis Hill, I only bought it this morning to wear to Kendal," she exclaimed, hurt.

He hadn't been a bit sorry. "It looks exactly like your other one," he insisted.

A remark like that spoiled things. Not that Denny didn't care. Vaughn knew he did. Only she'd have liked him to notice her the way he had once, long ago, even if she was thirty-eight now, you might say, pushing forty.

Anyhow, the hat did do a lot for her. Denny, even if prodded, assured Vaughn of this finally.

"You'll wow them in Kendal," he declared gallantly, as he put her overnight case on the rack above her in the train. Then, the way he kissed her, Vaughn didn't mind any more his not noticing little things.

"I've simply got to impress the Ludlow man," she explained earnestly as Denny was about to leave.

Everything, she said to herself, now that she was speeding nearer and nearer toward this unknown person, depended on that. If she succeeded in making an impression on him, he'd let her poke around the place on his land where fugitive slaves used to hide, and she could collect material for a first-rate layout. But if, after she'd come all this distance, he wouldn't let her see it . . .

His answer to her letter requesting an interview on a week end because that was the only time she could get away, being tied up at the office, had been decent enough. Could Mrs. Hill arrange to come to Kendal this Friday evening? That would give her all of Saturday there and one of the New York trains stopped shortly after noon on Sundays. He sounded pleasant but noncommittal, and Vaughn knew that people who own historical gems don't always care to show them.

Watching the passing country, she realized that she must have seen it once or twice before, going to Boston, only she didn't remember. Now that her work was taking her to this backwater, she was eager to know what it was like.

But the view from the window seemed to withhold something. There were no mysterious mountains; it was a forthright landscape, disclosing its coves and ponds, woods and swampy spaces to anyone who cared to look out of the train. And yet there seemed to be a secret in the shoulders of the hummocks and the shadows of the trees, as if the earth knew what Vaughn was getting into, while she was forced to sit still wondering, growing jumpier with every passing mile.

What kind of person would this Ludlow be? Would he understand about advertising? What did he do? What *did* one do in a place like Kendal? Farm? Keep store?

Was there a hotel? Or would she have to stay in some shabby tourist place, as Denny feared? The minute she got to the station she'd inquire. At best, it would be grim. And what, she asked herself, was she going to do all evening long, tonight and tomorrow?

Seeing herself imprisoned in some cold, depressing room with nothing to do all evening but polish her nails, Vaughn felt her courage crumble. She wouldn't stay. She'd simply turn right around and go home the minute she got there. There must be a night train . . .

17

What's the matter with me? she asked herself desperately, opening and closing the snap of her handbag, opening and closing it again. *I wanted this chance more than anything. Now it's come and I'm almost there I've got cold feet.*

It wasn't like her at all.

What's the matter with me?

Worn out—that was it—dead-beat. The whole family depended on her for everything. It was too much. On top of her job it was simply too much.

She enjoyed her work. Denny even seemed to think, a little reproachfully, that she preferred it to keeping house and looking after the children. Maybe she did. But she was tired of being responsible for everything. Those awful war years—when she had to make a new home each time Denny got sent to another camp, caring for the babies in places where there wasn't any room, where they weren't wanted, struggling alone while he was overseas, and then the worst part of all—when Denny got out and his old job seemed so pointless to him that he wouldn't go back for weeks—after those awful years, why couldn't things be easier?

She felt like crying. *Now,* when she was almost in Kendal, where it was so important that she control the interview, in case that Ludlow person should turn out to be cagey—*now* she felt like this. Good Lord!

Here I am, she said to herself furiously, upset when nothing's happened. Unstrung, probably looking a wreck.

She opened her handbag again and fished for the mirror. Thank goodness, except for a grain of soot, her make-up was all right. It wasn't as if she'd really cried. Yet her composure, the most essential thing in business, had been ruffled.

She went forward once more to the smoking section. A cigarette would calm her.

But before she had a chance to pull herself together the conductor came through calling, "Kendal." Vaughn rushed back to her seat, took down her overnight case, straightened her suit, adjusted her veil, and put on her broadtail jacket and her gloves much more hurriedly than she considered fitting.

Three or four women had crowded into the vestibule by the time she got there. The train stopped. The women lurched against her, then moved forward slowly. A man standing on the platform observed each one as she came down.

Nervously gripping the overnight case, Vaughn got out and looked around. First, a place to sleep.

"Vaughn Hill?"

Instead of acknowledging her name, Vaughn drew back, startled. She didn't know the man. A perfect stranger calling her "Vaughn." She wouldn't even answer, and he turned away.

Then it dawned: this must be the man who'd written. What a fool she'd been. He'd come to meet her train! How could she know? In New York nobody would do such a thing. Vaughn almost ran after him.

"Mr. Ludlow?" The man stood still. "I *am* Mrs. Hill."

He turned, took off his hat, and smiled down at Vaughn.

She caught her breath, suddenly overwhelmed, unable to say anything more. It wasn't only his coming to the station that took her by surprise. It was the man himself.

2. He was completely different from what she'd expected—quite certainly not a storekeeper, not a farmer, either, with that easy manner. His hair was gray but thick, cut close to his head like a college boy's, so that he looked old and young at the same time.

What surprised Vaughn was the outreaching friendliness of this stranger. It radiated from his eyes and crinkled his mouth in a cordiality so exceeding politeness that she was instantly attracted to him.

"Welcome to Kendal," he said, shaking her hand. His voice,

though quiet, was eager, and conveyed the sentiment better than his words. Taking the overnight case, he escorted Vaughn around the depot.

The place smelled earthy. There'd been a shower and now the sun had come out and was drying the puddles on the ground. This was the way it used to smell at home, in East Bolton, early in spring. Vaughn sniffed the country freshness happily as Mr. Ludlow helped her into his car.

He got in without speaking. She expected him to inquire about her trip or comment on the weather, but he made no effort to deny the strangeness which stood between them. Only, before putting his key into the ignition, he turned and looked at her a minute. The warmth and gentleness of his smile were like little feelers reaching out to Vaughn.

Smiling in return, she felt suddenly easy in spite of his silence, at home with him, as if they'd known each other for years and had already exchanged that knowledge of personal tastes prerequisite to friendship.

She was the first to say something. "Sorry I didn't answer when you spoke to me," she told him, surprised to find herself opening a business interview with an apology. "You see, I wasn't expecting anyone, so when you said, 'Vaughn,' I thought it must be somebody who knows me well, but as I didn't recognize you——"

He looked puzzled for an instant. Then he laughed. "It's an old Quaker custom," he explained, "using the whole name without any title. Not an indication of familiarity, simply the way we address everyone *except* our closest friends."

"Oh!" Vaughn exclaimed.

An odd person, religious. That sort of thing was out of her line, and as for Quakers, she knew nothing about them, only that they dressed and spoke peculiarly. But this one looked quite normal in his herringbone topcoat and gray felt hat. The sedately striped tie was exactly what any well-dressed man his age would wear in town. There was nothing unusual, either, once she got used to the New

England accent, about his way of speaking—except what he'd called her and, after all, that was her name.

"Nowadays," he added, smiling at her, "Friends hardly ever use plain speech except with one another. It was a slip, my speaking to you that way. I hope you don't mind."

"I rather like it," she told him shyly.

He gave her a grateful glance. "Then I'll continue," he said, and turned his attention to the road again.

Looking sideways at him, Vaughn realized that there was an unusual vivacity in the man's face, as if he were unafraid of showing feeling.

I'm so used to the deadpan everyone wears downtown, Vaughn said to herself, I guess that's why I'm struck by him.

Kendal looked like one of those little old places whose massive trees and white houses, fanlights and columns Vaughn admired whenever she had occasion to drive through, wondering, at the same time, how anyone could bear to live there. Even a week end would be deadly.

Mr. Ludlow was pointing out landmarks. Over yonder, he was saying as they passed the village green, Roger Williams had made friends with the local Indians.

Heavens, did the man think just because Vaughn had come all this way for the Underground Railroad material that she had a yen for history? Didn't he realize it was purely a matter of business?

Suddenly she remembered that she should have inquired at the station about a room. He'd whisked her away so fast.

The devil with Roger Williams, she exclaimed to herself. What I want to know is, where am I going to sleep?

"Is there a hotel?" she asked aloud. "I didn't know where to wire."

Mr. Ludlow gave Vaughn a reassuring glance. "Mary Lancashire has a room for you," he said. "That's her house we're heading for upstreet." The vivacity which charmed Vaughn suddenly went out of his face. "Sorry I can't entertain you," he murmured. "I live alone."

Vaughn drew a quick, surprised breath. "I didn't expect——"

21

"But," he went on, brightening again, "my housekeeper has counted on you for supper. Will you come?"

This had ceased to be a business interview before it had even begun. In New York, Vaughn thought, what this man was doing would seem absolutely crazy. On an expense account, one might take a client to lunch or put oneself out for a buyer. But to treat a stranger as one would a friend, when there was nothing to be got out of it—worse than that, a person who wanted something from you—well, it was the most extraordinary thing she'd ever come across.

Would she come? And not spend the whole evening doing her nails?

When she said, "Thank you, I'd love to come," though the phrase was prim, like a little girl's accepting an invitation to a party, she meant it as truly as any she had ever spoken.

The house she was ushered into was white and stately, surrounded by a beautiful lawn. The setting sun, shining full on it, sparkled in the little panes of the tall downstairs windows. Mary Lancashire came to the door herself, and once more Vaughn was received with that amazing friendliness.

A kindly soul with a wide bosom, Mary Lancashire had five young daughters who crowded around, staring at Vaughn as if they thought her something out of *Glamour* or *Mademoiselle*.

My Lord, Vaughn exclaimed to herself. *Ten pigtails!*

The middle girl looked Susan's age. She had the twelve-year-old's shyness and rounded elbows. Otherwise, she was so different. More like the child Vaughn had been than Susan. It was easy to see that she'd never painted her toenails nor had a permanent.

"Alice will show you your room, Mrs. Hill," the mother said graciously, and the tallest daughter stepped forward.

Nice features, Vaughn thought. Fifteen, maybe. When she grows up, she'll be a knockout.

Silently taking the overnight case from Mr. Ludlow, the girl led the way. Even on the stairs she turned back to gaze at Vaughn, obviously unable to conceal her admiration.

Mr. Ludlow waited in the parlor, twirling his hat in his hands, joking with the little girls.

"It's going to be chilly tonight," Mary Lancashire called from the foot of the stairs, when Vaughn had nearly reached the top. "Alice, thee'd better give Mrs. Hill the quilt from thy cupboard."

Vaughn stood in the room assigned to her, waiting for the girl to return with the quilt. The room was shockingly plain. Comfortable, perhaps, but it had no color. A creamy paper, white ruffled curtains, white counterpane and bureau scarf. Anybody, Vaughn thought, anybody with the least taste for decorating would see that was all wrong.

But she didn't want to act superior just because she came from the city.

"This counterpane," she said, when the girl came in. "I had the twin to it on my bed back home when I was a kid. Haven't seen one like it in years."

She took off her hat and looked at herself in the mirror, fluffing up her hair. The girl was reflected in the mirror, too, and Vaughn watched impatiently as she fussed with the quilt, her pigtails banging against the brass bars at the foot of the bedstead.

If only she'd get out, so Vaughn could think.

Why was Mr. Ludlow so friendly? Did he want something from her? she asked herself, opening the overnight case. Or was he simply lonely, here in this neck of the woods—a bachelor, widowed, divorced maybe—what?

The girl left at last, with a curious glance at the top layer in the overnight case.

There was something unreal about this place, Vaughn decided as she hung up her suit. This thee and thy and all those pigtails and the oldtime hospitality—like the stories about quaint little girls which Susan had a craze for reading.

She turned to the mirror again, wondering how she'd look with the new short hair. On the whole she'd never cared for casual childish styles. She was too small, and a quantity of carefully set dark hair made a good frame for a pale face. No, she wouldn't change her type. Only, she wished she could find something to remove those strained lines around her eyes.

What I need now, she said to herself as she made up, is a drink.

Cocktails before dinner—a "must" in civilized society. Something told Vaughn she wasn't going to get one, not in this setup. And right now, she thought enviously, Denny was probably fixing himself a marvelous concoction.

Darling Denny. What would he do all evening without her? Wouldn't he howl if he could see her in this all-white room after the fuss she'd made combining color schemes when they furnished the apartment?

And wouldn't the boys at the agency razz her if they could just see the screwy outfit she'd landed into running after that railroad account! Wow!

When Vaughn went down in her turquoise-blue dinner dress with the fur jacket over her shoulders and saw Mr. Ludlow waiting for her at the foot of the stairs, she felt like a prom girl. She looked nice. His eyes told her so. It was good she'd decided at the last minute to take off those pendent earrings.

Sitting beside him as they drove away, she wondered again why this man was so interested.

But I'm interested, too, she admitted to herself. There's something about him——

It had grown almost dark. The town that had been all green and white in the setting sun was dull.

As her new friend stopped his car before what looked like an old farmhouse, low and gray against the twilight, with a lantern shining brightly at the door, Vaughn turned questioningly to him. "Mr. Ludlow——" she began, but he broke in.

"Won't you call me Philip Ludlow, like other folks?" he asked. Though he smiled encouragement, he was appealing to her too.

It was odd how happy this request made Vaughn. She knew he was admitting her, not, as he'd explained before, into his intimate circle, but into the larger framework of his life, and this inclusion pleased her quite disproportionately.

"Philip Ludlow," she repeated after him softly. "How did you guess which I was? A lot of other women got off the train. Yet you spoke to me first. How did you guess?"

He turned to her with an expression of the most endearing humor, the kind which would never wilfully hurt. "I think," he said, and stopped, as if fearing the explanation would seem a little bold. Then he went on, speaking in a grave, courteous tone, yet with laughter in his eyes. "I think—yes—I'm sure—it was your hat."

Her hat! Vaughn gasped.

"You see," Philip Ludlow added, smiling openly as he helped her out of the car, "nothing like it ever got off the train in Kendal before."

3. Vaughn had quite forgotten how delightful it is to be made to feel charming. As she entered Philip Ludlow's house, the courtesy with which her host received her demanded the response of a leisurely lady.

There never seemed time for such graciousness at home, where Vaughn was always darting away from Denny in the middle of a meal or a sentence to answer the phone or keep an appointment. At the agency the men treated her like an equal, a fact which till this minute had given her great pride. Yet now, as Philip Ludlow ushered her into his parlor with a welcome which made Vaughn feel nothing less than queenly, she realized that she adored attention.

The room had obviously been furnished by someone who thought of it mainly as a vantage point for the view. There was a long window seat, and all the armchairs were turned so that they faced the windows. But it was dark now and Vaughn couldn't see beyond the lighted parlor.

One wall was solid with books. In a recess a lady's writing desk, a delicate piece made of some unusual wood, caught Vaughn's eye.

On it a tiny bowl of hepaticas stood before a photograph in an oval frame.

This is no farmhouse parlor, Vaughn said to herself, curious about the man who lived here. She'd just naturally supposed, because he belonged in this backwater, that he'd be something of a hick, so that the highbrow selection of magazines on the gate-legged table by one of the armchairs surprised her. They were political, religious, musical, and not the usual ones, either, but several she'd never even heard of.

I wonder what he does, she thought.

Philip Ludlow went to the little desk and took up the photograph. "My wife," he said, holding it under the lamp for Vaughn to see.

The vivacity went out of his face again the way it had when he'd spoken of living alone, but tenderness animated the unadorned words: *My wife.*

Vaughn studied the picture. A thin face with large grave eyes, a soft mouth—the trusting face of a deeply cherished person.

"She died last year," Philip Ludlow explained, replacing the photograph. "This was her desk." He straightened a pile of papers under an old-fashioned paperweight.

Acting on some odd impulse, he suddenly took up the paperweight and gave it to Vaughn to hold, as one might put a beautiful object into a child's hand.

Vaughn felt the smooth roundness of the glass with her fingertips, looking down through it at the wreath of china roses encrusted in the base, then up at Philip Ludlow appreciatively. Smiling at her with his touching friendliness, he took his treasure back, carefully replacing it on the desk.

As she watched him, Vaughn was struck by his hands, a workman's hands, brown and knobby, but very clean.

And again she said to herself, I wonder what he does.

He was calling her attention to two pictures which hung above the desk. George, he pointed out, and John, both in foreign service. They had nice faces, like their father's, but the expression in them

reminded Vaughn of men in Denny's outfit when they were about
to go into combat.

"State Department?" she asked.

"No. Friends' Service. George—that's the elder one—he's setting
up an agricultural project near Nazareth. Arab and Jew, working
together on the land, maybe in that way they can become reconciled. John's in China," he went on, indicating the other picture.
There was anxiety in his tone. "Helping treat kala azar where people are suffering from it, regardless of their political ties. He was
due home long ago."

Vaughn looked inquiringly at Philip Ludlow. There seemed to
be some tragedy.

"You see, it's impossible for replacements to get there," he explained, answering her unspoken question, "so John's staying. It's
a long time since I've heard from him."

Though his voice was anxious, Philip Ludlow's face expressed
contentment, and this contentment overlay the love in his eyes as
he spoke of his sons.

Seeing such satisfaction enjoyed by another parent, Vaughn felt
her own discontent laid bare to envy. The long-suppressed worry
about Neil rose in her. Before she knew what was happening, it
had overflowed into speech.

"My Neil's a problem," she admitted impetuously. "Sometimes I
wonder, will he ever be a real boy—you know, able to hold his own.
He's thirteen and sweet, but so afraid of hurting another fellow
that he won't defend himself. I don't think he's a coward,
exactly——"

She stopped. What possessed her? To discuss one of her children
in a business interview with a man she'd never even seen till an
hour ago!

She glanced up quickly to see whether he was annoyed. His
expression baffled her. It wasn't at all an expression of annoyance;
it was a look of appeal, a look a child might give a parent about to
drown a cat.

It stumped her.

To cover her perplexity, Vaughn talked on rapidly, so bewildered now that she grabbed unthinkingly at phrases she was always using on Denny.

"We want to send him to a good prep school," she blurted out. "And he must go back to camp. Last year he hated it, but that just goes to show. He needs to learn to hold his own."

What Philip Ludlow asked then baffled Vaughn even more than his expression. "Why do you want him to?"

Such a simple guy.

"Because we live in a rotten world," Vaughn answered, smiling indulgently, as if her host, too, were a child. Back to generalization, away from the personal, she felt sure of herself again.

His reply was characteristically gallant. "People like Neil," he said assuredly, "will make our world better."

Vaughn dismissed the subject, telling Philip Ludlow about Susan now—what a cute little thing she was and how her greatest ambition was to become a dancer. She didn't tell him much, just enough to sound poised, so he wouldn't think her simply an oversolicitous mother.

Yet, as he was escorting her in to dinner, Vaughn wondered: *was* it gallant, what he'd said about Neil? Or could he possibly have meant it?

Nuts! Vaughn exclaimed to herself, as he was pushing in her chair. Nobody could be that naïve.

He took his place at the head of the table.

Seeing him bow his head reverently, Vaughn did the same, waiting an unbelievably long time for him to say grace till, to her surprise, she found on peeking through her lashes that he was looking up and smiling at her, his thanks having apparently been given silently.

He asked no questions, either about her work—she was expecting this—or about her family or background. And yet he gave the impression that he would welcome with interest anything she cared to tell.

Vaughn, on the other hand, was full of curiosity. She took note of the fine silver, the dainty linen, the flower arrangement in the center of the table. It was all quite different from what she'd expected.

She stared at the woman who came in to serve, wondering just how much she did in this household. Did she clean as well as cook? Did she plan the meals? What about the laundry? And Philip Ludlow's clothes—who sent them to the cleaner, who did the moth-proofing? Who saw to it that the poor dear put on his heavy overcoat when winter came?

He caught her staring at the maid. Vaughn quickly looked down into her plate, afraid that he had read her thoughts. Where did she come in to be curious about this man's private affairs?

They're not my lookout, she told herself, embarrassed.

He restored her equilibrium as he pointed out with relish that the peas and corn were home-frozen, the strawberries had also come from his garden. He told her about Kendal and the many queer yet lovable characters in the town, till it sounded like the most amusing and delightful place to live. The gusto with which he told his stories, the innocent humor that could make the little dump sound so attractive, charmed Vaughn. But suddenly, in the middle of something he was saying, she remembered the purpose of her visit, and the joy went out of everything.

What if he had no intention of showing her the hiding place? Suppose with all this kindness he was simply trying to break it gently to her that it wasn't open to the public? Suppose——

The strawberry shortcake, so delicious a second ago, turned sour in Vaughn's mouth. She put down her fork.

It was only with the greatest difficulty that she managed to control her impatience. Would the leisurely meal never end? She was dying for a cigarette.

When they were in the parlor again, she took one from her bag. "Mind my smoking?" she asked, looking about in vain for an ash tray.

"Not at all," Philip Ludlow answered. There was no reservation in his voice, but somehow, sitting with him beside the fireplace, in which he had lit a cheerful fire, Vaughn didn't relish the cigarette and after a few puffs threw it in the flames. Then she was sorry; she had nothing to do with her hands.

He'd offered Vaughn a low, old-fashioned chair with a rush seat, just the right height. She settled back comfortably in it a minute, but then she leaned forward again. She was too tense.

This was the moment to speak up. Vaughn jumped in headlong. "You've been treating me like a guest," she began awkwardly, sliding her rings up and down her finger. "Maybe you didn't understand I was coming on business." That was a poor way to put it. She wasn't in command of the situation here, out of her office.

"I do understand," Philip Ludlow answered. "A business interview can also be an opportunity for making friends, don't you think so?"

She nodded agreement, but what she thought was: what a simple person! Still, there was a dignity about him that made Vaughn, in her turquoise-blue chiffon from Madison Avenue and her carefully matched accessories feel a little countrified, a little young.

His quiet hands made her feel that way. Hers always had to be doing something when she was sitting still. In the office she could have played with a pencil or spread a paper clip. Now she'd even thrown her cigarette away.

He was looking at her gravely. His expression encouraged her. "You tell me," it seemed to say, and something more: "Don't think that I shall judge you."

"You see," she explained earnestly. "It's a spread we want to do for one of the railroads. We've been trying to get their account for a long time." She stopped, regretting she'd put it this way. He would think she wasn't successful.

"I mean," she went on, fidgeting a little, "we've been looking for a new angle to advertise travel. The public is sick of streamlined cars—not to ride in, of course, but in the ads."

Though he sat relaxed while she was talking, his hands lying on the arms of his chair, quite still, except for the fingertips which reached out a little now and then to feel the wood beneath them,

30

Philip Ludlow watched Vaughn's face so intently that she first thought he might be deaf. Then she realized that he was simply listening with more regard than people usually gave her, and she went on eagerly.

"Contrast's what we're after," she informed him. "Primitive, venturesome travel. People like to read about others doing that sort of thing, though, naturally, for themselves, they ask the last word in comfort."

He nodded.

"Something with historical fiavor," she continued. "The Pony Express, for instance, was once used very successfully." She added ruefully, "By our competitors."

They both laughed.

He was such a delightful mixture of seriousness and fun. The old caution, the resolve not to count on a thing till she had it in her hand, forsook Vaughn then. This man wasn't going to let her down.

"I'd been trying to think up something really good," she went on, feeling now that she was talking to a friend, "when suddenly I had this marvelous inspiration about the Underground Railroad. I didn't know a thing about it," she confided, "except what I remembered from school."

"Not much," he put in.

"No," she agreed, and they laughed again. "But the name sounded romantic," she continued, "so I asked around and discovered there were still one or two places in New England which had served as 'stations,' only, I was told, they're hard to find. Well," she exclaimed, emphasizing the statement with a shake of the head, "they are."

"Surprised you located us at all," Philip Ludlow told Vaughn. "Hardly anyone knows what happened here a hundred years ago."

So it really was virgin ground. No one had come here before to popularize the place. She would have it all to herself—original material for her layout!

"It took a lot of hunting in the Forty-second Street library and correspondence with the chamber of commerce in dozens of little towns. I had a couple of false leads first," Vaughn went on. "So you can imagine how I felt when I found out about your place. When you actually answered my letter I was just thrilled."

"I'll take you there in the morning," Philip Ludlow promised.

Vaughn sank back, too relieved to thank him. He would take her—— Didn't he have anything else to do?

"It wasn't really necessary," she added, "for me to come. One can imagine things and write perfectly good copy. But I thought, if the railroad people asked me, I'd like to be able to say I'd been here. Anything to get the account."

A shadow passed over the man's face, only fleetingly, and for a moment Vaughn wondered whether she'd said the wrong thing.

"I'm very glad you did come," he remarked. "It's doubtful whether anyone enjoying freedom can imagine the tenseness of that drama, even seeing the place."

Vaughn, staring dreamily into the fire, wasn't listening. She was thinking what a lucky break she'd had. This stranger had given her a wonderful dinner. Tomorrow he'd take her to the hiding place. She was all set.

"So you're going to interpret the Underground Railroad to everyone who rides the trains," he mused. Then he looked very pleased. "What a help," he exclaimed. "Way opens so strangely sometimes."

Help? Vaughn was flabbergasted. Why should he care? There was nothing in it for him. Or did he think there was? Good Lord!

"Trained experts like you," he was saying, still looking pleased, "who know how to overcome indifference." Suddenly he looked at her searchingly. "This means a lot to you personally, doesn't it?" he asked. "Getting that account."

Except for that odd thing about Neil it was the only direct question he put to her all week end.

Instinctively Vaughn became the businesswoman.

"We're a very busy firm," she began, starting the old formula of the agency's having more accounts than it could handle, but Philip Ludlow was looking at her steadily, and she dropped her eyes.

Nothing short of truth would do for this man, so she told him, though not everything, not nearly everything. Not about the long time Denny had taken after he got out of the service to settle down at his job, so that in exasperation she'd gone and landed one herself; not about the hard, unspoken stubbornness that stood between them ever since, only of her fear that Denny might lose the work he had because of business falling off. That, she explained, was why it was so important, her getting on.

It was a relief to say even that much.

"Competition's so keen," was the way she put it. "It's expensive, living in New York," she added with a certain envy, as she looked around the simple room.

The man whose taste it expressed, sitting in the armchair on the other side of the fire, watching the flames spring between the logs, was, obviously, uncomplicated too. His simplicity, like his friendliness, extended toward Vaughn so that in the company of this person, whom she'd never even seen before, her own knotted self gradually unraveled.

Leaning back, she felt relaxed and happy.

She was still in this mood when he drove her back to Mary Lancashire's, bidding her good-by on the doorstep, formally, and yet with such touching friendliness that she experienced again the excitement she'd had coming down the stairs, the illusion of being on a date. It had been a lovely one.

The little pigtails were presumably in bed. Only Alice sat in the parlor with her mother. She was doing her homework, slumped in her chair, arms and legs untidily thrust from her. In her eyes was a faraway look, less, Vaughn supposed shrewdly, the mark of concentration than of irrelevant fantasies spinning in the child's mind.

Vaughn could remember how she herself, holding a pencil, leafing through a book, had slid into dreams. While a lesser part of her brain automatically followed through the stages of a formula, she fancied herself in turn a fashion designer, an important executive in a busy establishment, and maybe in other roles she didn't remember any more. Woolgathering, her mother used to call it, when she rudely summoned Vaughn back to her work.

Mary Lancashire said nothing to Alice. Having invited Vaughn to sit with them, she sewed on placidly.

"Thank you," Vaughn answered. "It's been a long day. I think I'll turn in."

She didn't feel like talking. It was very kind of her hostess to be so friendly, but she wasn't used to making small talk, and it bored her. Besides, she was dying for a smoke, and she wasn't sure the woman would like it.

Once upstairs, she sat down on the edge of the bed and lit a cigarette.

She'd never been allowed to sit on her white counterpane when she was a child. Even now, in this place which meant nothing to her, where she didn't give a darn what Mary Lancashire thought, sitting on it made her feel so guilty that she finally got up and stalked about the room. The whiteness of everything in the poorly shaded lamplight gave her the creeps.

It had been sweet of Philip Ludlow to bring her here. The old dear probably thought she'd love it. But at a hotel she'd have been able to get a drink, she could have sat in the lobby and smoked, instead of having to sneak off to her room. The overpowering virtue of Mary Lancashire, the stillness outside, made more horrible by the wistful whistles of trains streaking through the town without a stop—it was too much.

Still, one couldn't just walk around three sides of a bed all night. Vaughn got in and switched off the lamp, yet for hours and hours she lay awake, looking out at the frosty stars.

If I only hadn't taken so much coffee in the diner.

The bed was full of lumps.

What's the matter, anyway? she asked herself. I had a nice evening, didn't I? Why am I so edgy?

It was being away from Denny—that was the trouble. She could never bear being by herself. She turned over on her stomach, sighing miserably.

As she smothered in the pillow, Vaughn understood in a sudden flash why she hated the quiet and solitude: they were driving her

34

to admit that it wasn't the bed, or the coffee, but something in herself, something . . .

Toward morning, her body exhausted, Vaughn dozed off, but only to sleep without rest, for in her dreams there was no peace.

4. It was, Philip Ludlow explained to Vaughn as he drove her through Kendal the next morning, a little river port, accessible to the ocean, yet snug in a storm. At high tide the channel was deep enough for good-sized vessels. They had sailed up to the town docks in the old days, whalers and coastwise schooners—even the three-masters—with merchandise from every quarter of the globe. Until the turn of the century as many as twenty of these large ships and any number of smaller ones would take protection here during the winter. He could remember how fine they looked, riding at anchor or standing frozen at the wharves.

There were only a couple of little fishing boats in the river now, and Vaughn wasn't interested in Kendal's past. But she liked watching Philip Ludlow's face as he spoke of his childhood. Mischief played over it when he told her how he used to go to school by jumping from deck to deck up the river instead of walking primly along the street.

He must be sixty now, Vaughn figured, and yet it wasn't hard to imagine him a boy the age of Neil. There was something about him that reminded her of a child, not innocence—the realities of life hadn't escaped him—but an uncomplicated, uncompetitive ease that few boys carry into manhood.

He had driven away from the river into a street that ran between the lawns of handsome old houses. Slowing down, he brought the car gently to a standstill, without turning off the ignition.

"That's our Meetinghouse," he said, and by his tone Vaughn could tell that he was showing her another of his treasures, like the glass paperweight with the wreath of roses.

Looking over, she saw a small frame building, set back from the street in a yard shaded with trees. The double door was square and homely. The plainness of the clapboards, painted the color of the sky on a dull day, was so stark that to Vaughn the place looked anything but inspiring.

She liked fine architecture, especially in a church. You might not believe in what they preached there, but Saint John the Divine, Saint Patrick's, Riverside Church—they moved you by their beauty and grandeur so that you felt yourself reaching upward with their spires.

But this! Stealing a glance at Philip Ludlow, Vaughn saw that he was regarding his little Meetinghouse with some of the affection he had been unable to conceal when speaking of his family. Association probably made the place beautiful to him. To Vaughn, though, viewing it objectively, this little church was downright ugly. How could anyone with taste go there?

"I've never known any Quakers," she observed, as Philip Ludlow drove on into the country. She was rather hoping with this remark to coax some interpretation from him.

All he said was, "You'll know a good many by the time you leave Kendal."

It was months since Vaughn had gone driving in the country—not since last summer. Things were still wintry, but there was promise of life to come, a hopefulness about the fields and trees. The willows on the opposite bank of the river were already a sun-touched green.

She sat back and let herself have the full pleasure of watching the scenery. Rhode Island had something.

"It's awfully nice of you to take me," she said, without turning her eyes from the river. "I didn't expect it. As a matter of fact, I was afraid I'd feel like a traveling salesman." Turning to him with a grin, she saw that her remark puzzled him. "Stuck in a small town over the week end," she explained, and he caught the joke.

Leaving the highway, they entered a rocky dirt road. On either side stones covered the fields like a crop of Hubbard squash.

"Must be a headache to the man behind the plow," Vaughn said, and was surprised to find that Philip Ludlow understood her meaning, though she'd only spoken half the thought.

"Father used to tell about a farmer who tried to cart off the stones from his field every fall so they wouldn't hatch young ones in the spring," he answered, laughing. "This place I'm taking you to," he went on, "is the old homestead. I don't know whether I told you that last night."

Vaughn shook her head.

"We were all born on it," he related, "back as far as the minutes of the Meeting go. Friends fled to Rhode Island, you know, during the seventeenth century, to escape persecution in the Bay Colony. Father was principal of the academy, but he farmed too. I moved to Kendal when I married, to be nearer my work."

His work—— Vaughn was dying to know what he did. Until now he'd seemed almost to avoid speaking of it. She hadn't been able to place him.

Suddenly she had the answer. Silly that she hadn't seen it right away.

"You're a minister, aren't you?"

"Not I!" he exclaimed emphatically. The idea seemed to strike him as extremely funny. "Friends like us don't have ministers."

So now Vaughn knew no more about him than she had before, but she was rather relieved to find that she wasn't riding around with a minister. She had no chance to inquire further, because as they came to a very old farmhouse Philip Ludlow slowed down.

It was a shingled house, so old and weathered that it might have been in that field as long as the stones and the elms which framed it. The two people who stood on the porch smiling in greeting were old too. Dogs and ducks swarmed in the dooryard.

Waving to the old couple, Philip Ludlow stopped his car beside the barn, at some distance from the house.

The river made a bend here, and it was very shallow. One could easily cross it on the flat steppingstones that rose above the water. Vaughn noticed a little cottage farther up the bank, an old clapboard house with a wide chimney. The small panes of the front windows faced the river.

"What a lovely place," she remarked to Philip Ludlow, glancing back at it when they were walking toward the first house.

"Our farmer used to live there," he told her, "when the land was still being worked. Young couple named Brown in it now. The people we just passed, whom you're about to meet, are Edmund and Alberta Mansfield. We moved them to our homestead temporarily when the hurricane washed away their house over by the ocean, and they stayed."

"They look like a picture," Vaughn observed, when the old couple was once more in sight. "You know—on a New England calendar or something."

Philip Ludlow smiled in agreement. "You'll have to shout a bit," he warned. "Edmund Mansfield's getting deaf. He's very old."

They were a sweet couple, but there was less the manner of country people about them than Vaughn expected. In bearing and diction they were very much like Philip Ludlow. A Park Avenue hostess couldn't have received Vaughn with easier grace than did Alberta Mansfield in this farmhouse. Her husband expressed pleasure that Vaughn had come to see the "station." He had, apparently, had everything explained to him beforehand.

"I knew some of those 'conductors,' as we called them," he told Vaughn. "They liked telling about their 'passengers' on the Underground Railroad years afterward, when I was just a boy. Thee sees, I was born on the day that the Amendment to the Constitution which abolished slavery was passed. That morning, while my father was sitting in Meeting, the silence was suddenly broken. Bells rang joyfully all over town, and the cannon was fired. A nice day to be born," he observed, turning to Vaughn with a smile, "wasn't it?"

She had no chance to answer, because just then Jeanie Brown came in, trailed by her little girl, and they were introduced. She was tall, good-looking, with dark hair and high coloring, probably in her early twenties, and she was pregnant.

38

Alberta Mansfield explained to Vaughn that Jeanie was a neighbor.

"Thee knows, of course," the old lady assumed.

Vaughn knew, of course, nothing about Jeanie, and she didn't care either. She was intent on watching Philip Ludlow as he talked to the girl. He stood by the window with her, and even across the room his eager frendliness was apparent.

Was he that way with everybody?

Old Mr. Mansfield was warming to his subject. "If the slave was caught he was returned to his master, and the man who tried to help him escape was fined and imprisoned. But nothing," he declared with admiration, "could stop those liberators."

Vaughn wasn't listening. She was still watching Philip Ludlow. And then she laughed at herself and looked away. Goodness, she wasn't jealous of Jeanie, was she? Of course not! How could she be? She simply hadn't realized that Philip Ludlow was the same with everyone.

"A very dramatic moment in history," the old gentleman was saying, apparently not noticing that Vaughn's attention had wandered.

She nodded. Obviously, she thought. Hadn't the dramatic implications of that moment brought her to this place, to these peculiar people? She intended to make the most of that drama too. Her layout was going to be good. She just had that feeling.

Looking around the simple farmhouse parlor at the Franklin stove and the old portraits of ancestors dressed in drab-colored clothes but with rosy cheeks and very bright eyes, Vaughn could hardly wait now to write the copy. It was on the tip of her mind's tongue.

"But then," the old man added apologetically, as if he knew that he was inclined to be garrulous, "thee knows that."

It seemed funny, but rather nice, to be included in the Mansfields' thee and thy. No doubt another "old Quaker custom."

Philip Ludlow must suddenly have remembered why they'd come, for, smiling at Vaughn, he began to push the davenport

aside and turned back the rag rug. Set in the flooring was a trap
door just wide enough to admit a man. Philip Ludlow knelt down
and tugged at its iron ring, but the door wouldn't budge.

"Hasn't been opened in years," he muttered, pulling with all his
might.

Suddenly the door gave way and, with a grin of satisfaction as
he looked up at Vaughn, Philip Ludlow pulled it back, revealing
a deep hole.

Vaughn bent over and stared down into the darkness. There
was nothing there. Just a hole. She'd come all this way and it was
just a hole!

"Six by six by twelve," Philip Ludlow was saying.

Vaughn tried to see something in there, to imagine something,
at least, but she felt let down. What good was this to her layout?
The damp cold struck her face. The hole smelled.

Edmund Mansfield stood looking down into the blackness too.
Suddenly he began to sing:

> "Go down, Moses,
>   Way down in Egypt Land,
>   And tell old Pharaoh
>   To let my people go."

His voice was quavery, but there was something appealing about
the gentle face. His very carefully brushed formal clothes contrasted
oddly with the words of the song.

Vaughn straightened up and listened.

The old man seemed to be moved by something as he contem-
plated the hiding place, something Vaughn couldn't see in it at all.
He looked a little comical, but one couldn't laugh at someone who
was obviously so sincere.

Philip Ludlow was still on his knees. He waited until the
song was finished and then he explained the hiding technique
to Vaughn. "Father used to tell how, when he was a boy, a slave,
smuggled out of Charleston or Savannah in the hold of one of
the tramps that put in at Kendal, would be secretly hustled over

here. His father would lower the slave into the hiding place, provide him with plenty of food and water, close the trap door, spread out the rug, and get Grandmother to sit on the spot in her rocking chair with the baby in her lap."

"Not even the sheriff would have suspected thy grandmother, thee may be sure," Alberta Mansfield said.

Philip Ludlow smiled at the old lady. There were family jokes between them evidently. "They had to wait till dark, you see," he explained, sitting back on his heels and turning to Vaughn, "before they could take the fugitive to the next 'station' on his way to Canada. They traveled in the wagon, of course, and it was twelve miles. Even in the dark the slave had to be hidden under sacking."

Vaughn looked down once more into the hole. Then she turned away. The damp smell nauseated her.

Seeing she was no longer interested, Philip Ludlow got shakily to his feet, replaced the door and the rug, moved back the davenport, and dusted off the knees of his trousers.

What a letdown, Vaughn thought.

Could she have expected better though? She didn't know, but certainly this wasn't worth all the trouble.

There was no romance, no glamour, just hard facts about a risky, illegal traffic. What had made her think, back there in her office, that the idea had possibilities?

"Grandfather had a close call once," Philip Ludlow was saying. "The sheriff knocked on the front door before there was time to lower the slave into the hiding place. The poor starved-out soul was eating in the kitchen. But Grandfather passed the time of day with the sheriff long enough to allow Grandmother to put his Quaker coat and beaver hat on the fugitive, who walked out by the back door and escaped."

The two Friends chuckled over this.

"I wonder what made those people do it," Vaughn said thoughtfully. Seeing an expression of surprise come into Philip Ludlow's face, she added quickly, shouting, so Edmund Mansfield would hear, "Oh, I know they felt sorry for the slaves. But I mean, after all, they were breaking the law."

"They were bound by a higher law," the older man said quietly. "It's never easy to obey that, and always dangerous. But some men can't do otherwise."

Was he rebuking her? Vaughn bit her lip. And then she was angry, because her lipstick was probably smudged. And how could she fix it here? Maybe there wasn't even a bathroom.

Alberta Mansfield and Jeanie had been busy in the kitchen. Now Vaughn found that she was expected to stay for lunch.

It was simple food, unceremoniously served, and yet there was something in the relationship of these people to one another that gave the meal a certain air, something puzzling to Vaughn. They were gay, delighting in anecdotes which, more often than not, poked fun at the very one who was telling them. But there was also a dignified gravity, a gentleness between them, less, Vaughn thought, like the intimacy of old friends than that of people who have shared an uncommon experience.

Whatever their tie might be, they never let Vaughn feel like an outsider, so that, already forgetting the old man's remark, she couldn't help but enjoy herself. Seated between him and Philip Ludlow, she felt young and carefree. Her plate was constantly being filled by one of them.

"Jeanie's brother is going to Germany," Alberta Mansfield announced. "Friends are undertaking to help in a village for homeless boys."

At the same moment Edmund Mansfield, who apparently hadn't heard his wife speak, turned to Philip Ludlow and asked, "Has thee heard from George?"

"Yes. Last week. The American machinery is beginning to arrive. The first modern plowshare in Nazareth."

He sounded so happy.

Vaughn ate placidly, gazing out through the little windowpanes to the field beyond, where ducks were following one another down to the river.

They left after lunch, she and Philip Ludlow. He drove slowly, taking the longest way round so she could see the countryside. When they reached town, he drove right through and out again.

"And now," he announced, his eyes sparkling, "I'll show you the finest sight in Kendal."

"What is it?"

"Wait and see," he said. "It's impossible to describe, but I think it's the finest thing that's come to this town in many years."

Vaughn was curious. The old mansions with handsome doorways which, so far as she knew, made up the whole of Kendal, had disappeared. Here, on the lower river, there were mills of blackened brick and shanties surrounded by truck gardens. Farther along some boats had been hauled up on a strip of beach.

It was there that Philip Ludlow stopped the car.

A young man stood working on a small sailboat. Three or four slummy-looking boys were watching him, handling his tools, grinning and chattering.

As Philip Ludlow opened the door of his car for Vaughn and led the way over a path of crushed clamshells, the young man looked up. Seeing Philip Ludlow approaching, he brightened with pleasure, but the crowd around him edged away.

"Stick around, guys," Vaughn heard him say, and the boys stayed where they were, all except one. The others stared at her just as the pigtails had stared, but not with the same appreciation.

"Vaughn Hill," Philip Ludlow said happily, "this is Bart Brown. I wanted you to meet him. And," he added, smiling at the boys, "his entourage."

The young man wiped his hand on his trouser leg and greeted Vaughn. He had a nice smile, but he was homely and decidedly in need of a shave.

"Meet the fellows," he said, standing aside and introducing them as formally as though they were on the reception line of an important function. "This is Tony Torino, Bill Becker, Louis Kovaleski. Where's Joe?" He looked around.

"Went home," one of the crowd answered, and the others giggled.

"Bashful," another one explained.

Bart Brown handed them the sander. "Work awhile for me?" he asked. "Time out while I speak to the folks."

The boys grasped the sander and set to work on the boat.

"We're on our way back from the homestead," Philip Ludlow explained. "Saw Jeanie and the baby there. Vaughn Hill's interested in the Underground Railroad station."

The young man nodded. "Exciting, isn't it?" he asked Vaughn.

She didn't answer him. She was trying to figure out why Philip Ludlow had brought her here. As far as she was concerned they could pull out right now. This Bart person—something about him got on her nerves.

When they were back in the car, heading for Mary Lancashire's, Philip Ludlow turned to Vaughn.

"See what I mean?" he asked eagerly. "There's always a crowd like that down there, hanging around Bart. Older boys, mostly, too old for compulsory school, six, eight of them, often. The hardest lot of boys, some with court records."

But Vaughn didn't see. "Is that," she asked incredulously, "what you were referring to? You said, 'the finest thing in Kendal.'"

"It is," he assured her gravely. "Didn't you think so? But you couldn't really tell in that short time. Bart's doing something for those boys no one else could do—the Y, their church. No one could reach them. They simply wouldn't go. But they come looking for Bart. He has a way of communicating his faith and ideals without words. Simply the way he shares his tools, lends his things, helps the boys fix their radios. They know they have a friend in him."

"But what—what's so fine about it?"

"Bart," Philip Ludlow answered quickly. "It's because Bart's so fine. His love of people—it can change those boys' lives, you know. They're accustomed to having their weaknesses underscored, but it may be the first time that anyone has answered that of God in them."

Vaughn felt uncomfortable. She hadn't liked Bart, and when

44

Philip Ludlow mentioned God, she tried to deflect the conversation. "What does he do?" she asked. "For a living, I mean."

"Right now he's putting those boats in condition. In the fall he hopes to find something like that, where he can earn just enough to get along and still be accessible to the boys. He has his family to look out for."

"Then why," Vaughn asked, really angry with Bart now, "doesn't he get a job, a real job?"

"What about those boys?" Philip Ludlow asked her. "They're his real job. His wife is behind him, you know. She asks for almost nothing. Didn't you like her?"

Vaughn nodded politely.

The pair of them sounded crazy, and she wasn't interested. She asked no more questions.

Suddenly Philip Ludlow said: "Your Neil would get on famously with Bart."

"No!" Vaughn cried, surprised at the anger with which she spoke. "Neil isn't hard. Just the opposite. Don't you see what we want is to toughen him up?" She began laughing foolishly.

"I do see," Philip Ludlow answered evenly. That was all.

But Vaughn was annoyed. Neil and that fellow! The idea! She didn't really understand Philip Ludlow half the time. "Well," she said at length, "I suppose you can do that in the country, grow your own food and live on very little. In New York, with competition so keen, we have to be on our toes all the time or someone will snatch our bread and butter away from under our noses."

He seemed unimpressed by all this. Business was evidently a thing with which he had had no contact. It was some time before he spoke. He sat looking into the fire, obviously engaged with his thoughts.

"What Bart really hopes for," he told Vaughn then, "is to start a little worker-owned factory with those boys—some undertaking in which they can share the responsibility and the profits, make decisions themselves, be morally accountable for everything that goes on. It's the one type of organization he believes in."

"But that wouldn't work!" Vaughn insisted. "It's a nice idea, but it simply wouldn't work."

"Maybe not," Philip Ludlow replied in a strained voice. He looked worried too.

Vaughn was no longer able to conceal her curiosity. She had to know what the man did. A person with these peculiar ideas. "Do you farm?" she asked.

He laughed and said: "My little garden couldn't be called a farm by any stretch of the imagination, even," he added, giving her a mischievous look, "if you were writing an advertisement about it. But by working in the late afternoon, I do manage to keep Agatha supplied all season. She puts stuff away in the freezer and——"

"What *do* you do?" Vaughn blurted out.

Her curiosity seemed to surprise him. "I go to business," he said, as if he assumed she'd known this even before she wrote.

Business! Vaughn couldn't have been more startled.

"But how"—she began—"what I mean is—all you've been saying about Bart Brown is—well, visionary. If you're in business, you must see it's something one could never make go."

"I'm not sure that we are what you call 'making it go,'" he answered gravely. "But we haven't lost hope."

Was this his own business he was talking about now? Heavens above!

"You!" she exclaimed. She didn't care what happened to that Bart person, but Philip Ludlow——

"Don't you think," he asked, turning to her as they approached Mary Lancashire's house, "that everyone ought, as far as possible, to choose work in which he can be morally responsible for his actions? That's hard," he went on, without waiting for her answer, "in a large concern or factory, where he works on a part and sometimes doesn't even know what the finished product is going to be, to whom it will be sold, for what purpose, at what profit. It is hard."

"It's impossible," Vaughn broke in.

"No," Philip Ludlow answered with firmness surprising in one so gentle, "not impossible, merely a new departure. It's up to us who are engaged in business to share the management as well as the profits with those who share the labor. We can only hope to achieve peace with our neighbors and our own consciences if we all know exactly what we're about."

Vaughn was flabbergasted. What kind of little business could this be, for goodness' sake? "But what is it you do?" she asked again.

He turned to her with obvious surprise. "Haven't you ever heard of us down in New York?" he asked shyly, "Kendal Radio? We do pride ourselves on more than a local reputation."

"Kendal Radio! Of course I've heard of that. You mean you——" She didn't try to hide her astonishment.

"I and a group of associates," he answered. "It's worker-owned."

5.   Once, years ago, on a cruise to Bermuda, Vaughn met an English boy with whom she hit it off perfectly. He had a girl in London, and Vaughn was getting engaged to Denny at the time, so they both knew there was no future in it, but all day long they sat on deck, looking across the sea to the horizon and telling each other things—things they wouldn't have shared with people they were close to at home. Just because they knew they'd never meet again after the trip, they plunged into this friendship, momentary but more intense than if they'd had a month of dates ashore.

Vaughn didn't remember much. She'd forgotten about it long ago. But the speed with which she and Philip Ludlow were being drawn together over the week end made her suddenly think, after all these years, of that boy on the cruise.

She wasn't surprised to find that she was invited to supper again. Convention seemed to demand that she hesitate before accepting, but it would only have been a pose, and Philip Ludlow would have seen through it. No use pretending Vaughn wasn't eager to be in his company, and she was sure he'd have been disappointed if she declined. Maybe he had that cruise feeling, too, knowing they would never meet again.

They spoke little during the meal. Being out in the air all day had made Vaughn healthily tired. Her host seemed content, too, to be quiet. They were old friends now, under no compulsion to be entertaining.

Kendal Radio, Vaughn thought, taking a second helping of johnnycake. So that's what he does.

She never would have guessed he was in business. How did he make out, with his queer notions, competing against larger firms? There was something she'd heard about Kendal Radio. Something—she couldn't remember.

When, well fed and at ease, they were in the parlor again, seated before the fire, Philip Ludlow began to talk. What he said showed that he'd been thinking about Vaughn.

"I hope," he told her, "that our Underground Railroad station came up to your expectation. You traveled a long way to see it."

"Well," Vaughn answered slowly, "there's nothing very glamorous about an old hole." She had taken the same low chair beside the fireplace which she had had last night, and she was feeling at home in it, as if she'd sat there many times before.

"Still," she went on, gazing thoughtfully into the fire, "that's just what the copy writer's job consists of—making dull, uninteresting matter sound romantic, attractive, irresistible; praising products to the sky which we wouldn't dream of having truck with ourselves. We do a lot of that." She laughed.

But Philip Ludlow didn't seem to see the joke.

"I don't know what I'd expected, really," Vaughn went on, serious again. "More romance, I guess. The fact is, that Underground Railroad business was nothing but bootlegging. Wasn't it?"

Philip Ludlow looked a little stunned. "It depends," he answered gravely, "on your point of view."

Vaughn shifted in her chair and fumbled for a cigarette. She wasn't quite hitting it off with the man now. She mustn't be flip like that again. Maybe he had less sense of humor than she thought.

48

As for what he was driving at—it was a mystery to her. They were talking past each other.

She tried to think of something that would get them on the track again. It was no longer necessary to impress him. He'd done ten times more for her than she'd hoped for when she came, and this had no connection with business. She simply wanted to understand him.

"Philip Ludlow," she asked, leaning forward a little, "did those Quakers really believe it was right to break the law like that?"

"Quakers never believed it right to break the law," he answered emphatically. "Only, when forced to make a choice, they have always tried to obey God rather than men."

It was hard to argue with a person who talked this way. "How did they know they were obeying God, as you call it?" Vaughn asked. "I mean—if every individual were to think he knows better than the lawmakers——"

"Friends are convinced that God's will is directly revealed through the inner light," he answered simply. "When a man believes brutality is contrary to the will of God, he must try to prevent it, even if it is sanctioned by law."

Vaughn studied Philip Ludlow's face. It was a long time since she'd heard anyone speak about God. Her friends, the people in the office, might have some private belief, but nobody ever spoke of it.

There was nothing sanctimonious about him; it wasn't as if he were trying to convince her. A little hesitation even slowed his speech, so that Vaughn guessed he wasn't repeating some lesson learned long ago, but arguing the issue with himself on the basis of his faith.

Vaughn wondered, watching him, what it was like to be that way—so simple and trusting, yet, at the same time, hardy. For the lines about his mouth showed he must have received some blows. He'd done tough things too. As a young man just out of college, he'd told Vaughn when they were driving back from the farm, he'd shipped in the Merchant Marine in order to sail around the world. Got his seaman's ticket, too, he'd proudly added.

49

No, Vaughn thought, looking at him, there was nothing soft about this man. He was just nice.

He got up to put a log on the fire. "Would you like to see my grandmother's dolls?" he asked over his shoulder.

His grandmother's dolls! The question struck Vaughn as funny. The Merchant Marine, and now his grandmother's dolls!

But when he led her to an old sea chest standing under the window in the dining room and opened the lid, her amusement turned to appreciation. For there lay a row of the most beautifully carved little wooden figures, men and women dressed in gray.

"Grandmother made them," Philip Ludlow explained, holding up a lady in a long dress, bonnet, and shawl, "for Mother and my aunts. Naturally they're all what we call 'plain' Friends. That was the only sort of doll those little girls could play with. Isn't this one nice?" he asked, picking up a tiny gentleman. "That's John Woolman."

"The clever little beaver hat!" Vaughn exclaimed, as he laid the doll in her hand.

"Yes. And notice the Quaker coat. See, it has no collar. Friends wouldn't wear them. These are Lucretia Mott and Elizabeth Fry, I believe, and here's William Penn."

Vaughn looked at the little figures with genuine pleasure. "Susan would love them," she told Philip Ludlow, smiling up at him. "She's too old for dolls, of course, but miniature things—she has a whole collection. And these are so perfect—the beautifully carved hands and faces, the tiny bonnet strings." Delighted, Vaughn handled the dolls a long time before giving them back and watching Philip Ludlow put them away in the chest.

With dreamy reluctance he shut the lid. "She was a beautiful woman, my mother," he said thoughtfully, less as though he were talking to Vaughn than to himself.

"What did she look like?"

Vaughn was curious. She'd wondered once before this evening what type of beauty this man admired.

"It was her spirit," he said gently, "I was referring to."

The clock in the hall struck eleven. Vaughn couldn't believe it was that late.

"I must go," she said regretfully.

Philip Ludlow followed her out of the dining room.

Glancing at herself in the hall mirror, Vaughn noticed that her mouth needed doing and reached in her bag for her lipstick, but changed her mind and let it go.

This was the moment to thank her host. After tonight she wouldn't see him again. Standing in the hall, fussing with her jacket and purse, Vaughn tried to think of something to say which would show she appreciated his friendliness as well as the chance he'd given her to succeed in her work.

But her mind was blank. She felt that sting of the eyeballs, which was the closest she ever came to tears. She, Vaughn Hill, the least sentimental of persons—how could she possibly feel this way, saying good-by to someone she'd only just met?

He's a dear, she thought, and I'll never see him again.

"I wish," she said aloud, looking down at her purse, opening and closing the catch, "this weren't such a little job, already finished. It would be nice to have something to come back here for some time."

"Maybe you will have," he answered. His tone sounded almost as if he hoped so.

Vaughn shook her head. "Not in Kendal," she exclaimed, laughing. The ridiculous idea had restored her composure, and she looked up at him. "Mine's all inside work, you see. This was just an idea I happened to get."

"And a good one," he commented chivalrously.

"Thank you," Vaughn said, adding with sincere cordiality, "If you're ever in the city, be sure to stop in at the agency. Mr. Hamilton, my boss, would be thrilled to meet you. This layout is going to be a big thing for our firm."

Philip Ludlow smiled but said nothing. It was only a polite smile, Vaughn decided. He would never come.

They hardly spoke as he escorted her back to Mary Lancashire's for the last time. Only, as he helped her out of the car and they stood in the lighted doorway, he looked at her as he'd done yesterday at the depot, smiling again with that warmth and gentleness which made Vaughn think of little feelers reaching toward her, so that her eyeballs began once more to sting.

"I'll come for you in the morning," he said, as Vaughn held out her hand for the final good-by. "Meeting's at eleven."

"But I'm leaving!" Vaughn cried. It hadn't occurred to her that he'd ask this.

He didn't press her. "Meeting breaks promptly at noon and your train doesn't go till twelve-fifty," was all he said. Yet he stood in the doorway, waiting almost humbly, she thought, for her acceptance.

Again she felt the welcoming warmth that had surprised her since the minute she came. He would share even this. Nevertheless, she was panicky. Quaker Meeting—men and women on opposite sides of the room, she thought she remembered hearing. Did they really quake? Their language was different. She wouldn't understand. He had said they didn't have a minister. How would she know what to do?

Yet while she stood weighing her fears, trying to put down her distaste, her lips had already given an answer. "I'll come," she said. And recalling the self-pity which had overtaken her in the train, when she pictured herself forlorn all week end, she felt a rush of gratitude for the unwanted invitation. "Thank you," she added, looking at her new friend happily.

Then, when he was gone, Vaughn realized with a bang what she'd let herself in for. It wasn't honest, she thought, to attend a religious service if one had no faith. She was dying to run after him down the dark street and take it all back. Why had she promised?

But the way he'd looked, waiting for her to accept—— She turned slowly and entered Mary Lancashire's front hall.

Going up the stairs, standing in the white room, she remembered the little Meetinghouse Philip Ludlow had pointed out as they drove by. It was the plainest building she thought she'd ever seen, its austere front relieved only by a wide door and tall, color-less windows.

Well, she might as well be in church as here in this room, Vaughn supposed, getting into bed and turning out the light. But to join in a service she didn't believe in, to repeat prayers with doubt and reservations drying up the words in her mouth—she'd done with all that long ago.

It had broken her mother's heart at the time. That's what her mother had said. But suddenly Vaughn hadn't been willing any longer to go to church. There was no reason, at least none that she could furnish then, and she hadn't thought about it since. There were other "notions," as her mother called them, little things, yet they split Vaughn further and further from her parents. She was crazy to go out with boys, but they felt she was too young. Worried, they sent her to boarding school, where there was daily chapel and where she almost died of homesickness.

She'd got over it finally, but even now, after twenty years, just because she was lying in this strange bed without Denny, Vaughn could feel the bitter surge of aloneness that used to strangle her in her dormitory cot. The queer thing was, once she got over her home-sickness, she didn't want to go home any more. College, New York, her first job—she went back less and less.

And then Denny. Those wonderful dates they'd had, the wed-ding, their first apartment—that funny little place in the Village which she'd managed to fix up quite attractively with Kemtone and monk's cloth. It was cramped after Neil came. They always had to climb around his bathinette to get into the tub. When it turned out, six months later, that Susan was on the way, they finally moved.

Those few years on Ninety-first Street were nice. Vaughn wheeled the children to Central Park. Nobody believed there'd really be war. Suddenly Pearl Harbor. Denny enlisted and went off for basic training. They were never so happy again.

Vaughn sighed and turned over.

It was funny. She could see herself as if someone else were lying here, in Mary Lancashire's brass bedstead—an outside observer—and the real Vaughn was at home, curled up beside Denny.

But even that Vaughn at home wasn't a single person. There were two of them, acting at the same moment in opposite ways. Sometimes, when her body was loving Denny, at the very moment when he was seeking her, her mind would be off somewhere else, in the agency, usually. Then, when she really intended to be separate from him, like after a spat—when she turned her face away and wouldn't talk to him—if he wanted her then, chances were she'd be so overwhelmed by love that she'd remember that night weeks later.

Most of the time, though, she and Denny weren't so intense.

Ever since he got back from overseas, he'd been terribly remote. He loved her just as much, she was sure, but he was enclosed in a world of his own and showed no desire to let her in.

When you began to think about it, though, wasn't there something almost immoral about two people sharing a bed but not their thoughts?

Now that she was looking at it this way, as an outsider, Vaughn suddenly saw that maybe she, also, was too preoccupied. But wasn't that a natural reaction to Denny's aloofness? He left her alone even when he was with her. And how else could she have done her work so successfully? Probably some people closed a door in their minds at five o'clock. They simply couldn't have as much motivation as she had—getting ahead for the sake of a husband who wasn't very secure.

How still it was here, when one was used to New York. Vaughn stayed awake a long time, looking at the stars. One never really saw them in the city. You wouldn't think they were bodies swimming in the universe. They seemed more like pinholes in a curtain stretched across blinding brightness.

A new wishfulness slowly expanded in Vaughn as she lay there, her eyes closed—not physical longing, but an undefined, pressing desire to achieve, to make her life count, to give the children something she'd missed, to get along better with Denny.

Who knows? she thought, opening her eyes to look out at the

54

holes of light in the dark curtain, then shutting them again. There might really be something back there. Scientists don't know. Something . . .

If one could tear away the curtain.

She felt strangely peaceful.

Lying quietly on her side, gazing at the trees outlined against the moonlit sky, she seemed like a child, who always slept alone like this, who stood at the very beginning of life, instead of nearly halfway through, at best. It was as if she could really start now, forget her worries, avoid her mistakes, begin all over again, making herself more of a person, much more of a person.

She wouldn't toss tonight. She felt reassured by the sense of approaching sleep. That plain little Meetinghouse. The wide door had been shut when they drove past, Vaughn remembered, but tomorrow at eleven it would be open, and she would enter with Philip Ludlow.

6. It wasn't like any church she'd ever seen or heard of; it was, she thought, sitting in it and looking around at the bareness, just nothing. There wasn't even a flower.

From the second Vaughn sat down, even before that—from the second she passed through the wide door, she was aware only of a heavy stillness. Philip Ludlow had ceased to notice her. As they entered the building a change came over him, a withdrawal which left his face almost expressionless.

He led her to the front bench and sat down beside her, bowing his head. She'd been wrong in thinking that men and women would sit apart. A young man had taken the place on her left. He was staring into space, very still. All along their row and in the facing ones people seemed gripped by this strange intentness.

The Mansfields were here. So was Jeanie and that peculiar character who cared more for playing with boys than doing a man's

55

job. Their little girl sat between them, looking at a picture book. Mary Lancashire was in the next row, surrounded by her brood.

There were old men, obviously farmers; women with house-worked hands lying quietly in their lap; high school kids whose faces, less withdrawn, showed that they were wrestling with something.

And there was Vaughn Hill of Hamilton Company, unwillingly stuck in the middle of this strange silence.

Tucking a half dollar into her glove so she wouldn't be embarrassed rummaging during the collection, she had stepped out into the bright tranquillity of the Kendal Sunday with Philip Ludlow—First day, he called it. And this seemed particularly apt, since the early spring freshness and the clarity of the sky gave the day a feeling of firstness, of new beginning, which Vaughn sensed as soon as she stood in the sunshine.

Philip Ludlow was gay, confiding to Vaughn that he always suffered from spring fever, just as though he were still a youngster.

"The sea——" he began, but Vaughn interrupted him.

Suddenly the enormity of what she was doing had hit her again, and she stood still. She had meant to be suave, to go through with this graciously, as a politeness due a host who had entertained her so warmly. Then all her poise forsook her. She wasn't a cool, competent representative of Hamilton Company working on a layout, she was little Mary Vaughn Stevenson of East Bolton, Illinois, who suddenly knew she didn't want to go to church, and though she was ashamed of losing her grip and acting like a little girl, she simply couldn't go on.

"I—I—you shouldn't be taking me," she burst out, feeling her throat tighten as she spoke. "There just isn't anything in me of what you call——" She couldn't finish.

He was immediately grave, standing still with her, clearly waiting for Vaughn to decide whether she wished to go back. She knew without his saying so that if she did, it would be all right.

"There's something of God in everyone," he said, looking thoughtfully at the pavement.

What he said wasn't the thing that decided Vaughn to walk on. It was merely that the panic had left her.

"For some of us," he observed, accompanying her again, "it's easier to realize this truth in quiet waiting together." He pointed up to the sea gulls flying over the river, and his gravity was gone. "They follow the tide to Kendal," he explained.

She had realized then, when they were still walking up the street, and now, sitting in the Meetinghouse, she was even more certain, that his faith wasn't something static, but that he was constantly working to renew it. The thought made her feel better.

Yet when she found herself stuck inside this place, she wished it would at least offer her something beautiful to look at or some music, now that she had come. It was terrible just sitting still with nothing to see or hear, and she couldn't keep from fidgeting.

Vaughn wondered when, in the name of reason, the thing was going to begin. Her watch said eleven-twenty. They hadn't even sung a hymn yet. Was this what was meant by "quiet waiting together"? Waiting for what? It wasn't really church at all.

After a long while people shifted in their seats a trifle, and the little girl leaned her head against her mother. Otherwise, nothing happened. Outside, a train whistled far away, but in the Meetinghouse there was only this uncanny silence. Even the children were still.

Suddenly Vaughn felt that if someone didn't move soon or say something, she'd scream. She'd been afraid to come lest she be required to confess words she didn't believe, but this was worse than saying things. She was being forced to listen to a voice within. There was nothing else to listen to.

I don't want to, she cried to herself. There's enough on my mind already. Denny, Neil, the office . . .

Fighting the pressure of the silence, she tried to concentrate on the work that had brought her to Kendal. At least, then, the hour wouldn't be wasted. She had all the facts now that she needed for a first-rate layout, thanks to Philip Ludlow. He'd been wonderful to her. Vaughn moved her head a little and stole a look at him from under her lashes, but quickly turned away, for his very soul showed in his face. It was like spying on a naked person to observe him now.

Oddly embarrassed, Vaughn pushed her thoughts back to the layout. She could go home and write it this evening. Not that the hole had inspired her, but then she'd known all along that it wasn't necessary to see it, except for the prestige it would give her with the railroad. Details would occur to her on the train this afternoon. Tomorrow in staff conference she'd lay the preliminary sketch before Ham.

Ham Hamilton. He ought to come here, Vaughn said to herself.

The thought struck her as funny, for she was thinking of the way Ham was always running around the office holding his head with both hands because he couldn't think. "If I could just think," he'd wail desperately.

This was certainly the place for Ham.

"Faith is the substance of things hoped for——"

Vaughn jumped. The voice that spoke these words came from behind her somewhere. The unexpectedness of it and the comical picture of Ham Hamilton in Friends' Meeting set off a nervous giggle Vaughn was powerless to control.

Horrified, she put one hand to her mouth, squeezing the half dollar in the other and waiting for the laugh to issue from her into the awful stillness. But only a small noise, like a well-bred burp, got past her fist. She sank back, weary with relief.

"Faith is the substance of things hoped for," the speaker was saying quietly, "the evidence of things not seen."

It sounded like the old gentleman from the homestead. Curious, Vaughn began to turn around, but the deep concentration on the face of the young man on her left rebuked her, and she looked into her lap again. She listened, but the voice had ceased.

Things hoped for. Vaughn could think of so many: the railroad account, possibly a raise, a good vacation this summer. She and Denny hadn't had a real one in years.

58

The old gentleman's voice jolted Vaughn back from her dream.

"The evidence of things not seen is what brings us here," he said slowly, thoughtfully, "into the gathered meeting. It's God's will which we try to understand when we center down."

This didn't sound like preaching, rather it was as if the old man were confiding to a few intimate friends an idea that had just occurred to him.

"The substance of things hoped for together is greater than what each of us seeks for himself," Edmund Mansfield declared. "We are joined in trying to grasp our real function and leaving here are"—he hesitated, as if searching for words which could express a sentiment so deeply felt—"once more turned toward that way of life which alone can make us satisfied with ourselves."

Only the last words had much meaning for Vaughn. The rest seemed difficult to grasp. But the phrase, "That way of life which alone can make us satisfied with ourselves."

What is that way of life? I'd like to know, Vaughn thought.

She was far from satisfied with herself. Forced to sit here quietly, she realized how she was raring to go, get on with things, improve her position, her appearance.

But of course the old man was talking about a more high-minded kind of self.

I'm not satisfied with that, either, Vaughn admitted.

Still, how was just sitting here going to change anything? One had to get into action.

She glanced secretly again at Philip Ludlow. His soul still showed. But Vaughn didn't turn away. She wanted to study this person who had said, "There is something of God in everyone." Now that the usual gaiety wasn't lighting up his face, it looked drawn. The folds around his mouth seemed pressed in more by sorrow than laughter.

Watching him, Vaughn saw that in his case, at least, what he had said was true. There was undoubtedly something special about Philip Ludlow, and even if you weren't in the habit of talking that way yourself, you might as well call it something of God as anything else.

Vaughn tried to think of God, too, but the picture which came to her mind was a childish picture of a capricious old man with whiskers, sitting on top of the universe. This was the way He had appeared to her when she was a little girl, and this was the concept she'd revolted against when she grew up. Nothing of an adult nature had come to take its place.

She didn't want Neil and Susan to be disillusioned like that. Better not to have any religion to start with, she'd often said to Denny, than to discover with shame, as you were growing up, that all you held sacred was nothing but a bundle of childish ideas. She had had a pretty unhappy time about this in her teens.

No, she couldn't pray. She couldn't even think about God. And as for Jesus——

Here in this neck of the woods a man might still be able to believe in turning the other cheek or loving one's enemies. That was only because a person like Philip Ludlow didn't know. If he'd been in the war, if he'd heard the stories Denny's buddies told—well, nothing was more impossible than to love those enemies. Everybody wanted to be a good Christian, naturally, but you couldn't take every word literally, or you'd be wiped out. Forgive them, yes. She wasn't against rearming Germany, if that would mean security. But love—*love*. Even if you tried and tried . . .

Someone on the bench opposite cleared his throat. Looking up, Vaughn saw that a younger man had got to his feet and was rubbing his hand nervously along the back of the bench before him as he began to speak.

" 'Give over thine own willing, give over thine own running, give over thine own desiring to know or be anything,' " he said, and it sounded as if he were reciting poetry. " 'Sink down to the seed which God grows in thy heart and let that be in thee, and grow in thee, and breathe in thee, and act in thee.' "

Vaughn felt so moved by these words, not their meaning, but the measured cadences, the simple phrasing, that she didn't even notice the speaker.

"'And thou shalt find,'" the hushed voice went on, "'that the Lord knows that and loves and owns that, and will lead it to the inheritance of life, which is His portion.'"

No, Vaughn thought, as the speaker took his seat again and everywhere around her heads were bowed, the words had no meaning for her, but the sound was beautiful.

She settled down into the silence. It had become more comfortable, now that she was used to it a little. She was even thankful that no one else said anything, because she had a lot to think about.

If you could make contact with God alone, as these people seemed to think, without help from anyone, without spoken words or ceremony, couldn't you maybe figure out all religion for yourself? Start from scratch. If God was really in everyone, so near . . .

It was a very unusual idea, and Vaughn wanted to think about it, but since those last words were spoken, she seemed to feel an undercurrent in the silence, which made it hard to think. It wasn't like the quiet in a library, where everyone could concentrate by himself. There was something general in the silence that seemed to draw her out of her private mind into a larger one.

She tried at first to hold on to herself, to resist, but the current was becoming too strong for her. Slowly she gave up, let herself go, carried along on the stream of silence.

She'd been managing things for so many years now, had so much on her shoulders, it was a relief to let go this way, to be the one who was managed, carried along, her will absorbed into a stronger will. She leaned back and shut her eyes, overwhelmed with the delight of not struggling, of surrendering to a force she didn't even try to understand.

It was for only a moment that she felt this wonderful, mysterious sense of being cared for. A church bell striking twelve somewhere in town brought her back to the world. But as the moment passed, she turned instinctively to Philip Ludlow, because she was glad now that he'd asked her to come.

61

Grateful, she wanted to reach out and touch his hand, to let him know, so that she was startled and a little confused when, the very same second, he turned and actually did extend his hand to her.

As Vaughn looked into his face, she noticed that the sorrowful folds had smoothed into peacefulness, that with the smile which he now gave her the gaiety was slowly coming back into his eyes.

But as he grasped her hand in his, Vaughn felt a shock of horror, for something very hard pressed between them. The blood rushed hotly to her face; she was still clutching the half dollar.

Part 2

1. "How was it?"

Denny bent to kiss her and took the overnight case from her hand.

"Very nice."

Glancing at him quickly, Vaughn hurried along by his side.

He was wearing his old mustard-colored Harris tweed and the green tie she'd always hated, though, of course, she'd never told him so, and his topcoat still had that frayed buttonhole she kept resolving to mend when they were out and forgot about at home.

Funny, she thought, how one never really sees one's husband till one's been away, even just for a week end. I didn't know he's so thin.

His face had lighted with happiness the minute he'd caught sight of her coming up the ramp, yet as soon as he got used to being with her again, it relaxed into its usual inscrutability.

Vaughn stayed close to Denny. She never could be in this vaulted station without feeling the terror which had attacked her the first time, when she arrived from the West to hunt for a job—the sensation of being in the stomach of a perfectly enormous whale.

But a man trying to make a train dashed between them. When the man had passed, Denny took Vaughn's arm.

"Kendal isn't such deep country as we thought," she told him, as they squeezed through the crowd coming down the wide staircase and pushed their way up. "What I mean, it's really a little town. Manufacturing. But the hiding place is on a farm. Some old people live there."

"Did they treat you all right?" he inquired, turning to her. "Not snooty or anything?"

So he'd worried.

"Denny, they were wonderful. I might have been a friend down for the week end. They didn't ask me whether I'd stay to lunch—just took it for granted. And Philip Ludlow—that's the man I wrote to for permission to see the place, remember?—he had me to dinner. In fact," she added, "I spent both evenings at his house."

"And you were so afraid!" Denny exclaimed, grinning. "Know how you said when people have some historical gem in the family, they won't let anyone come near it?"

Vaughn laughed. "It wasn't a bit that way," she said.

"What's the hiding place like?" he asked.

"Well," she admitted, hesitating, "well, it's—just a hole." Seeing Denny raise his eyebrows, she dutifully repeated Philip Ludlow's dimensions, as if she hoped thereby to endow the hiding place with more significance. "Six by six by twelve."

"Think you can make something out of it?"

It struck Vaughn all at once that she'd never even thought about the object of her visit on the way home, though Friday, when she left, it had seemed the most important thing in life.

Now, questioned by Denny, she realized that her work had slipped her mind and she had no answer for him. Riding back in the train, she'd only been thinking of the man she'd met over the week end, aware not only of an unaccountable excitement, but of other vague, extraneous emotions.

While Denny drew her forward, she had a sudden desire to stand still, right in the station, and recall details before they became blurred: Philip Ludlow's little old house the way she'd seen it that first evening, set against the twilight, with a lantern shining brightly at the door, and the quiet room where she'd sat with him talking by the fire.

If I could just catch hold of each thing, she thought.

Once surrounded by the children, geared into her routine, she'd forget. And she wanted to remember.

But Denny was striding ahead.

Not in the middle of Grand Central, Vaughn said to herself sternly, as if she were talking to Susan or Neil, and her unwilling feet went on.

In the street she tried to come back to Denny. "Children all right?" she asked. It was only to make conversation. If there'd been trouble he'd have said so.

"They're at the movies," he answered. He wasn't thinking about

Vaughn any more. The way he looked now, she knew he didn't care to talk.

It was always like that, once they'd skimmed over the surface of their experiences. Vaughn felt a little hurt. She wanted to tell Denny many things—about the Friends' Meeting she'd been taken to this morning. But he wouldn't have understood. And about Philip Ludlow, how strange it had been to find someone like that in Kendal, someone who'd made her feel . . .

They sat like strangers in the bus. Denny stared past Vaughn, looking out of the window with, Vaughn was sure, unseeing eyes.

To her, Fifth Avenue had the drained-off appearance of Sunday evening—like a ghost town, with hardly a soul. Nevertheless, the stores were alluring. As the bus stopped for a red light Vaughn noticed a very handsome suit in Bonwit's window. Navy with accents of brick red. The wide collar and fluid lines would do a lot for her. A smallish person needs important clothes, especially in business.

"See that?" she asked quickly, nudging Denny.

He was so far away in thought that by the time he returned to her, the light had changed and the bus was already several blocks uptown.

"What?"

"Never mind."

Obviously relieved, Denny settled back into himself again. Vaughn looked out along the Avenue, but what she saw now was in Kendal.

There was a long copper pan filled with pots of begonias on the wide sill above the window seat. His hobby, Philip Ludlow had explained, giving the name of each variety. Vaughn couldn't remember the names, only the affection with which he spoke them and the enthusiasm in his face as he turned toward her, holding up a blossom-covered plant for her to see.

Denny shifted his position but said nothing, and Vaughn didn't turn.

She was thinking of the genial, almost loving way Philip Ludlow had looked down at her when she held out her hand in farewell, as the train was coming into Kendal, and the peculiar thing he'd said when she thanked him.

"It was nice of you to entertain me," she told him, "a stranger——"

"Some have entertained angels," he answered, laughing, "unawares."

Angels, she thought, as she and Denny walked home from the bus. What a strange thing to say. And again, as they were going up in the elevator of their house, the word echoed. *Angels*—he wasn't referring to her, was he?

Denny pulled out his key and let Vaughn into the apartment. Even her living room she saw, as she'd seen Denny in that first moment of meeting, with new eyes. The squared-off lines of the modern sofa didn't please her any longer, and she wondered how she could have chosen that big peony pattern for the drapes. The room looked smart and new, the way she'd intended it when she furnished, but it lacked the kindliness of Philip Ludlow's rather shabby little parlor.

Vaughn went around noticing everything. She was a bit blue. "I hate not finding the children when I come home," she told Denny.

"Guess they were lonely," he observed.

As she was putting her things away, Vaughn held the hat up for an instant and stared at it dreamily. "Philip Ludlow liked the fruit on my hat," she reported to Denny. "He said the little bananas reminded him of the plantains he used to have for breakfast in Bali."

"*Bali?*"

"He was in the merchant marine."

"Oh. What's he do now?"

"Kendal Radio. Did you realize," she asked eagerly, "that that's in Kendal? Know anything about it?"

She looked at him anxiously, but Denny shook his head.

"I never would have believed," Vaughn exclaimed, "that he's in business. He's such a terribly idealistic old gentleman—visionary, really, with the most beautiful manners—you know, old-fashioned courtesy. It made me feel like a *grande dame*."

Denny stared at Vaughn in obvious amazement.

"I liked it, Denny," she insisted. "Nobody ever treats me that way here, except you, of course. But at the office——"

"You don't want them to," Denny broke in. "You're always telling me——"

"I know," Vaughn answered, before he could finish. She was smiling. "I'd forgotten how nice it is to be made to feel charming."

Denny said nothing for a minute. Suddenly he asked, "Isn't there any Mrs. Ludlow?"

"She died last year."

Vaughn changed into her negligee and sat down at the dressing table to begin her ritual.

In that aimless way of his, accomplishing nothing, Denny fussed around the room. Now he came and stood behind Vaughn, jiggling the coins in his trouser pocket. His hair was growing thin. Maybe the new tonic wasn't right for it. And his cheekbones were showing more and more.

He has a nice face, though, Vaughn thought. If only——

Suddenly their eyes met in the mirror. Vaughn smiled, but Denny didn't respond. He was preoccupied.

"For an elderly gentleman, old-fashioned and all," he remarked presently, watching her tie up her hair in the azure veil, "this guy got you on a first-name basis pretty fast, didn't he?"

"You don't understand," Vaughn said quickly, rubbing cream into her face. "He's a Quaker. Seems Quakers don't believe in handles. Saying the whole name's formal. He explained it to me."

Denny heaved a puzzled sigh. "That thing around your head makes you look like a madonna," he remarked then, adding, as he went into the living room, "Guy sounds goofy to me."

Like a madonna—well! It was a long time since Denny'd said anything like that. Still, Vaughn had been right, absolutely right, thinking he wouldn't understand. After all, how could he? She

69

didn't blame him. She wouldn't have taken anything about Kendal seriously herself, if it hadn't been for Philip Ludlow.

Giving her face its final inspection, she got up and joined Denny.

"I hope there's something for supper," she murmured.

She was peering into the virtually empty refrigerator when the children came home.

"Hi," they said, seeing her, "hi," as casually as if she'd been here when they left, but Vaughn knew there was a lot of meaning behind the senseless syllable.

She was so happy seeing them. How could she ever have gone away?

Neil stayed just inside the door, a little shy, even with his mother. Susan hung on Vaughn's arm, her bright hair falling back in a mass as she tilted her head to speak, her face lighting with what she had to say even before she opened her mouth. There was something about the child—an extraordinary charm. It had come out only lately, as if there were a seedling in her soul, a hidden unfolding quite apart from her dawning puberty. She had a life of her own, secret imaginings, which she shared with no one, at least not with Vaughn.

"What did you do while I was gone?" Vaughn asked.

"Went to church," Susan said hesitantly, "with Angela." It was almost a confession.

To church, with Angela? Vaughn couldn't go away for a week end without Susan's trying some adventure. Last time it was the Bowery. That had upset Vaughn so that she'd punished the child severely. Now it was church. Couldn't punish her for that. After all, hadn't Vaughn——

"So did I," she told her.

"You!" Susan exclaimed.

"Yes, I. Why not? You make your mother sound like a heathen. I went to Quaker Meeting.'

"Wasn't it beautiful?"

"No. Well, in a way, yes."

70

"It gave me goose-pimples," Susan whispered, letting Vaughn's arm go. She went to her room and turned on the radio.

Her every movement is beautiful, Vaughn thought, watching the child as she walked out of the kitchen. I wish I knew what made her go with Angela.

Neil stayed, saying nothing, just, it seemed, lapping up his mother's presence.

"What'll we have for supper?" she asked him, looking into the discouraging refrigerator again. "Waffles? Huh?" Then, feeling the day's fatigue, she added, "They're so much bother."

"Oh, let's just have cereal and a hunk of bread," Neil said.

"Well," Vaughn decided, "I'll make some peanut-butter sandwiches, anyway. Hand me the jar."

When he'd given it to her, he stayed close, trying to catch her eye. "Pop Miller called up yesterday," he told her in a strangled tone. "Dad said to wait till you got home to decide whether I'm going back." He turned to her with big, hopeful eyes, but they weren't really trusting. It was a last-ditch glance.

"There's nothing to decide," Vaughn said, her voice rising. "Now, look, Neil"—she was angry at him for making it difficult—"of course you're going back. Boy your age belongs in camp, doing things with other fellows——"

"I've been there. I've done them. Why do I have to keep on? I don't want to be an animal."

"An animal?"

"You know—last year I was a muskrat. This year they might let me be a beaver—maybe. And I'd have to work for my letter all summer. I want to live."

She turned to him in exasperation, her mouth tense, but then she relaxed, for she saw the humor of what the child was saying. "*Live,*" she repeated. "You don't know what you're talking about."

He seemed to think he'd gained an advantage. "Yes, I do, Mom," he insisted. In his excitement his voice wavered between falsetto and bass. "Come a nice hot day I want to be able to paddle up the creek."

"But isn't that just what you do do at camp?" Vaughn asked, surprised.

"First couple of weeks, yes. Then we have to start practicing for the track meet and the play and learning those songs for Parents' Day, and we never have time to do anything we want."

His eyes pleaded with Vaughn. But she knew that, whether he liked it or not, camp was the best thing for the boy. Maybe next year they could take a trip.

"Don't let's talk about it any more," she said. "It's all settled. I'll call Mr. Miller tomorrow."

Neil's face and shoulders crumpled.

"I know it's hard to make summer plans so early," Vaughn said soothingly, as she unscrewed the pickles. "One isn't in the mood. But with the first spell of hot weather, you'll——"

"No, I won't," Neil said firmly.

And, remembering other times, Vaughn knew he wouldn't.

2. *Sunday-night supper at the Denis Hills'*, Vaughn said to herself, watching her family eat.

The spread didn't look very filling, but Denny and the children presumably had had a good dinner, and Vaughn was too tired to want much.

Susan sat on the tall stool, dangling her bare legs, dreamily stuffing her mouth. The others wedged themselves around the kitchen table.

It was a pretty scrappy meal, Vaughn admitted to herself, taking a pickle with her fingers and wincing as she put it in her mouth. But if she were writing for a woman's magazine, she could make something of it.

Sunday-night supper at the Denis Hills' is always a festive occasion, she thought, smiling inwardly as she composed. Color photographs: well-groomed, gay young people serving themselves at an elegant buffet supper, which their hostess had tossed off at a moment's notice, merely by spending all of Saturday in the kitchen.

There are special dishes, part of the family tradition, simple but enchanting, which Mrs. Hill whips up in no time.

Neil was helping himself to cereal, his pet brand. Vaughn found it particularly revolting. It was crumbly and always spilled over. He put the box down on the table and patted the cereal into a mixing bowl with his dubious-looking hands. All the nice china they owned, and Neil never ate his cereal out of anything but this old mixing bowl. Would she never civilize him?

The Hills are a typical New York family of the professional—— No, she didn't care for that. They might be typical of thousands of other families, economically, culturally even, but Vaughn didn't intend to be lumped with them. She began again. *The Hills are a——* The suitable adjective failed to suggest itself.

Denis Hill, an up-and-coming research chemist in a—in a—— In a what? You couldn't say it was a soap factory. That would take all the glamour out of the whole article. Household supply house? Maybe it was enough just to say a research chemist.

Vaughn, his wife, is a fabulously successful advertising woman. Enterprise, imagination, a flair for clothes—Vaughn has all these, plus that indispensable something which has made her, in just a few years, one of the leading copy writers in her agency.

Well, she thought, laughing to herself, that really is putting it on thick.

The children were arguing about the top from the cereal box. It was Neil's, but Susan fought till she got it.

Why does he give in to her? Vaughn wondered. He ought to stand up for his rights.

The Hills have two children, she went on, composing again. *Neil, thirteen, is tall and skinny with a broad freckled nose and a smile——* How could she describe it, the way his mouth curled softly, betraying all his gentleness and sweetness, and the look in his eyes that sometimes went with it, a left-out look, which was the reason why Vaughn felt so strongly that he needed to be thrown

73

with boys his age? *Neil is clever with his hands, musical, and passionately interested in boats. Susan at twelve is an accomplished little ballet dancer. She has her mother's small features, her father's fair hair, which she wears cut simply, level with her ears and straight across her eyebrows, like a medieval page.*

The Hills live in a two-hundred-a-month apartment on East Eighty-second Street. Their living room is modern in tone with a few priceless heirlooms.

That took care of Aunt Ethel's highboy and the old sofa they'd had shipped here and reupholstered when Denny's mother died. But she was leaving out the peonies on the drapes.

Sunday nights the Hills enjoy informal, charming little suppers in their rock-maple dining room. Though they may be all by themselves the simplest food is made to look exquisite, served on fine Spode dishes. The old Stevenson candlesticks in the center of the table, brought over from Wales by Vaughn's maternal grandmother . . .

"Children should be taught the social graces early," Vaughn says, looking lovingly at Neil and Susan as they come up for a second helping of soufflé. "That's why, even when we're only family, supping on leftovers, I always insist on a certain formality. Grace and elegance aren't just born," she adds with one of her delightful smiles, "they must be ingrained."

Suddenly it dawned on Vaughn that Susan had for some time been asking her a question, patiently repeating it at intervals. "What else did you do?"

So the child was still thinking of church.

Vaughn tried to remember something that would interest her. "Philip Ludlow," she said—"that's the gentleman who showed me around Kendal, where I was, you know?—he has the most wonderful collection of dolls."

"Gee!"

"Didn't you see anyone but him the whole time?" Denny asked.

"Dozens of people. I told you about the Mansfields. You weren't listening."

74

"I remember," Denny insisted. "Anyone else?"

"The woman I stayed with had five daughters—imagine!"

This seemed to impress Susan even more than the dolls. "Gee!" she repeated, awed.

"She wouldn't let me pay for the room," Vaughn told them. "Just the same, I didn't care for her. The bed had lumps. And, Denny, the whole room was white, every single thing in it, white. They don't even do that in hospitals any more."

Denny smiled, but not very sympathetically.

"Oh," Vaughn recalled, "then there was a fellow who—— Well, I don't know what you'd call it. He just seems to spend his days playing big brother to a bunch of delinquents. I didn't like him, either. Everyone else was nice."

"All Quakers?"

Vaughn nodded. She was surprised at Denny's interest.

They had stacked the dishes and were moving into the living room. Susan and Neil went away to do their homework, having, as usual, left it till Sunday night, though Vaughn had *told* them, the very last thing before she left for Kendal——

Sighing, because she never seemed to get anywhere with the children, she turned on the lamp and took out a foolscap pad.

"How come she wouldn't let you pay for the room?" Denny asked.

Vaughn shrugged. "Oh, I don't know," she answered absently. She was wondering how she would begin the layout. "Look, dear," she said as tactfully as she could, "if I'm to present this at staff conference tomorrow I'll have to work all night, so please don't speak to me now."

Denny was very quiet as he lay down on the sofa and smoked. *The Underground Railroad*, Vaughn wrote boldly at the head of the sheet before her. Then she stopped and fiddled with the pencil.

She knew a lot about it now, yet the few succinct phrases, the arresting catchword which would ensnare the public, eluded her. Denny was still as a mouse. It was Philip Ludlow who kept interfering.

All those little details Vaughn had wanted to recall began crowding back, not things which would help her to write the copy, only about the man personally. She couldn't remember when she'd met anyone she liked so much. Had he liked her also? He'd seemed to. Or was he that way with everybody? Wouldn't he have ushered a runaway slave into his house with the same warmth? But he really did like her. Vaughn was sure.

It was useless to try writing any longer. Maybe tomorrow, at the office—— Vaughn never worked well at home.

Turning in her chair, she saw that Denny was gazing out of the window into the darkness, rather sadly, she thought.

He made her think of Neil, the way the boy had looked in the kitchen. Why was everyone around her dissatisfied, when she was trying so hard to do what was best for everyone?

It couldn't be that Denny——

No, she said to herself, startled. He couldn't—— No, it isn't possible! What made me think such a dreadful thing?

Something bothered him, but he loved her. She was sure he loved her. She did love him so. Coming back after being away always made her realize this more. She loved him. If only he were different.

"Denny," she said suddenly, laying down her pencil.

He turned and looked questioningly at her.

"I wish you'd been along."

Annoyance rushed into his face. "I don't mix in your business affairs," he said coldly. "You know that."

It was unreasonable of him. She felt her tenderness give way to temper.

"Where would we have been when you came back," she asked with rising fury, "if I hadn't gone into business? What would have happened to the children? It took you a long time to settle down in your job."

How rotten to remind him, when he was so touchy about that, anyway. Vaughn wanted to take it all back, to tell him she didn't mean it, but of course it was a fact and he knew it. She got up and started toward him with her arms outstretched, though she was half afraid now that he'd brush her off, he looked so hurt and angry. But before she could reach him, to her surprise she burst into tears.

He jumped up and sprang toward her. "Why, honey," he cried, gathering her in his arms and drawing her down onto the sofa. "What's the matter? Disappointed in Kendal? That's nothing to feel so bad about. Honey, I haven't seen you cry since I went overseas." He held her tightly till the sobs subsided. "What's come over you?" he asked softly.

"I don't know," she said, nestling against him. "I feel like when I went away to boarding school."

He pushed her gently from him far enough to see her face. "How do you mean?" he asked. "Homesick?"

"I guess so." She started to cry again.

"You can't be homesick," he reasoned. "When you've *come* home to me and the children."

"That's how I feel," she answered, sobbing. "I—I miss Kendal."

He laughed at her lovingly. "How can you be homesick for a place you'd never even seen two days ago?"

She clung to him. "I don't know," she answered, wiping her eyes. "It's just that everything seems so wrong with us sometimes, and there I felt something—something I wish we had."

He was immediately serious. "Like what, for instance?"

She didn't know how to explain. "A different world," was all she could say.

Denny looked at her wonderingly. Then he got up and turned off the desk lamp.

"You're tired," he said, drawing her up from the sofa. "Let's go to bed."

Denny was right. Vaughn hadn't realized how exhausted she was till she lay down. The warmth of his body comforted her.

"Don't mind me," she said, blowing her nose. "I didn't sleep much there."

"You know," he said playfully, as if she were one of the children whom he was trying to cheer up, "if you hadn't told me that that man's old enough to be your father, I'd think you'd fallen for him."

She tried to chuckle, to sound amused, but the joke was too feeble. "Sorry I was so mean," she whispered, rubbing her cheek against his shoulder. "I shouldn't have said what I did."

"It's true," Denny answered.

In the dark she couldn't tell whether he still felt hurt. Probably not, because he was soon asleep. But Vaughn stared out at the oatmeal sky above the city for a long time, remembering how clear the stars had been in Kendal, those nights she lay awake.

3. Vaughn was mistaken when she feared that her recollection of Kendal would grow dim, once she was meshed in her New York routine again.

As she stepped into the agency the morning after her return, she hugged to herself the feeling she had had at Philip Ludlow's, the consciousness of an almost forgotten charm. Now, walking past the desks that lined the outer office, some of this charm clung to her as country smells might still be clinging to her clothing. She held her head a little high, remembering how she'd felt in Kendal.

Her boss burst in only a minute later. Rushing for his private sanctum, he gave Vaughn more than his usual greeting. There was a hint of approval in the way Ham stopped to speak with her, an interest she'd never noticed in him before.

"Go to the country?" he asked.

Judging by the Monday-morning sag of his mouth, Ham had had quite a week end himself. That Marilyn was said to drag him around a good deal. The skin beneath his eyes reminded Vaughn of a pricked balloon. He was often that way, but it struck her more today because she was feeling elated herself.

Such a good-looking fellow, too, she thought. It's a shame.

There was a lot to do.

"Don't buzz me for anybody," Vaughn told the telephone girl. "I'm busy till ten, then there's staff conference."

The girl nodded languidly as Vaughn hurried by.

Then Katie Martin blew in and stopped to chat with Vaughn.

Go away and let me work, Vaughn wanted to say, but if there was one thing you learned in business, it was to let your superiors talk when they felt like it.

"Wouldn't you think," Katie said to Vaughn, "there'd be some kind of insurance policy a person could take out so if he should suddenly lose his job—— What I mean is, if you're sick or disabled, you can get compensation and the life insurance companies will waive your premiums, but if you're not sick, just fired——"

"I'd never thought of that," Vaughn answered.

"Neither did I till last Friday."

Katie gave Vaughn her usual wide-mouthed smile as she went on to her own office, but there was a little pucker between her eyes.

Now, what in the world made her think of that? Vaughn wondered. Katie's no worrywart.

Naturally, though, when your husband was dead, like Katie's, you had no security. That would be enough to make a person jittery.

Well, Vaughn thought, I don't have any too much myself. The way Denny acted about getting a job, when he first came back——

Katie'd always been very nice to Vaughn, especially in the beginning, when Vaughn had to get the hang of things in the agency. Ham was always blowing his top, but it was a pleasure to work for Katie.

As soon as she was out of the way, Vaughn sat down at her desk and began jotting down little slogans that popped into her head:

You, too, can escape from slavery by the railroad—take a vacation at the shore or mountains.

Our conductors will serve you with the same devotion as the "conductors" on the Underground Railroad.

Our stations are more comfortable than those on the Underground Railroad.

79

These were corny, but one always began that way, polishing a trite phrase till it took on personality. Still, none of them would do. They lacked a catching quality.

What's more, Vaughn thought, some of it isn't true.

She was a little surprised at herself. After all, a lot of things she wrote weren't true, exactly. She'd never had scruples before.

Throwing the sheet into the wastebasket, she decided to start afresh, and was just beginning to have that explosive feeling, which always heralded an idea, when the door opened. Ham.

"Just wanted to know how you made out," he said. Instead of standing with one hand on the doorknob, the way he usually did, he came in, shut the door carefully, and sat down on the edge of Vaughn's desk.

The minute I start working on this thing, she thought, sighing and putting her pencil away, somebody comes and talks to me.

Then she laughed at herself, because, of course, last night nobody had talked to her at all. Denny'd been still as a mouse the minute she asked him to let her work. It was Philip Ludlow who had interfered, yet it wasn't accurate to say he'd come and talked to her.

She told Ham a little about Kendal, careful not to say too much —just why, she didn't understand. She liked Ham. He spoke her language. He'd given her a break after the war.

"You have to be willing to put everything you have into the agency," he'd warned her when he took her on.

Well, she had. She certainly had. Everybody was kept on a make-good basis, and she was still here. That proved it. She'd worked her heart out for Hamiltons'.

"Yes," Ham was saying, and Vaughn knew by the tone that he was only making conversation, though what he was leading up to she couldn't imagine, "I always think, when Marilyn and I drive through some of those old towns, it would be nice to stop and——"

Vaughn interrupted him. "Know anything about Kendal Radio?" she asked, looking up at him intently.

"Kendal Radio?" he repeated, sticking out his lower lip.

That was enough for Vaughn. You could always tell how Ham felt about a thing by watching his mouth.

"It's made there, you know," she added, "and I wondered——"

"Lousy outfit," Ham said flatly.

"You mean," Vaughn asked, "shaky?" She felt injured by his unfeeling attitude.

Ham shrugged. "They're solvent all right," he answered, "far as I know. But the cheapskates do their own advertising. Do everything themselves. Bosses take over the machines, even if there happens to be a bottleneck. Firm like that, large capital and all, they ought to feed their stuff into the agencies."

Vaughn nodded. Ham was right. If the good-sized firms went in for writing their own copy, where would the agencies end up? Still, she couldn't see Hamilton Company handling Philip Ludlow's account. If he was as pernickety about advertising as about everything else——

"Very high-principled gent in the firm I met up there," she remarked dreamily.

"What's principles got to do with it?" Ham asked. "They got a product to sell—radios. So they go and write their copy themselves, and who wants to read it? Full of facts, like an encyclopedia, but no emotional appeal. That was all right after the war, while there was a shortage of consumer goods, but now—— Wait and see. They're going to get what's coming to them."

Vaughn winced. If Philip Ludlow—— She was afraid to meet Ham's eyes now. He might see how she felt. But he wasn't looking at her.

"Reason I came in," he was saying, sticking his chin in the air and tightening the knot of his necktie, "is, we're making up the vacation schedule in staff conference this morning. I thought we could talk about it first, Vaughn." He leaned a little toward her and looked at her fully for the first time since he came in. "I mean, you know, not in front of everybody."

She looked up at him in surprise. Since when was Ham so confidential with her?

"What I wondered was," he went on, fussing with his tie again, "how would you like the first two weeks in August?"

Vaughn sighed. "Gosh, Ham," she said, "I don't care. We aren't planning to do very much. And I don't know when Denny's getting his time off."

You, too, can escape from slavery by the railroad—take a vacation at the shore or mountains, Vaughn repeated to herself inanely. *Our conductors will serve you with the same devotion——*

"Well, how about it then?" Ham asked, almost pleadingly. "The first two weeks in August?"

"Say," Vaughn exclaimed, "isn't that when you'll be away? Wouldn't you rather have me here to keep an eye on things?" Maybe she was sticking her neck out, assuming that much importance.

Ham pursed his lips. "Katie can do it," he said, shrugging. "How about it, Vaughn?"

Now she knew by his tone that there was something special on his mind. She looked up questioningly.

"You see," Ham explained, "I thought maybe we could make a foursome in that hole we go to up in Maine, you and Denny, Marilyn and me. We get kind of tired being by ourselves. Not that there isn't a good crowd there and all. It's never slow. But you know what I mean—people you meet like that aren't the same as your own friends. After a while you get sick of listening to them tell about their business and their bulbs and their children and their diets. Know what I mean?"

Vaughn nodded. She'd never been to a place like that. Twenty dollars a day per had never been within the Hill budget, but she had imagination.

"Wouldn't you like it?" Ham asked hopefully. "Marilyn and I'd show you around."

Speechless, Vaughn nodded again. To be asked by Ham, as if they really were friends—to be asked—— She could scarcely believe it.

"Wouldn't you?" he repeated coaxingly. "I'd get you the reservation. It takes drag—you know what I mean. Place like that, they want to keep it for the right kind of people. I don't want you to think it's snooty or anything. Just slacks and a flannel shirt is all anybody ever wears. But it's more congenial if there's the right crowd." He was very serious.

"Thanks, Ham," Vaughn said feebly. She was too thrilled to say more.

He picked up a rubber band off her desk and started snapping it against his fingers.

"Think Denny'd like it?" he asked, suddenly frowning at her.

"Sure, Ham. Sure, Denny'd like it," she answered, knowing perfectly well that Denny—— "It's wonderful of you to ask us."

Ham was still frowning at her. "Denny's not fun like the rest of us," he said frankly. "In other words, he doesn't seem to care for some of those parties we have. That's the only place I've ever seen him, you know."

"Denny's quiet," Vaughn admitted, "but he'd love it up in Maine."

After all, a chance like this—Denny would go through with it for her sake. Besides, she thought, bristling a little, why shouldn't he put himself out? It was good business. Spending those two weeks with the Hamiltons would move Vaughn up onto a special footing with them which no one else in the agency enjoyed, so far as she knew, except Katie Martin. It was the surest way of advancing.

Ham's frown had disappeared. "It's a swell old place," he said, smiling happily now. "Golf, tennis, fishing, swimming—if you like the water. Marilyn won't go in. Gee, Vaughn, I certainly am glad! What I thought," he continued eagerly, "you and I could maybe plan some of that Redbrook Furnace campaign. Can't spend all one's time running around after a ball or shuffling cards."

He stopped and looked out of the window. There was more on his mind. Vaughn could tell.

Redbrook Furnace—— Wait a minute. Wasn't that the account Katie was handling?

Ham turned and looked at Vaughn again. He read her thought.

"You see," he explained, "Katie Martin's leaving in the fall and I thought maybe you'd——"

"*Katie Martin's leaving? No!*"

"Yep," Ham assured Vaughn, looking very serious. "She's going. Seems her sister's having a baby or something."

"But that's no reason for leaving," Vaughn exclaimed. "I mean, she could take a week. From what I hear, she hardly took that much time out to have her own."

Ham looked fussed. "Well, it's more than just the baby," he admitted. "You see, Katie's getting on in years. Must be forty-five, every day of forty-five."

"What of it?" Vaughn cried. "She's good, isn't she?"

"Darned good. Aren't many copy writers like her. But she's getting on."

Katie Martin—fired for old age. Vaughn couldn't believe it. In his roundabout way Ham had told her the truth.

Well, Vaughn said to herself grimly, that gives me just seven years. I'll have to make a lot of money.

Ham had recovered his composure. "So what I was saying," he went on, "if you make good, there might be a chance——"

"I'm trying, Ham," Vaughn broke in.

He looked at her thoughtfully. "Up there in Maine," he said, "when we're not doing anything special, I could give you a line on Katie's accounts. Of course it depends how your record looks—what you can produce between now and then."

"I'm trying, Ham," Vaughn repeated meekly. "This railroad layout I'm thinking about is going to be something. If you hadn't come in and interrupted," she said, smiling archly at him, "just when I had a good idea, it'd be finished. But it's just as well for me to take a little longer polishing it up."

"Don't take too long," Ham warned. "It isn't only up to me, you know. Dad and my uncles——"

The bosses!

Ham reached out and patted her arm. "If it were——"

84

She dropped her eyes, feeling constrained, uncertain how to respond to this advance. He wasn't just bantering now.

"I like you, Vaughn," he said softly. "I always liked you. You know that." With a sigh he stood up and started for the door. "We've got to get to that conference," he said, his tone usual again. "Now don't say anything, just that you want the first two weeks in August."

Vaughn was doing some rapid arithmetic in her head. Neil's camp. And she'd need clothes, no matter what Ham said about slacks, et cetera. And Susan. What about Susan? She felt suddenly scared. "How much is it a week, Ham?"

"Well, it all depends," he answered negligently. "Some space is higher than others. I'll write to the manager. Coming?" He opened the door and stood holding it for her in a way she couldn't remember his ever doing before.

But Vaughn wasn't ready to go. She wanted a minute to get over the surprise. She was so happy, she was afraid everyone would read in her face that Ham wanted her along on his vacation.

"I'll be in in a minute," she answered.

When he'd left, Vaughn took a deep breath and looked at herself in the mirror. It was a long time since she'd felt as charming as this.

4. Yes, Vaughn had been quite mistaken in thinking she'd forget Kendal.

All that spring, in the most unexpected and inconvenient moments, when she was interviewing a client or trying to make a decision, suddenly she would find herself miles away in Rhode Island, not paying a bit of attention to business.

Kendal was as familiar to her now as New York. Like a story repeated over and over, it probably retained very little truth, but this didn't bother Vaughn, since there was no danger of her going back and being disillusioned. The daydream was satisfying.

It was a retreat into which she escaped when things grew difficult. This was something new. She'd always faced life and stood on her own feet, ever since boarding school. Now there were these moments when she turned to Philip Ludlow.

"That layout isn't going well, the one I spoke to you about," she would tell him, sitting before his imaginary fire. "Something doesn't click. I don't know what it is."

While she could rarely answer for him, she nevertheless pictured his face quite clearly—the extraordinary interest which was concentrated in it when he listened to her, the impression he gave of never passing judgment, even in the privacy of his own thought. In fantasy she saw his quiet hands resting on the arms of his chair, only the fingertips moving a little to feel the grain of the wood beneath them. Somehow, pretending this way did Vaughn good.

She started several times to tell Philip Ludlow how unco-operative Denny had been about going to Maine with the Hamiltons—not angry, exactly, but hurt and unhappy, which in turn had made Vaughn angry. They had had an awful scene about it when she came home with Ham's suggestion. She didn't confide this to Philip Ludlow, partly because she had no business telling a stranger about her troubles with her husband, not even in a daydream, and partly because thinking about Philip Ludlow at this point always made her uneasy.

He didn't, of course, judge Vaughn, but on this occasion he did speak to her. Though she had absolutely refused to tell him about Denny and the trip to Maine, he had asked—it was really nothing but an echo of the question he'd put to her that night at his house, when she told him Neil must learn to hold his own—"Why do you want him to?"

Well, of course the man mustn't be expected to understand these things. What did he know of a woman's problems, a professional woman, trying to raise a family and get on in her job? After all, while she did daydream about him this way, Vaughn never lost sight of the fact that Philip Ludlow was very human.

But she enjoyed talking to him, though probably by this time he didn't even remember her.

Woolgathering, that's what she was doing. Not since her high school days had Vaughn been guilty of that.

Maybe it was the fault of spring, she thought one evening as she got out of the subway and walked toward the house. Now that the clocks were turned forward, she came to the surface in daylight.

After all, she wasn't too old yet to be stirred that way, though you'd hardly know, in this neighborhood, that May had come. Down in the Village, she remembered, men used to appear around this time with farm wagons, selling plants—geraniums, begonias (Philip Ludlow's hobby). Vaughn had always rushed out in those days to buy something.

She wondered how Kendal looked now. Very pretty, probably. Mary Lancashire's lawn must be green.

Here, one could hardly tell it was May, Vaughn realized, as she stopped at the store to pick up a head of lettuce. The only difference the weather made was in her clothes. Sometimes it was too cold for her spring suit; sometimes it was too hot. It rained a good deal, so that she had to wear rubbers and carry an umbrella, which was a nuisance.

But, thinking of Kendal, of the gardens in town and the fields at the homestead, of the promise she had felt there in March of life to come, she was aware, for the first time since she moved to the city, of the importance of weather to anything but her personal convenience. Not that she hadn't always known that sun and rain make things grow, but the food she bought was processed by elements so far away that her only index of their clemency was the price she had to pay.

She remembered how Philip Ludlow had kept scanning the sky when they were out together, and how he and the old gentleman at the homestead had talked of a wet moon. Weather affected their lives as though they, too, were growing things, and their dependence on it seemed to root them in the earth.

That week end in Kendal a window had been opened in

Vaughn's mind. It wasn't, she told herself, walking on and entering the dark foyer of the house, that she'd discovered anything she hadn't known before, only that facts had come home to her which had passed her by till then.

There was a letter under the door of the apartment. Vaughn picked it up as she let herself in, experiencing that vague excitement at the sight of mail which was left over from youth, though of course no one very interesting wrote to her any more. She had Denny; there were no folks left at home. Bills and appeals were the chief things nowadays. And still, Vaughn was always a little fluttery when she saw a letter. An old reflex——

The letter was for Neil—*Mr.* Neil Hill. Vaughn was curious. Who would write to the boy? There was no secret about it, she saw as she moved nearer to the light. The sender's name was printed on the envelope: Nicholas Company, Detroit. How did they get his name? Was Neil up to something? She'd have to find out.

But he wasn't in, though it was time for him to be home. This was Susan's dancing-class day, so she couldn't be here yet, but Neil—— Well, it was really too early to begin worrying.

Kids his age were always answering ads, Vaughn thought as she put the letter on his desk, sending for free samples, which usually involved money in the end. She remembered a few unpleasant experiences of her own.

A nice room, she thought, as she was leaving it, a boyish room, with the hunting-dog picture she'd got at a sale, the anchors on the bedspread, and the points of the compass worked into the rug. If only Neil would learn to pick up his things. She kept after him about neatness all the time, but where did it get her?

Settling herself, exhausted, on the living-room sofa with a drink, looking out at the windows across the street, Vaughn began for no reason at all to think of Jeanie Brown in Kendal. It must soon be time for Jeanie's baby. She'd been pretty big in March. Somehow Vaughn felt sorry for the girl. She seemed very young.

But how silly—to feel sorry for her. Yet, with that husband who didn't provide properly—that Bart. What was he doing now? Still playing with those boys when he ought to be getting down to work? Vaughn was impatient with Bart. She disliked him. But Philip Ludlow had seen something in the man, and now Vaughn wondered a little whether . . .

Here she was sentimentalizing about people she didn't really know, people she didn't care about, whom she'd never see again. What had got into her?

She was worried, too, really worried about Philip Ludlow. Kendal Radio wasn't doing well. The company's earnings in the first quarter of nineteen fifty had been alarmingly below those of the same period in previous years. Vaughn had made it her business to find out.

It made her sick. Why was Philip Ludlow so pigheaded about advertising? Naturally amateurs couldn't do the same job as specialists. If she'd known about this when she was in Kendal, she'd have spoken to him. If he'd only come to New York now and see what was going on, if he'd just look over some of the graphs and charts which proved the value of Hamilton Company's methods.

Vaughn sighed. She wished she could help him.

And then she laughed to herself bitterly and gulped down the rest of her drink. Because she wasn't getting along any too well herself. How could she help someone else? If she didn't pull herself together soon and show what she could do, come fall she'd be out on the street, like Katie Martin.

That old Underground Railroad. Why, for goodness' sake, had she ever thought she could do something with that? It had looked so good to her in the beginning. The week end in Kendal, it seemed just within reach of her imagination. Yet, as soon as she got back, the spark cooled. She'd worked and worked without producing one draft good enough to show to Ham. It wasn't as if she could chuck it, either. After talking so much, if she didn't come through with a good layout, it would be much worse than if she'd never tried. The whole office knew about it now.

That was why it was so important for Denny and her to go to Maine with the Hamiltons.

If I can't get ahead on brain, Vaughn thought despondently, I'll have to do it on charm.

Neil had come home, but instead of joining his mother and telling her about his day, as she wished he would do, he stayed in his room. Maybe he was reading that letter.

Vaughn got up and went in to him. She'd like to know——

The boy was sitting at his desk. He looked up as Vaughn came in, and there was such overwhelming happiness in his face that, somehow, all her worries and fears, not only for him, but for the others, for herself—all the weight of life anxiety suddenly dropped from her. Neil was radiant and, seeing him so, Vaughn caught a flash of his happiness in her own heart. Yielding to a burst of uncontrollable emotion she knelt beside his chair and kissed him.

Then she was afraid that, in his budding manhood, he might resent what she'd done, but he accepted the kiss as naturally as if he were still three instead of thirteen. Something very, very wonderful must have happened to Neil, Vaughn decided, getting to her feet again.

He had only given her that one fleeting glance, then he returned his attention to the paper before him. It was, Vaughn saw, looking over the top of his untidy brown hair, a very capable spread, first-class printing and cuts, for a little sailboat. Neil was so absorbed that she suddenly understood why he hadn't resented her kiss: he'd been insensible to it, hypnotized by the ad.

"Somebody seems to think you're a tycoon, *Mr.* Neil Hill," she said, resting her hands on his shoulders. "I suppose you're going to succumb to sales pressure and buy a transatlantic liner?"

He was too intent on the spread to respond to her banter. "Look," he told her, pointing to the picture of a boy in a white T-shirt sitting in a little sailboat, happy as a clam, "complete kit just fifty dollars—all the lumber sawed and ready to put together, hardware, caulking compound, mast, boom, rigging—everything. Well, the sail's extra, but——"

"I see," Vaughn said, playing along with him. "I suppose you'd launch it in Central Park?"

"No," Neil answered, dead serious. "Jim Wilson—you know that kid at school lives in Rye?—he said I could moor it at his place. They have a dock. So, could I, Mom?"

"Of course not," Vaughn said, "you know you couldn't. Darling, you ought to wash your neck better right back here."

"Don't think I can't put it together," he begged. "I've been staying after school and helping Mr. Hughes in the shop, and we talked it all over. He's sure I can do it."

"He is, is he?" Vaughn exclaimed indignantly. What right had a teacher to put ideas in a boy's head that his parents would have to pry out again? "And how does Mr. Hughes think you're going to pay for it?"

"Well, you see," Neil burst out, turning to her eagerly, "I figured, instead of you and Dad paying all that money to send me to camp, which isn't worth it, really it isn't, Mom, I thought, after you'd deducted what it costs to feed me at home, there'd be fifty dollars left over. There would, wouldn't there? You see," he went on, without waiting for her answer, "my uniform would pay for the sail. So it wouldn't cost you and Dad a cent. It's simple."

"Very simple," Vaughn said scathingly.

"And you're always saying I should get in with other boys," Neil went on, his eyes shining. "That's why you wanted to send me to camp, wasn't it?"

"Yes."

"Well, there's nothing makes a man so popular as owning a boat," he assured her. "Fellows will be on my tail once I put this together. I bet I won't even get a chance to take the tiller." The thought cast a momentary shadow on his face.

Vaughn was getting tired of this. It was time to point out the ridiculousness of the scheme. She hated hurting the kid, but it was better to open his eyes now than to wait till the thing had gone too far.

"Where would you build it?" she asked, knowing this would bring Neil down to earth. "There isn't a room in the house big enough." She had him there.

"That's all right, Mom," he said, unruffled, ecstatic. "It's all fixed. I spoke to Joe about it, and he was very nice. You know that passageway by the dumb-waiter where he keeps the garbage cans? Maybe you've never been in the basement——"

This was too much.

"Look, Neil," Vaughn said, feeling her temper rise. "It's all very well to make believe. I even do it myself sometimes. But at your age you have to be able to tell the difference between reality and——"

She stopped for breath, exasperated. Why was it that mothers were always having to make their children take medicine? She resented being put in this position and she was annoyed with Neil for forcing her to be harsh.

"You mean," he asked, his face quivering, "I can't do it?"

"You're going to camp, big boy," Vaughn answered. "It's better for you to be supervised, and you'll have other activities, not just water sports. Besides," she added, trying not to sound reproachful, "your father and I need a vacation too. Ever think of that?"

He stared at her without answering.

"No," she answered for him, "I don't suppose you did. We haven't had a vacation in years, and now there's a chance to go to Maine——" Her voice trailed off. She was too upset to speak.

"What about Susan? She going with you?" Neil asked. His face was tense.

Vaughn didn't answer. She didn't know what to do about Susan. That had been on her mind ever since Ham had proposed the arrangement. If the Hamiltons liked it, then it was definitely not a place for children. There would be a lot of drinking. Besides, this Maine trip was really business, not pleasure, and how could Vaughn concentrate on it if she had to take care of Susan too?

They couldn't afford to send both children to camp. As it was, Maine would cost them much more than they had a right to spend. What in the world was she going to do with Susan?

Vaughn was in a state. She knew it. And Neil was just making things worse. She wanted to get away, go to the kitchen, start supper.

But the boy was looking up at her, staring as if he was unable to believe that she would do this to him. And suddenly, without any warning, Vaughn remembered the way Philip Ludlow had looked at her when she told him about the need to toughen Neil up—like a child appealing to a parent who was about to drown a cat.

Now I'm getting maudlin, she said to herself furiously.

She was just about at the end of her rope.

To Neil she said, as evenly as she could, "It's all settled, so let's not talk about it any more. I sent in your registration fee months ago."

He didn't hide his disappointment. "Don't you like having me around?" he asked, gulping. Then he got up and rushed out of the room.

It was a good thing he went. The way Vaughn's nerves snapped then, she might have struck him.

5. Sometimes June is the hottest month of all in New York. Or maybe it's just that I haven't got used to sweltering, Vaughn said to herself.

There was a fan in her office, but it seemed only to circulate hot air. Vacation was still two months away and Vaughn wasn't even looking forward to it. Things had changed since Ham proposed that she and Denny go to Maine. Three months ago she'd been on the make. Now she was practically in the doghouse.

It wasn't enough to plod along, keeping one's accounts going. One had to be original, creative. That railroad idea—at the time it had seemed to Vaughn almost a touch of genius. To catch a new client, one for whom all the advertising agencies in the country were angling—a copy writer who could do that would be indispensable.

She had come very near bringing it off too.

That was the worst of working in this place. You had to do more than your best all the time; if you started coasting, just once, you were through. People outside had warned her about Hamiltons' when she first came, saying that the prestige of working for a firm like that wasn't worth the price. There was no heart there, as many previous employees had learned to their sorrow. But Vaughn had been equal to it. Until now.

In the beginning she'd wondered whether she belonged in such an establishment. They had a way of writing copy that was misleading, though, if it came to a showdown, they could prove that they'd stuck to the facts. But she told herself then that that was her job, and she'd got used to it. She learned to write this kind of copy herself; she was a whiz at it, Ham had said once.

The Redbrook Furnace business, though, had made her gag. "Cheaper in the long run," Ham had wanted her to say of it, and she had, knowing perfectly well that it was not only the most expensive product of its kind on the market, but that it wasn't performing well in preliminary tests. There had been a lot of complaints. Yet Hamiltons' was going to back it, leading a lot of little householders to invest their savings in the most expensive furnace they could get, which wasn't even going to keep them warm come winter two or three years from now.

It was routine to Vaughn. She never inquired into the actual merits of a product. But for some reason she'd got to thinking about this one. She'd even gone so far as to argue with Ham about it, which was never a good idea.

"You mind your own business, sister," he'd said with surprising good nature, "and finish that copy by this afternoon. That's the way I want it."

She'd complied, but now, weeks later, she was still thinking about it. That was funny, because usually she forgot a problem the minute it was finished.

She sat at her desk where there were a million things piled up waiting for her attention, yet in thought she still dallied over that Underground Railroad.

There must be something I can do, she said to herself, some way to get back the glamour I saw in it once. I'm stale, the way I've been working on this the last three months. Stale on life too.

It had no savor.

Ham was standing just outside her office. She could hear him speaking to someone, and through the ground-glass door she could see his outline. Beside this was the bulk of a tall man's shape. Something about the elderly set of these shoulders made Vaughn's heart jump. *Philip Ludlow.*

He'd come! He remembered her! She looked at her watch. They'd go out to lunch together. She rushed to the door.

Of course it wasn't. Even before Vaughn opened the door a crack, enough to discover that it was someone who wanted to sell Ham insurance, she knew it wasn't. But just for a minute she'd thought——

She went back to her desk and flopped into the swivel chair. What had made her imagine that Philip Ludlow would ever come to New York? She couldn't see him here. He belonged to Kendal with the massive elms, the old homestead, the river, and the Meetinghouse.

For the first time since she'd been working Vaughn threw her arms across her desk and dropped her head on them.

Seeing Philip Ludlow again would have touched off the spark which the layout needed, she thought sadly. He was her link with the whole thing. If he had come——

She sat up and took a pencil in her hand, compelled to maintain an appearance of working, in case someone should come in, but she was only doodling.

Maybe, she told herself, drawing swirls across the paper, maybe in Kendal, if I went back——

The idea was so startling that she stopped the pencil and held her breath an instant. *Could she go back?* Why not? If she looked at the hiding place again, maybe then—— Last time she'd seen only a hole. But the old man singing about Moses and Pharaoh had obviously seen something more. That Bart Brown had called it "exciting." Perhaps there was something down there at the bottom of the darkness which her eyes had missed.

Could that be it? She jumped up and went to the window, pressing her face against the corner of the pane, from which she could glimpse a slit of sky between two buildings. *Could that be it?*

She stood there a long time, feeling her heart beat and searching for a cool patch of glass with her forehead.

After all, it wasn't so far—only a week end——

Still, she couldn't just hop on a train. First, she would have to write and ask Philip Ludlow whether she might see the place again. And he would have to arrange about her staying with Mary Lancashire. Now, in June, the all-white room would be cool and fresh. Vaughn could picture herself there, could see the ruffled curtains moving with the breeze blowing off the river. Now, stifling in city dust and heat, she longed to find herself in that room, opening the overnight case, stretching out a minute on the counterpane.

She remembered how peacefully she had lain in the brass bedstead the second night she was there, gazing out at the moonlit sky, feeling like a child, who always slept alone like that, who stood at the very beginning of life. Lying there, she had had the feeling that she could really start then, forget her cares, avoid her mistakes, begin all over again, making herself more of a person, much more of a person.

She had felt expanding within her a new wishfulness to make life count, to give the children something she'd missed, to get along better with Denny.

Vaughn sighed.

She couldn't just write to Mary Lancashire and ask if she might come again, because she hadn't been very nice when she stayed there. Polite, yes, but not friendly, as the older woman had been. And when Mary Lancashire refused to take payment for the room, explaining that it was a pleasure for her to accommodate Philip Ludlow's guest, Vaughn had been almost rude, insisting that she'd come on business.

Why, when she'd been offered kindness?

Maybe it was the counterpane, she thought suddenly, moving her forehead to another part of the glass. It reminded me of when I was a kid, and I was always being told not to lie on it.

She turned from the window, suddenly convinced that there was something in the hiding place that she'd missed, some essential factor.

With a swiftly overpowering impulse, she sat down at her desk again, took out her pen and a sheet of letter paper, and wrote.

Dear Philip Ludlow, she began. But it looked too personal. After all, she hardly knew the man, she was asking him to let her come on business. Crumpling the sheet, she threw it away. Then she started afresh on the typewriter.

Dear Mr. Ludlow. No, it didn't look right. Hadn't he made a point of asking her to address him "like other folks"? Wasn't it bad enough that she had to admit she wasn't able to write the layout, that she was hopelessly stuck?

Dear Philip Ludlow, she typed on the third sheet, and this time she let it stand. She wrote hurriedly, simply asking whether she might come again this week end. It was, she realized, short notice, but she needed more data. Would he arrange for a room at Mary Lancashire's? But this time she must insist on paying. It was a businesslike letter, and yet, as she sealed it, for one delicious moment Vaughn relived the feeling she'd had in that brass bedstead of standing at the very beginning of her life.

6. His answer, which arrived Thursday, was so friendly, and the cryptic sentence at the end was so characteristic that Vaughn could almost hear Philip Ludlow's precise New England accent.

Come by all means, he wrote. *I shall expect you on Friday, but Mary Lancashire mayn't have you this time. I want you to stay with me, as my cousins will be here for Quarterly Meeting. We'll be unable to linger very long at the homestead. Nevertheless, in your quest for the spirit of the Underground Railroad, way is, I venture to think, more likely to open in the sessions.*

Vaughn was at first so happy with the invitation that all the stuff about "Quarterly Meeting" and "way opening in the sessions" escaped her. But when she reread the letter, she wondered suddenly what sort of situation she was getting herself into. Maybe she ought to refuse.

Though she'd never heard of Quarterly Meeting it was undoubtedly another of those Quaker things. He'd expect her to attend. Why was he mixing things up?

Religion and business, she thought impatiently, are two distinct matters.

She was going back to Kendal to get a new slant on the layout, not to be talked to again about God. She'd explained in her letter that she needed more data. Was it that he wouldn't believe she could fail at her job?

Vaughn smiled, considering this flattering implication. Then she came down to earth.

What difference does it make, what he thinks? she asked herself, putting the letter away in her desk. Philip Ludlow isn't the one who's going to give me Katie Martin's job.

But she was going, even if she had to sit in church. She was ready to do anything for the layout. Besides, it hadn't been so bad in that bleak Meetinghouse, once she got used to it. At least she hadn't had to kneel or repeat prayers, or do anything she didn't sincerely mean. She hadn't had to do anything except keep still. There had even been that one moment when she'd had a wonderful sense of relaxation. It had forsaken her again, and she'd forgotten about it till this minute. But, harassed and driven as she felt now, she remembered that moment wistfully.

She was going. Philip Ludlow expected her tomorrow. She would take that same train.

What should she wear? Something less dressy than the pure silk suit she'd worn the other time, certainly. And a cocktail-length dress, like that turquoise job, wasn't at all necessary. Thinking back to that first visit, Vaughn wondered whether she hadn't looked a little too-too for Kendal. That hat——

What had he meant, anyway, when he said that nothing like it ever got off the train in Kendal before? At the same time she'd taken it for a compliment. Now she wasn't quite sure.

Rushing out of the agency, she took a taxi to that little millinery shop on Fifty-second Street. She felt eager and excited as she stepped down into its deftly shaded fluorescence.

It was such a high-class place that no hats were displayed. The restrained greeting of the saleswoman implied that Vaughn's taste might be worthy of her creations.

"Faille, madame?" she asked. Her French accent didn't sound synthetic, but Vaughn couldn't really judge. "Baku? Leghorn?"

Vaughn seated herself at a dressing table and took off her cloche. Before answering she considered herself in the mirror. What would do most to give her importance and, at the same time, charm; to hide her discouragement, make a feature of her white skin and large gray eyes?

Seeing her face in this uncompromising light, she had a sudden shock, for she looked haggard, absolutely haggard. No wonder——

The saleswoman, without waiting for an answer, had retired backstage and was now emerging with a little saffron straw turban, carrying it like a consecrated crown upon her hands. Gently her fingers molded it to Vaughn's head.

Vaughn sat submissive, watching in the mirror, waiting for the moment when the woman would step back and leave her to study the effect.

No, there should be a brim. I'd have to wear a veil with it, Vaughn said to herself, a nose veil, anyway.

Aloud she asked if she might see something else.

The saleswoman didn't argue. She took off the turban and went for another model, quite a large shape of stiffened black veiling, with a forward swoop. In the sunshine, Vaughn thought, it would cast interesting patterns of light on her face. With her rhinestone earrings——

It did something for Vaughn. The drawn look disappeared. She was more vital. But also very sophisticated. Was this really the effect she wanted to create?

How would she look to Philip Ludlow?

She tilted it, level with her eyes, then off the face a little. But it was still a very worldly hat.

"No," she said slowly, taking it off, "that's not quite—not what I want."

"What was it you had in mind?" There was controlled impatience in the saleswoman's voice, the merest insinuation, overlaid with a French accent, that Vaughn's taste was less cultivated than she'd originally supposed.

Vaughn couldn't say what she'd had in mind, for she didn't know. She stared in the mirror as the woman removed the hat, stared at her own face, scanning it for some hint of that quality which should be drawn out. Heavens, didn't she even know what kind of person she wished to appear?

The saleswoman waited with long-suffering patience, but Vaughn didn't answer. "Is it for a special occasion, madame?" the woman asked at length.

Vaughn smiled. Wouldn't she be convulsed if Vaughn were to tell her that what she wanted was a hat to wear to a Quaker Meeting—Quarterly Meeting—something suitable, yet becoming, quiet, but capable of attracting appreciative notice from a rather elderly, unworldly gentleman?

Maybe, she thought suddenly, those cousins of his wear bonnets, like his grandmother's dolls.

At that Vaughn laughed out loud. Those sugar-scoop affairs with strings tied under the chin—— The whole situation was too ludicrous. How did she ever get started this way?

The saleswoman smiled dutifully and went away. She returned with a little off-white organdy bonnet with wings, like a Sister of Charity's, only that it had streamers of navy velvet. Simple, ingenuous in effect, yet really artfully dramatic. She patted it down on Vaughn's head, then cocked her own thoughtfully.

"It's kind to your face," she declared at length.

Kind to—— Well, I like that, Vaughn exclaimed to herself indignantly. For two cents I'd walk out of the store. *Kind to my face!*

But, apart from the implication that Vaughn's face cried out for compassion, it wasn't a bad hat.

Ignoring the woman, Vaughn examined herself in the dressing-table mirror. This floating-on-air effect was rather good for her profile, she had to admit as she inspected it both ways with the hand glass.

She tried to imagine herself against the Kendal background. Was this the impression she wanted to make when she walked through the Yard of the Meetinghouse with Philip Ludlow? Would his admiration for her be genuine, or only a phase of his old-fashioned courtesy?

I don't have a bad nose, she said to herself, looked at sideways. But my chin's too long. Just an eighth of an inch is all.

That other time his courtesy had made her feel charming. She'd loved it. But she saw now that it might not be anything special about her which had evoked that sympathetic manner. Hadn't he been the same with everybody—Jeanie, the old Mansfields, and all the people they'd shaken hands and chatted with after Meeting that Sunday?

This manner was more than a mere social grace, she realized, tilting the hand glass a little to see herself from another angle. It was Philip Ludlow's way of showing what he felt for people. His grave interest in what they had to say, his little quick moves to help weren't just the politeness of a well-bred man.

It's almost, Vaughn thought, forgetting the hat for a minute, a reverence that he seems to have for other people. He really cares. Like his meeting me at the station and getting me a room, though I was just coming on business and he didn't even know me yet. And so many little things—I expect them from those who love me, but from a perfect stranger——

No one she knew was like that, not even Denny, who was the most kindhearted person in the world, but so wrapped up in his own problems that he hardly noticed anyone else. Their friends and the people they worked with were frankly out for themselves.

No one Vaughn knew was like Philip Ludlow.

Remembering the way he'd appeared to her in that very first moment when she'd practically run after him to say she actually was Vaughn Hill, the way he'd looked down and smiled, radiating friendliness, she felt suddenly so overwhelmed with desire to see him that she wanted to start immediately—get out of the store, rush home, pack her bag——

"I'll take it," she told the saleswoman without another glance in the mirror, without inquiring the price. The main thing was to get to Kendal.

The minute she arrived home, Vaughn went to the closet and rummaged through her clothes. Did she have anything to wear?

No, it was the same with her dresses as with the hats in the shop. Nothing was just right for Kendal. Either a dress wasn't plain enough—Philip Ludlow was always speaking of things there as "plain"—or it didn't do enough for her, and she couldn't help remembering how he'd looked at her that night when she came down the stairs at Mary Lancashire's, so that she'd felt like a prom girl.

She considered the lemon surah, holding it at arm's length before her. With the eight-button gloves and her big pearls—yes. Simple, yet dressy. And the muted green shantung? With her new bag and orange lizard pumps——

Perhaps, to travel in, the tucked sheer, if it was as hot as this tomorrow. Those floating panels were becoming. Gave her more height. Suppose it turned cold? She slid aside one dress after another till she found the Irish linen suit.

I definitely need clothes, she thought, glancing quickly through the remainder of her things. Next week I'll have to put my mind on getting things for Maine.

Spreading the dresses on the bed, Vaughn opened the hatbox and put the lovely organdy bonnet beside them. She'd wait and ask Denny what looked best. Not that he ever noticed what she wore.

When Denny came and Vaughn announced she was going to Kendal for the week end, he seemed first startled and then angry—actually angry.

"What for?" he asked. "It was a flop the other time."

"I know," Vaughn answered. "That's why. I've tried so hard to write that copy and it just won't come. So I thought maybe if I went back and had another look at the hiding place——"

"Another look at——" Denny stopped in mid-sentence, the thought left unspoken, but so much bitterness in his voice that Vaughn looked up swiftly.

"What do you mean?" she cried.

"What do you think I mean?" he answered angrily. "I'm not a writer, but don't you suppose I know how much inspiration anyone could get out of staring at a hole in the ground? That's not the look you're going all that way for." There was a nasty edge to his voice which Vaughn had never heard before. "I thought you hated it so," he went on. "The awful bed and that woman you stayed with——"

"I'm not going to stay with her," Vaughn explained hastily. "Philip Ludlow's invited me. His cousins——"

"So I was right!" Denny cried with a catch in his voice, almost as if he were about to break down. "That's what's been upsetting you all these weeks. That's what's kept you from doing your work. I thought so!"

"Denny!" Vaughn cried, horrified. "You don't know what you're talking about, Denny."

But Denny didn't hear her. He had left the room. A moment later he had left the apartment.

Vaughn threw herself down on the sofa, breathing hard, staring dumbly at the cigarette box that stood on the coffee table. So Denny really thought——

She couldn't believe it. Now she remembered what he'd said the night she came home from Kendal, about thinking she'd fallen for Philip Ludlow. But it was crazy, just crazy. She'd never looked at any man but Denny. And, anyhow, that wasn't why she was going. This layout had her so worried, and now, when she'd finally figured out something she could do about it, here was Denny making a scene. The whole thing was one big mess.

How could Denny? Why, even when Ham made passes at her at parties, which he always did after the second cocktail, Denny never minded. They'd always laughed it off afterward. He understood. And now—— Why didn't he see that Kendal was business too?

She suddenly sat upright on the sofa.

All right. She wouldn't go. If that was the way Denny felt about it, she simply wouldn't go. She'd just stay home. Then he'd see what a fool he'd been, suspecting her of falling for an old man in the country, interfering with her progress at the agency. She'd just show him.

Going into the bedroom, she snatched up the dresses and the linen suit with their hangers. Her hands were shaking as she suspended the things in the closet.

"There!" she cried, slamming the door on them.

That was the end of that. She tried to settle down, now that she was staying home, to rearrange the direction of her mind. There was that buttonhole of Denny's to be fixed before she put his topcoat away for the summer. Rushing to her sewing case, she pulled things out. It just showed how much she really cared for Denny, that she'd mend his clothes even when he was so ugly to her. Only, her hands shook so that she couldn't thread the needle.

But if I don't go, she suddenly exclaimed to herself, throwing the topcoat down, won't Denny be even surer?

How could he? she asked herself, growing more and more angry. *How could he?*

Then she broke down and cried.

The children, she wailed to herself, collapsing on the bed. What about the children? If Denny really—— At least Neil and Susan hadn't heard. They were both in their rooms. But if Denny didn't turn up for dinner, what was she to say to them?

Wouldn't you think, she asked herself, sitting up, he'd at least consider the children?

He came back, though. As they took their places at table he looked stern, yet it was obvious that he was making an effort to act as if nothing had happened. He even tried to be nice to Vaughn. But she wouldn't so much as look at him. Though she pretended to be gay with the children, to cover up the debris of quarrel that cluttered the air, nobody laughed for her pains.

Had the children heard? The thought gave Vaughn such a queer pain she couldn't eat. They probably hadn't, but she saw that they knew in their bones what was going on.

Everyone was glum.

After dinner Denny took a book and read. The only time he spoke was when the children came in to say good night. At eleven o'clock Vaughn went into the bedroom.

She could hear Denny out in the hall putting the chain on the door, the way he did every night when they retired, locking the four of them in, safe and snug.

But were they snug really, since Denny had upset them all with his silly nonsense?

It was in that moment, when Denny put the chain on the door, that Vaughn made up her mind. She was going. Yes, she was going. The whole thing was ridiculous. If Denny wanted to make up lies and ruin their happiness, she wasn't going to let that stop her.

She dragged the overnight case from the closet and began nervously to pack, taking the clothes out again with hands which shook the way they had when she put them in. Denny, coming to bed, watched her. His expression was hard.

They undressed in silence. The coldness between them froze their lips, so that they couldn't speak, and their arms, making them incapable of reaching out to one another.

But when they were in bed, to Vaughn's complete surprise Denny kissed her. Then he turned over and went to sleep.

They had made up. With that kiss they were once more on speaking terms. In the morning everything would be as usual. He would see her off at Grand Central.

Yet Vaughn knew that the misunderstanding between them wasn't dissolved. On the contrary, with that kiss it became completely established. With that kiss Denny was declaring as clearly as if he'd spoken the words that even if Vaughn had fallen for someone else, his love for her remained unchanged. His forgiveness of what till then had been only a shadow, a ridiculous surmise, still open to question, made it a thing of substance, an existing situation.

She didn't know what to do. Lying there, aching, she knew only that to protest—and how could she protest, when he was asleep?—to protest would be the same as admitting that there actually was reason for Denny to be jealous.

The thought went spinning on and on until suddenly it made her sit bolt upright.

Could there be? Could what he said, perhaps, be true? *Could it?*

She felt her eyes dilate as she stared into the darkness. Perspiration ran down her arms.

How could it be true when she'd seen this other man for only one week end in her entire life? She was merely going back to Kendal because it meant so much to all of them that she shine at Hamiltons'. And anyway, *anyway*, he was just an old Quaker. Didn't that *prove* Denny was wrong?

But, she admitted honestly, there had been something else there, something which had nothing to do with business, that she had found nice. It was a feeling of being important, not, though, in the sense she'd intended when she arrived, hoping to impress the natives with her position. It was as if just the fact that she was a human being mattered more than anything else in the world. This was a new experience.

Yes, now that she thought about it, maybe it was this which drew her back more than the hiding place, the need to be in a place where she didn't have to be better than she actually was, achieve more than she actually could. Philip Ludlow had made her aware of this human importance the minute he'd met her at the train, making her feel that she didn't have to *do* anything in order to rate with him, she didn't have to be successful or bright or beautiful (though he obviously preferred her beautiful) or—and this seemed very strange—good, even. This simple guy would like her no matter how she was, just because she happened to be a person.

Yes, he was a dear. She'd been afraid of crying when she said good-by. Still, that didn't mean——

Denny, she cried, *Denny!*

But the cry was in her heart, not hurled against the deafness of his sleep.

Suddenly she began to tremble, and a chill ran over her arms and stomach, so that she crawled down quickly under the covers. She had in that instant realized that though Denny might have told himself with the kiss that he would always love her, if he suspected her of loving someone else, his wouldn't be the old love. With time it wouldn't be any love at all.

She pressed nearer to him, shivering, trying to draw warmth and comfort from his quiet body. But while they lay so close now that nothing separated them, actually, she knew, they were both alone.

In her distress she wanted to talk to him, to draw an answer from him, reassurance. Yet, if she were to speak, he wouldn't hear her.

He wouldn't even hear me now, she said to herself, sobbing.

Their bodies might press together all night long, but in their hearts they were worlds apart.

Part 3

Part 5

1. He opened the door and ushered her into his house as if her coming were a great occasion in his life.

"My cousins haven't yet arrived," he told Vaughn, "but I expect them any moment."

Vaughn wondered whether the cousins would come driving up in a buggy, their bonnet strings tied under their chin, their shawls streaming in the breeze.

Susan would just love this place, she thought, smiling to herself.

Philip Ludlow kept the overnight case in his hand, asking whether Vaughn didn't wish to go directly to her room. Perhaps she'd like to rest before supper.

She assented amiably, but she knew she wouldn't rest; she was too excited.

Now, in daylight, this seemed more than ever a little old farm-house, Vaughn thought, noting the dull green wainscoting and the small colonial pattern in the hall paper. Glancing through the door of the parlor, she saw that the rear windows looked out upon the river.

She remembered how her eyes had pricked when she stood in this hall the last time, saying good-by to Philip Ludlow, thinking she would never see him again. Yet, here she was, back once more, with nearly two whole days to spend: tonight, tomorrow, and half of Sunday. As she followed him up the narrow staircase, the promise of these time spans repeated itself rhythmically in her mind on each successive step: tonight, tomorrow, half of Sunday; tonight, tomorrow . . .

He led the way to a room over the ell and, putting her case down, left, shutting the door softly.

It was a little mansard room, a boy's room, for there were books on the shelves Neil would have appreciated more than Vaughn did, and a cabinet of treasures—arrowheads and rocks and bones, which had obviously been collected in the owner's childhood.

A stripe of sunshine lay across the spattered floor and glistened in the jar of larkspur and pink roses that was standing on the writing table. The high bedposts, worn and nicked and polished over till they shone, the little braided rug, and the sharp cleanliness and plainness of everything harmonized with the rest of Philip Ludlow's setting.

To Vaughn, who'd always thought a room should express either a period in furnishing or one's tastes or hobbies, this bare sanctum under the eaves with a view of the river seemed to be nothing but a background. She wondered, feeling her personality, like her luggage, stand out against it, whether in such a room one might not more easily find oneself.

Taking off her hat, she laid it carefully, with a pat of approval, on the bureau. Then she went to the open window and leaned her elbows on the sill, looking out over the slates of the roof and across the garden which ran down to the little river and breathing in the cool country air. It had been dark when she was here before, so that she'd never seen the view and she hadn't guessed that the river could be so close, or so narrow and wooded at this point. The sun was beginning to drop behind the trees on the opposite bank, making long shadows on the grass under the window.

Vaughn's chest ached with longing as she looked out and smelled the roses in the garden. She didn't know what it was she longed for, only that there was something that she wanted which her life didn't hold. And like a stone at the bottom of her heart lay the thought of Denny, of how he had left her in Grand Central with another of his magnanimous kisses on her forehead and the weight of their appalling misunderstanding in her heart.

What was going to happen? Would he still be like that when she returned? If he was—— But *why?* she asked herself. *Why?* Couldn't he understand that she'd come to Kendal for that material? This time she'd surely catch hold of it. Just being back here gave her that feeling again.

She'd dreamed of Kendal so long that all the way up in the stuffy train she worried lest the place prove to be merely a fantasy and she should be disappointed, not in external details, which wouldn't have mattered, but in that special thing she remembered having felt here before. If this should prove to be only illusion, the bottom would drop out of everything.

But it was here. She knew, as she stood looking out of the dormer window, that it was here, real, as real as the fragrance of the newly laundered curtains, which had been dried out of doors and now gently blew against Vaughn's cheek. When Denny'd asked her that night what Kendal had, she couldn't tell him, but she recognized its presence all about her now. She'd felt it the minute Philip Ludlow looked up at her from the platform, as she stepped down from the train, not half an hour ago.

Relinquishing the overnight case, as his hand shot up to grasp it, she'd been suddenly shy, all her usual urbanity forsaking her, now that she had to explain why she was obliged to come back, to acknowledge her failure with the layout.

But Philip Ludlow looked so pleased, almost as if he'd been expecting her all along to return, and her own happiness in actually being face to face with the man who had been merely a daydream during the past few months was so overwhelming that nothing else seemed to matter. In the end she hadn't spoken about her work, only of the dreadful heat in town.

When they were in the car and Philip Ludlow was about to switch on the ignition, he turned and smiled at her gently. She knew then that he could see she was upset.

"If way shouldn't open for you this time," he told her, "just remember, you can always come back."

She'd started to blurt out that she could never come back because Denny—— But she'd caught herself and said nothing. She didn't even thank him.

Denny, Vaughn thought now, and the beauty of the garden below was suddenly painful to her. Maybe she shouldn't have come.

If Denny could only feel this, though, Vaughn thought, swallowing against the tightness in her throat, if he could only meet Philip Ludlow, he'd understand.

Would he? Would Denny find his troubled self unraveling in the older man's presence, as hers had done the other time?

She rested her face in her hands sadly, her elbows supported on the sill. The other time—— Yes, of course, she'd felt herself unravel the other time, but then she'd been full of confidence. Now, everything was wrong—her work, her marriage, and even her relation with the children. She couldn't get them to do a thing, no matter how she kept after them. Neil was all shut up and wounded-looking since she'd made him face reality about the boat, and Susan was off in a world of her own, just like Denny. They'd politely closed a door on Vaughn. She stood outside.

The sound of a car, more like the clatter of a small truck, brought her back to Kendal, and she hurried to the other window, from which she could see the driveway. A red jeep came rattling up and stopped at the garage. As its flimsy door was opened, a young man in a navy officer's raincoat jumped out, then turned to help a girl down.

Philip Ludlow came across the lawn to greet his visitors.

The cousins!

For Pete's sake, Vaughn exclaimed to herself. She laughed at the surprise. That loosened the tightness in her throat.

She'd known she was romanticizing when she pictured the cousins arriving in a buggy wearing bonnets. There'd been nothing like that when she was here before. Vaughn hadn't really expected bonnets. But for some reason she'd taken it for granted that the cousins would be pious, unmarried females, quite naturally the age of Philip Ludlow.

These people—obviously a couple—must be in their late twenties. Even from way up here, Vaughn thought, the man's resemblance to Philip Ludlow was striking. He had the same bearing, only looser in the joints, the same close-cut hair, though his was fair, and the shy, yet outreaching smile, which charmed Vaughn in the older man, was his too.

The girl, Vaughn decided instantly, was a knockout, not only her figure, her genteel, well-put-together features, but her clothes. One didn't have to be close up to appreciate the expensive cut of her

Sandringham reefer or the care that had gone into her simple hair-do.

The two newcomers chatted and laughed with Philip Ludlow as they walked toward the house, moving easily and, somehow, though they never touched each other, giving the impression that they moved in unison, responding to the same inner rhythm.

Denny and I moved like that once, Vaughn thought wistfully, as she turned away from the window and opened the overnight case. Or——

She stopped in mid-thought, stopped unpacking, holding the make-up kit and the jar of face cream in the air motionless a minute. Or were they ever? Like *that*?

Oh yes, her heart cried, yes, we were, long ago.

But if that were so, how was it possible that now——

A little row of books stood on the candlestand beside the bed. They didn't look like the juveniles on the shelves, but were obviously adult, thoughtfully placed there for a guest.

I wish I weren't too rushed to keep up with things, Vaughn thought, not recognizing a single title.

In a hurry now to go down to meet the cousins, she nevertheless dropped the make-up kit onto the bed for a second and picked up a volume.

She'd never heard of Isaac Penington, the author, but that didn't mean anything, she thought, opening the book. New publications kept coming out so fast.

The antique wording of the introduction was a surprise.

He that readeth these things, let him not strive to comprehend them, but be content with what he feeleth thereof suitable to his own present estate, and as the life grows in him, and he in the life, the words will of themselves open to him.

Vaughn shut the book over her finger and stood staring out at the shadows in the garden.

. . . and as the life grows in him, and he in the life, the words will of themselves open to him.

How was it that she'd let poetry slip away? When she was growing up it had been a world to her, a charm that overspread everything, like the sunlight in this room. But in her hurry to get ahead, she'd put it from her as unessential. Nowadays, even if she had the time, she'd never think of opening a book of poetry. Like her longing for home, this urge had been gradually smothered till it died.

What made me think of poetry? she wondered, putting the book back on the candlestand.

It was prose, seventeenth century, judging by the sound of it. But it had spoken to something in her which had once been moved by poetry.

Dreamily she reached for the make-up kit.

Standing before the bureau, rubbing cream up along her temples, she considered the face reflected by the tiny rectangle of mirror, in front of which Philip Ludlow's son had presumably knotted his tie years ago, before he became a man and went off to do whatever it was that pleased his father so. Vaughn couldn't remember what exactly.

She looked different.

Though it was such a tiny mirror it seemed to show her more of herself than she'd ever seen, a tentativeness of expression that was never there before, as if she were peering about, feeling her way. She'd always been such a positive person——

But of course, she told herself, briskly massaging her throat, without eyeshadow and lipstick, the grease high lighting her cheekbones, showing up the little creases in her forehead and at the corners of her mouth, she did look different. Still, didn't she see herself this way every night and morning at home? How could another person be looking out at her from young Ludlow's mirror?

Impulsively she wiped off the cream. Now she'd be able to see what she looked like in Kendal with absolutely nothing on her face, stripped down to her real self. She stared at it, half closing her eyes, skinning back the veil that held her hair.

How did she look to Philip Ludlow? Did he see through her make-up?

Furious for wondering, she pulled off the veil. What difference did it make how she looked to him? He was nothing to her but an uncritical elderly friend. But to Denny, to herself—— How did she look to herself?

She tried to see, yet nothing made any sense, only suddenly an irrelevant thought struck her.

So that's it, she realized with surprise, so that's why I thought they'd be old and would wear those bonnets—because then I'd be younger, and *my* hat . . .

She'd wanted first place in his attention. What a nasty little cat she was, deep down.

She spoke to herself severely as she buttoned the muted green shantung and put on her pumps. Starting down the stairs, she spoke to herself as severely as she would have done to Susan.

Remember, she said, you're only a stranger here, an interloper, really. These are his *cousins*. Remember!

But when she stood at the door of the parlor and Philip Ludlow and the two young people rose, smiling in greeting, such warm, impersonal love reached out to include her that she forgot.

2.

Their name was Ludlow too—Sally and Luke—and the minute she saw them close up, Vaughn knew she was going to like them. They'd driven over from Narragansett Bay, where they lived, Philip Ludlow told her, adding that Luke was the son of his cousin William.

The first thing Vaughn noticed was that they were smoking. So some Friends did.

Then maybe, she thought, for one single, hopeful second, maybe they'll have a drink too.

But no. Not in Philip Ludlow's house, anyway. Supper was announced, and they went in, Luke escorting Vaughn with an easy, modern version of his cousin's courtesy. She liked him more and more.

The dining room was cool, fresh. Faded daylight came through the wide-open windows.

Like yards and yards of pale silk, Vaughn said to herself, sitting down.

There was a bowl of white roses on the table and the most wonderful food: roast lamb with vegetables from Philip Ludlow's garden—peas and asparagus and little new potatoes.

It was the nicest dinner party, Vaughn thought, she'd ever been to. These distant cousins—distant most of all in years—seemed to find the most terrific pleasure in being together with one another and with her. Why was it, she wondered, that in Denny's and her crowd people hardly ever began to warm up to each other till they'd had a few drinks?

Sally and Luke assumed that she, like themselves, had come for the purpose of attending Quarterly Meeting.

"No," Vaughn said briskly. "I'm here on business." She was about to enlarge on this, to go into details about her work, when she happened to glance at Philip Ludlow.

He was looking right at her, and his expression made her still. It was a queer mixture of compassion and pleading, not intended to be seen. The moment their eyes met, he hastily withdrew this expression from his face, turning toward the window and observing that the sky looked as though there might soon be a break in the heat.

Oh, Vaughn cried to herself, moved without understanding.

Trying to appear casual, she addressed a noncommittal remark to Sally, then saw that she, too, had noticed Philip Ludlow's look.

What did it mean?

Only Luke seemed unaware of any emotional tension. He was in business himself, he explained now. What kind of work did Vaughn's agency handle?

She was delighted to tell him, but while she talked, expanding on coverage, readership, color processes as opposed to monotone, she kept wondering about that look of Philip Ludlow's. She didn't dare glance in his direction again.

It was as if he were trying to get a message through to her about a fugitive, as if they were fellow "conductors" on that railroad.

He—sure, Vaughn said to herself—he could be one of those people, but not I. I wouldn't care enough to take the risk.

Suddenly, sitting there, listening to Luke with what Vaughn hoped looked like attention, she wondered: Is that why I can't write it? Does one have to *care?*

It was a new idea. In advertising, one's own feelings played no more part than in acting, she always thought. The product had to be presented as enticingly as possible. Whether the copy writer cared personally about it or not was so immaterial as never even to have occurred to anyone. But maybe for a thing like this——

As they were leaving the dining room and entering the little parlor again she filed the idea away in her mind. There might be something to it.

"Thee doesn't mind, does thee, Cousin Philip," Sally was asking, "if Luke and I drop in on the Browns later?"

Philip Ludlow gave her a look of affectionate accord. "They're expecting you," he said.

"Do you know them?" Luke asked, turning to Vaughn.

She shook her head.

"The last time you were here," Philip Ludlow reminded her, "we saw Jeanie at the homestead. Later we went down to the beach where Bart works on the boats. Remember?"

"Oh yes," Vaughn answered coldly. "That man."

"What a guy!" Luke exclaimed. "What a wonderful guy!"

So he too—— What was there about Bart that these people admired?

Vaughn chose the low, rush-seated chair by the fireplace, the one she'd sat in the first time she was here. It was too hot now for a fire, but sitting here the other time, she'd felt uncommonly relaxed and happy.

"Yes," Philip Ludlow was saying, "Bart's doing a wonderful piece of work. Most of those boys he's helping were in serious trouble before he came."

"I don't see how he does it," Sally exclaimed. "I mean, he seems to look so much further than the rest of us. There's a definite picture in his mind of the way the people around him can be helped, not just wishful thinking, but actually living inside the difficulties of those boys and working his way out along with them."

"But why?" Vaughn asked. "Why does he do that, when he has a wife and——"

The three Ludlows were looking at her queerly, so that she felt as if she'd said something out of place. Was her reasoning cockeyed? Or was theirs?

"What about the baby?" she asked, to change the subject.

"A little boy," Sally announced. "Bartholomew the Third."

Luke turned to Vaughn. "You know, of course," he asked, "that Bart was a CO?"

Vaughn shook her head.

"Most of those boys felt the peace testimony wasn't only a stand they took in wartime," he told her, "but something they'd have to work for the rest of their lives. Easing tensions between races and hostile groups, relieving suffering, helping misfits adjust to society— these, they feel, are their principal jobs."

Vaughn was out of her depth. "A CO?" she repeated. Denny's CO——

"A Conscientious Objector," Philip Ludlow explained, seeing her puzzlement. "Like many young Friends, Bart couldn't square it with his conscience to go to war."

So that was it, Vaughn thought, that was why she didn't like that man! He was a coward. Without exactly knowing what it was, she'd sensed something. Her disgust probably showed in her face, because Philip Ludlow began to explain the religious basis for this attitude.

"We've always taken literally the command to love our enemies, to overcome evil with good," he said simply, "though far too often we've failed to uphold this testimony."

"But, Philip Ludlow," Vaughn cried, "you just don't know what it was like! Denny was in the Battle of the Bulge and——" She couldn't go on. The horror of those days, the fear of bad news, all she'd lived through—how could she describe it to this sheltered man? Anyone who hadn't known firsthand——

He looked at her intently. "Your husband?" he asked. "So was George. Their paths may have crossed."

"George?" Vaughn repeated, unable to place the name.

"Our older son."

"Then you do know what it was like," she exclaimed. "One could never love——"

"Yes," Philip Ludlow broke in gravely, "I know what it was like." He was silent a moment. "Our other son, John, was a CO," he said then. His voice was very sad. "We saw both sides, my wife and I."

Vaughn glanced quickly at the photograph on the little writing desk. Out of the face of that deeply cherished person the large, grave eyes looked back at her.

It seemed best to drop the matter and speak of something else. "Is it his room you put me in?" she asked. "George's?"

"No," Philip Ludlow answered. "Sally and Luke have George's room. You're in John's."

"Oh—John's." Vaughn couldn't quite hide her disappointment. She didn't care to have John's room. He was the one who was a CO, or whatever the letters were. Anyone who wasn't willing to fight for his country——

But how silly, she said to herself. It's really a nice room, with that view of the garden. Only, in the mirror——

She'd looked so different in that mirror—tentative—as though she weren't quite sure what she was.

"Don't you think," Philip Ludlow asked, turning to Luke, "Bart's war experience developed this gift for helping through friendship?"

"But I thought you just said he didn't go to war," Vaughn exclaimed. These people could mix her up better than any she'd ever known.

"He was in one of those volunteer units that cared for mental patients," Luke told her. "Just college kids, not trained for anything like that. It must have been grim. That's what gave Bart this understanding."

"That's all very well," Vaughn said, "but not to defend one's country—— Weren't you in the Navy?" she asked him. "That raincoat——"

"Yes, I was."

"I thought so," she said with relief. "You're a Quaker, but you wouldn't act that way. You're too brave."

"It sometimes takes more courage to stand out against the opinion of the majority than to go with it," he said, and he sounded very troubled. "I didn't live up to my religious conviction."

Vaughn said nothing.

"Look, Vaughn," he pleaded, "you're not the only one who can't see this thing the way we do. But just think—if every young man in the world had taken Bart's stand, there simply couldn't have been any fighting. The world wouldn't be in its present mess."

"But the Germans," Vaughn broke in, "and the Japs. And now the Russians—— It's purely self-preservation."

"In a physical sense, yes," Luke conceded. "But if war is wrong, even survival can't justify it."

Cripes, Vaughn thought, giving up, I wish he weren't so nice. Then I could hate him, the way I should, for thinking as he does.

"Say," Luke exclaimed, jumping to his feet, "it's getting late. Come on, Sally." He took his wife's hand and, grinning, dragged her off the sofa.

All four of them went out together through the dooryard to the side lawn.

Sally walked with Vaughn. "I wish you'd come to our place some time," she said. "Do you sail? We live on the water when Luke isn't working."

Her friendliness touched Vaughn. After all, hadn't they only just met? "I'd love to," she answered warmly, "but I haven't sailed since I was a kid. At home." And she wondered for an instant why she still called East Bolton "home." Wasn't her home the apartment in New York?

"We'd like you to come," Sally said.

"Neil, my fourteen-year-old, thinks he wants a boat," Vaughn told Sally, smiling as she remembered how she'd had to talk Neil out of the idea.

Standing beside the house with Philip Ludlow and watching Sally and Luke get into the jeep, Vaughn thought: Denny would like these two. They're our kind. And yet, so different.

3. "They're nice," Vaughn exclaimed with enthusiasm as she and Philip Ludlow stood on the side lawn watching Sally and Luke drive off.

"Yes," Philip Ludlow agreed. "I'm so glad you happened to come at Quarterly Meeting time so you three could meet. When you were here in the spring, I had a hunch you'd hit it off together."

"They're sort of like us," Vaughn remarked. "You know—Denny and me and our friends. Oh," she added quickly, seeing his surprise, "not really like us. Not even a little. But our kind—young marrieds trying to get on."

Philip Ludlow was taking her around to the back of the house. "Would you like to see the garden?" he asked. Without waiting for her reply, he said, "Yes, Sally and Luke are trying to get on. But they're deeply concerned, too, so that actually they're helping many others get on, along with themselves. Luke has many concerns."

"You mean," Vaughn asked, "he owns several firms?"

"No, I don't mean that," Philip Ludlow exclaimed with amusement. "Luke has only one business, but he has a lot of what we call 'religious concerns,' projects for helping needy people."

Vaughn burst out laughing. "Quakers talk so funny!" she said.

Philip Ludlow laughed with her. "We do."

They passed through a little latticed arbor covered with climbing roses, and he stopped to pick some beetles off the buds.

"Unhun," Vaughn murmured, nodding thoughtfully, her mind still on Luke, "he looks like a do-gooder—like you. Still, I can't understand what he sees in Bart. You—you're different. You like every-

123

body. But a guy like that—— He's wonderful, too, but one can see he's got a lot of ambition."

"Your son would, don't you think?" Philip Ludlow asked, still busy with the beetles.

"My son——?"

"Would understand about Bart." He turned and looked at her.

"Oh," she exclaimed, following him at last. "Well, maybe. Yes, I guess he would. Neil's a little like that himself," she admitted ruefully. "And he'd love the boats—wanted to make one of his own, a couple of weeks ago, right in our apartment house. I had an awful time——"

She stopped, suddenly flustered, remembering how Philip Ludlow had intervened when she lost her temper then. He must be remembering too.

Her mind denied this at once. How could he? Philip Ludlow hadn't even been there, it insisted. But her feelings weren't convinced. It was impossible that she'd only imagined, that evening . . .

"You think I'm wrong, don't you?" she blurted out, to her surprise. "About Neil?"

Philip Ludlow seemed puzzled, so that now Vaughn knew he couldn't remember. But he didn't demand an explanation.

Instead, observing her distress, he took out his penknife and, turning toward the arbor, cut a little red rose, already tightly curled in sleep. Smiling at Vaughn till she reached for it, he laid the flower in her hand.

"Oh," she exclaimed, touched, so happy. "No one's ever just given me something that way." And then she added quickly, "Except Denny, of course. But I mean a stranger——"

"We're not strangers any more," he declared, closing his knife.

She looked up at him gratefully.

"On Nantucket," he told her, "they had a rose, bloomed at this time, which they called Quarterly Meeting. My grandmother came from there, and when she was a young girl, she used to hide one in her kerchief. You see, in her day Quakers were so plain they weren't supposed to wear flowers. Seems funny now, doesn't it?"

Vaughn looked down at the tight little bud in her hand. "You said the first evening that a business interview could also be an opportunity for making friends. Remember?" she asked. "I didn't believe it then. Now that I know, I wish——" She sighed, unable to finish, suddenly not quite certain that Denny would see what she saw in this man.

Maybe Philip Ludlow guessed what was in her mind, for he quickly began speaking of impersonal things: tomorrow's sessions and the Friends who were coming from a distance to attend. "Friends from away," he called them.

"Meeting for Worship's in the morning," he told Vaughn. "Meeting for Business after lunch. I think there'll be time at the close of the business session to let you have another look at the hiding place."

The hiding place! Vaughn had forgotten all about going there. Imagine, she said to herself, imagine me forgetting that.

"We'll get back late," Philip Ludlow was saying, "but Sally and Luke won't mind waiting for supper. We can take our time. Unless," he added, a new thought appearing to strike him, "you have to leave. You were planning, though, weren't you," he asked hopefully, "to stay till First Day?"

"Oh yes," Vaughn assured him. "I told Denny First—I mean, Sunday. That same train. I *think*," she added, shocked that she could have any doubt, "I *think* he'll meet me."

Philip Ludlow shot a swift glance at her. The doubt must have communicated itself to him. When he said, "It's fine that you're staying," it was with a little hesitation.

Had he really noticed something? Vaughn wondered, glancing down at the rose in her hand. Did it show in her face, stick out all over, maybe, that she and Denny——

But if Philip Ludlow had noticed, he gave no further indication. He was scanning the sky. "Going to be good Quarterly Meeting weather," he predicted.

They walked around the garden slowly, Philip Ludlow naming

everything almost formally, as if he were introducing his friends to Vaughn: the alyssum in the border falling softly over their feet, the white petunias behind it, and the tall bank of larkspur from which, Vaughn supposed, the bouquet in her room had been cut. Twilight had bleached all the flowers of their daytime coloring and touched them with a strange glow.

Like figures in a dreamworld, Vaughn said to herself.

Glancing up, she saw that she was directly beneath the window of her room, the window from which she'd leaned out when she arrived, longing for something.

Philip Ludlow was bent over a rosebush, still looking for beetles, though it was really too dark, Vaughn thought, to see much.

Suddenly, standing there on the cool grass and watching this man bend over his growing things the way she herself used to bend over the children's cribs before she went to bed, Vaughn had the preposterous impulse to tell him everything. Now, while they were by themselves, she'd pour it all out—what Denny had said last night. It would be such a relief, getting the whole story off her chest. If Philip Ludlow really had noticed, maybe she should.

But no. It was unthinkable. A nice girl didn't discuss her marital difficulties with outsiders. Things like that—one might tell one's parents *maybe*. But no one else.

Vaughn sighed. She'd never wanted to tell her parents things.

I didn't want to tell them while I still could, she thought, staring at the reflection of the sky on the river.

They had always criticized.

Philip Ludlow wouldn't do that. But how could Vaughn tell her trouble to the very man who'd made Denny—— That kiss last night. And the one in Grand Central. A tremor of fear passed over Vaughn.

Philip Ludlow saw it.

"Chilly?" he asked. Before Vaughn could protest that she was warm enough, he'd taken her arm and was leading her through the deepening darkness to the house.

Lamps had been lighted in the little parlor. It looked cheerful and inviting, and as Vaughn took the low, rush-seated chair by the fire-place, she had a pleasant sense of snug, familiar ease, almost, she thought to her surprise, like coming home. She was happy again.

But then, glancing around the room, her eyes met those of Philip Ludlow's wife looking out from the photograph on the writing desk. Though Vaughn still held the rose, she was seized all at once with a startling, sickening envy. Remembering the tone of his voice, the tender movement of his hands when he showed her the picture, she felt this dreadful pang shoot through her—sheer, undisguised envy of the dead woman who'd had the knack for evoking such deep, undying love.

4. "As a small boy—six or seven," Philip Ludlow half whispered to Vaughn while they walked to Meeting that bright June morning—he might have been telling her a secret— "I was always hunting for something to look at in the Meeting-house. You know how it is; you've been there. Nothing but white-washed walls and plain benches. The maple tree by the south window was the only thing that was any fun for me, and I used to stare at it swaying in the breeze or shining in the sunlight or dripping with rain."

"You poor thing," Vaughn murmured. Yes, she could under-stand how hard it would be for a child to sit still so long. She herself——

"Autumn First Days were best," Philip Ludlow recalled. "Then the gold and reddish leaves dropped and swirled up again in great clouds before the window."

"You poor little thing," Vaughn repeated.

Philip Ludlow nodded. "After a while," he confided, "I learned to bow my head and yet stretch my eyes far enough to see people. I could guess by the way a man would fidget that he was about to get up and speak, or if a woman began untying the strings of her bonnet, I knew she was going to offer prayer."

There was such charm, such vivacity darting in and out of this man's face as he spoke that Vaughn guessed he had had a childhood on which he could look back with delight, in spite of having to sit still.

"We used to have Elders on the facing bench in those days," he went on, as they were nearing the Meetinghouse, "and sometimes, when they'd closed their eyes to center down, I thought they were dead. Really. I'd squirm so my mother'd have to lay her hand on my knee." He turned and smiled at Vaughn, but actually, she thought, it was at the far-off little boy that he was smiling, half in pity and half with longing for him.

"Suddenly," he went on, apparently still thinking of the Elders, "the body attached to the face would rise, life would return to the features, the eyes opened, the mouth spoke. I didn't understand, so I'd look for another dead Friend. And again I'd feel my mother's touch, though when I dropped my eyes her hands would be lying in her lap."

His hushed voice told Vaughn how deeply he cherished this memory.

"Only an illusion of touch, you see," he explained gravely, "the leading of her spirit away from outward things——"

"That was how you learned finally to—to——" Vaughn began. She didn't know how to put it.

"To center down," Philip Ludlow concluded for her. "Yes, and I came to love the plainness and the silence. But one has to be pretty well grown up for that. It was the same with our boys," he added thoughtfully as he and Vaughn mounted the steps of the Meetinghouse and passed through the door.

Now that Vaughn was here again, she noticed things that had escaped her before: the old-fashioned wooden blinds folded back from the tall windows and little Philip's maple tree patterning the sunlit glass with shadow.

She remembered how unwillingly she'd come that other time,

and resolved now to try to understand, to be fair to Philip Ludlow, but even as she entered, she felt the silence closing in on her, and she recoiled. Could she face what lay in wait behind it—her unknown, deeply buried self?

It was all right for these people. They had their inner light, whatever that was, which they were always talking about. But for Vaughn——

Philip Ludlow led her to the same bench they had occupied the other time, and as they sat down, Sally and Luke came and took the places alongside.

Sitting here again was like being in the low, rush-seated chair by Philip Ludlow's fire, Vaughn thought, savoring the familiarity. She didn't look around, for, like the child she'd just been hearing about, she knew there was nothing to see. There would be no music, either, no relief from the contemplation of her soul.

When Philip Ludlow bowed his head, Vaughn did the same, less in imitation of him than out of the habit of her own childhood. And without thinking what she was doing, for the first time in twenty years she silently repeated the Lord's Prayer.

She listened as each word echoed in her mind across the past, and each word was new, not at all related to the rigmarole she'd obediently reeled off in youth. It had a meaning which she'd never dreamed existed. As the timelessness of the last words broke upon her consciousness, she was carried through the silence, detached from all her known world, her thoughts, her cares, her ties of love, and the many duties she daily laid upon herself.

She was carried to a place where she'd never been before, where the quiet which had seemed to be an adversary, closing in on her as she entered it, had become a good thing—a refuge.

So remote was she that a voice speaking suddenly made her jump.

"We are met in the presence of God," it said softly.

Vaughn felt the goose-pimples rise along her arms. *In the presence of God.* For a second, in that detachment, that was how it had seemed to her: *in the presence of God.*

It was a woman who'd spoken, somewhere at the back of the room, but Vaughn felt no curiosity. She didn't try to locate the speaker. She was trying to locate God. A moment ago it had seemed—— Yet now, the more she tried, the further away she was getting.

She opened the snap of her purse, holding her fingers tensely over it so no sound would escape, then closed it again, opened, closed it.

The pure in heart were supposed to see God. She remembered that. If she couldn't, did it mean she wasn't pure in heart? Could it be true, what Denny thought? Could it?

No, she cried within herself, squeezing the purse till the snap cut into her palm. No, I'm sure it isn't that. It isn't that!

Then what? She really did try to be a decent person, to look out for her family, to be honest and, when occasion demanded, charitable. Could anyone in her position do much better?

Oh, she thought, I fall down on the job lots of times, especially after a hard day at the office. But on the whole——

Still, when, for the first time in her grown-up life, she really wanted to see God, she couldn't. Was it the same for Him, looking at her? Or could He see?

If He does, she thought suddenly, how do I appear?

It was terrifying to think of her soul without make-up—she'd never really seen it herself. She'd never sat before the mirror and applied cold cream to it, removing layers of cosmetics—the foundation, the lipstick, the eyeshadow, seeing herself in the skin of her soul like that.

She didn't even know where her soul was, how to put her hands on it.

The uneasiness in her mounted. She was being pushed by a sense of urgency, a driving need to find her self before the hour was up, to look at it while there was still time, so that she felt out of breath, as though she were running. Her heart pounded so loud that she thought surely the whole Meeting must hear it.

Running to catch up with her soul.

She looked wildly around the room at the rows and rows of quiet people, at Sally and Luke on her one hand and Philip Ludlow on the other, all completely oblivious to the commotion within her.

And suddenly she saw with relief that this was it, the place where all the anguish which she daily pushed back from her consciousness could be exposed—the whole nasty mess, which was always being crammed with more and more stuff. Here, into the bare room, into the quiet, she could empty it all out—the things she mustn't tell Philip Ludlow about Denny, about the children. Things further back—things she hadn't wanted to say to Denny, to her parents, though it would have been better to say them. And all the little hurtful things, so small in themselves, which had divided her from Denny, always a little more, because she'd never felt sorry till it was too late.

Not each separate event, for there were too many and they'd been crammed in and pushed down till they no longer existed as shapes in her memory, only in the marrow of her bones.

Tears rushed into her eyes as she recognized how hopeless it all was.

But she couldn't waste this precious hour feeling sorry for herself. She must find her soul and look at it, as God could do. It was a chance that would never come to her again. If she could only make use of this time, as these people did, if she could only draw from it that wonderful simplicity, which made their everyday acts important, not just to themselves—if she, Vaughn, could draw some of this out of the hour, she might be able to go home and——

She couldn't focus on what she would do then, for that drive in her to rush out and achieve was stilled for the moment. She couldn't even think. She could only sit and feel the quiet surround her, exposing the ache which was so great that it seemed all of her, her whole self, to the healing silence, and gradually the ache became absorbed in it.

There was a slight movement of the bench, a rustle against Vaughn's sleeve, and Philip Ludlow was on his feet.

Vaughn was so startled, she almost dropped her handbag on the floor. She'd completely forgotten Philip Ludlow. The past few months he'd been so much in her mind that he'd popped up at very inconvenient moments. Yet now, when he was here, right next to her, he didn't seem to exist. How funny. She'd been so far away in that strange new place, she'd forgotten him till she found he was standing up beside her, tall and still.

"All of us," he was saying, speaking very slowly, almost as if he were thinking it out as he went along, "come here sometimes feeling forlorn and empty of spirit. The inner light seems hard to see."

Forlorn! Vaughn jumped. He was speaking of her, telling everyone, right here in Meeting, that she—— It was exactly how she felt, *forlorn*. So he'd guessed about Denny and her, he *knew*——

She held her breath, looking up at Philip Ludlow, but though she could see the side of his face quite plainly, the personality behind it seemed to grow less distinct as he spoke.

Did he know? His eyes weren't on her. She was right here, next to him, yet they didn't seem to notice her. They didn't seem to notice anyone. As he talked, they had that gazing-within expression which seemed to go with "centering down."

"In some strange way," Philip Ludlow continued, "our lonely, empty spirit seems to transmit strength to someone else and receives it in turn from someone who had, perhaps, nothing to give to himself."

No, Vaughn decided, turning from him, he didn't know. He wasn't speaking about her. But what he said did have special meaning for her, just the same.

"Through this experience," he said, as though it were something quite fresh, a thought that had just struck him, "we seem to discover in ourselves both the impulse and the means to 'walk cheerfully over the world, answering that of God in every one.'"

He sat down with a minimum of movement and bowed his head.

The other people in the room seemed to turn their attention from him and to be meditating again.

As Vaughn bowed her head, too, resting her hands quietly in her lap, she had a sense of being joined by the words Philip Ludlow had spoken to everyone around her, joined by something even deeper than his words.

And suddenly she was overcome again with longing, as she'd been when she arrived at his house and looked out at the garden, smelling the roses, only now it wasn't a formless longing, but was shaping itself into his words: to be able to answer that of God in him. That, she saw now, was what she really longed for.

But the man beside her—she'd forgotten him again, so that she was taken unawares when she felt a touch on her finger and, turning, saw that Philip Ludlow had stretched out his hand to her.

5. "Thee came back to us," Alberta Mansfield exclaimed happily, as Vaughn walked down the aisle with the Ludlows after Meeting.

The warmth of the old lady's welcome was touching.

Edmund Mansfield remembered Vaughn too. "I ran across an entry in my father's diary the other day," he told her with what she could only think of as youthful enthusiasm, "and I said to Alberta: 'that young woman who was so interested in the Underground Railroad would appreciate this.'"

"Oh yes," Vaughn murmured.

The Underground Railroad—she'd forgotten again. Someone was always having to remind her why she was here. After all, she didn't come to Kendal to go to Quaker Meeting.

She was unexpectedly surrounded by a mass of swinging pigtails —the little Lancashires greeting her, but only with smiles, shyly. They seemed afraid to speak. The eldest girl wasn't there, but the mother came waddling up, beaming at Vaughn over her wide bosom.

The Ludlows were leaving the Meetinghouse. Vaughn stayed. She wanted to be nice, to show Mary Lancashire that she wasn't really so awful.

133

"I had a wonderful time with you last March," she said, hoping the woman didn't remember how ugly she'd been about paying for the room. "And I told Susan—that's my little girl—all about you," she said to the children gaily. "Susan thought it must be simply wonderful to have a lot of sisters."

"Hasn't she *any?*"

"How old is she?"

So easy to break through their shyness, if you put your mind to it, Vaughn thought.

"She just has a brother," she answered, smiling at the circle of faces as charmingly as she could, "and he doesn't care much to play with her."

"You must bring her to us," Mary Lancashire said, "and the brother too. We need a boy in the house."

Vaughn was taken aback.

Next thing, she said to herself, she'll be inviting Denny.

"And, of course, their father," Mary Lancashire went on. "We need a father too," she added softly.

Oh, Vaughn exclaimed to herself, I didn't realize her husband was dead. I knew that week end that there wasn't a man around, but I didn't stop to wonder——

She was horrified. How could she have stayed under someone's roof without taking that much interest? Could any decent visitor have failed to see the courage of this woman, coping singlehanded with five children?

I must be a very self-centered person, she thought with a shock.

Mary Lancashire had been talking on. "Sometime this summer," she was saying.

Vaughn's attention returned, appraising the tone of the woman's voice. This was no come-and-see-us-some-day invitation, extended without sincerity.

I bet she wouldn't say it, Vaughn told herself, unless she meant it.

"Thank you," she said aloud. "It'd be wonderful. Next year, maybe, if we don't take a trip. This vacation we're going to Maine with some friends, that is, my husband and I. Neil's going to camp——"

She didn't know what to say for Susan.

The little girls went running out into the sunshine.

"If way opens," Mary Lancashire murmured, starting after them.

Susan, Vaughn was thinking, as she moved along, *she* had goose-pimples, too, in church.

Suddenly, unaccountably, she longed for the child. Yet she'd seen her just yesterday and tomorrow she'd be home again, watching Susan skip through the apartment, her bright hair falling back from her head as she lifted her face to leap . . .

It isn't that, Vaughn thought, feeling the desire increase. It's not so much that I want to *see* her as that I wish I'd thought about her during the silence. About Neil and Denny too.

She didn't know why she felt this, only that, perhaps, holding them up before her when she was carried away like that, maybe she would have understood . . .

Mary Lancashire was saying something about having to go now and help with lunch.

In the vestibule Philip Ludlow stood waiting for Vaughn. As they went down the steps together into the Yard, other people came and spoke to her—Jeanie and Bart Brown, and some women whom Vaughn must have met the last time, though she didn't remember them now.

Like old home week, she said to herself, amused. But she was pleased, too, at being so warmly received.

"We're lunching in the Yard," Philip Ludlow explained, leading the way around the building. "We always do in Sixth Month, unless it rains." He looked up, considering the weather.

"It's perfect today," Vaughn said, looking up, too, at the country-blue sky that had only a few harmless-looking clouds floating on it.

Philip Ludlow shook his head gloomily. "Wind's shifted," he said. "I wasn't such a good prophet last night."

It didn't seem possible that the weather could change. Not a breath of air stirred the maples and elms in the Yard.

135

"I liked what you said in the Meeting," Vaughn told Philip Ludlow shyly, "though I guess it was over my head. It scared me, sort of, for a second. You should have warned me before we went in that you were going to speak."

"But I didn't know," he answered. "How could I tell you?"

She turned to him in surprise. "Didn't you prepare it?"

He shook his head. "Sometimes," he said, "one has a feeling that the group is joined in a common purpose and one seems called upon to put this purpose, this aspiration into words."

"Oh," she said, "I thought, because you don't have a minister, you took turns preaching."

How was *she* to know?

"There are times," Philip Ludlow added, "when no one feels moved to speak. It's no little thing to break the silence."

"You know," Vaughn said thoughtfully, as they walked on, "it's nice of everyone not to mind my coming, when I'm so—different."

Philip Ludlow looked down at her in that shy, affectionate way that had touched Vaughn the first time she met him. "Not so different," he answered. "'True unity is in the inward life, not in outward conformity,' an early Quaker said."

"But that's just it," Vaughn exclaimed. "The inward life. I never even thought about things like that before."

This didn't seem to shock or even surprise Philip Ludlow. "The same man spoke to the subject in another beautiful passage," he observed. "Would you like to hear it, or have you heard enough," he asked, adding with a grin, "on an empty stomach?"

"I'm not hungry," Vaughn assured him. "Tell me."

They stood still beside a flowering shrub.

"'He that keeps not a day,'" Philip Ludlow quoted, in his quiet, precise voice, "'may unite in the same spirit, in the same life, in the same love, with him that keeps a day; and he who keeps a day may unite in heart and soul with the same spirit and life in him who keeps not a day; but he that judgeth the other because of either of these errs from the spirit, from the love, from the life, and so breaks the bond of unity.'"

136

He spoke slowly, as if he realized that for Vaughn this was a foreign language. And he graced the words, she thought, with the spirit and life and love—whatever they were—he was talking about. These shone in his eyes and sounded in his voice so that Vaughn believed she'd caught the drift of what he was saying, not through the words, but through him.

She was reminded of the sentence that had struck her yesterday afternoon in that book she'd found by her bedside, about life growing and words opening of themselves. Last night she'd been too tired to read more. She'd put the rose Philip Ludlow had given her into the toothbrush glass and placed it on the candlestand. Then she'd gone right to sleep. But tonight, she decided, she'd make a point of reading further.

Tonight—— She wondered what Denny and the children would be doing tonight. Maybe they'd play Canasta or listen to that program. Suddenly she cried, "I wish they were here," and, seeing Philip Ludlow's surprise, she explained, "Denny and the children."

"So do I," he replied so quickly that Vaughn knew he must have had the same idea. How did he come to be thinking about her family?

"But they wouldn't understand," she assured him. "Denny wouldn't be caught dead in church." She looked up swiftly, afraid Philip Ludlow would be shocked by her speaking so plainly. He didn't seem to be.

There was a long carriage shed behind the Meetinghouse, a row of open stalls. In the old days, Philip Ludlow explained, horses were tethered there while their masters were in Meeting.

"Such a pity," he said sadly, "it's falling to pieces. Some Friends feel we ought to have it taken down instead of paying for repairs, since it's no longer used."

Tables had been set under the trees. Sally and Luke, the Browns, and other young people, including the pigtail set, were loading them with jugs and platters. The men had taken off their jackets. Sunlight fell brightly through the trees onto their white shirts and the gay dresses of the girls.

"Looks like a feast," Vaughn observed. "I think maybe I am hungry, after all."

Philip Ludlow laughed approvingly. "Glad to hear it," he said. "Friends have a reputation for not underrating the importance of food."

Old Edmund Mansfield came slowly toward them. "Philip," he called, "thee's wanted in the shed. Seems thee's the only one who knows how to unpack ice cream."

Philip Ludlow excused himself and hurried off, leaving Vaughn with the old man.

Seeing him again, she remembered how comical and yet earnest he'd looked singing that song about Moses and Pharaoh, the time she'd gone to the homestead. Suddenly she had an idea.

"Edmund Mansfield," she said eagerly, speaking as loud as she could, "would you tell me something?"

"Gladly."

"You remember the day I came to your house? It was so dark in that hole, I didn't get a good look. When I was home, I got to thinking that maybe I'd missed what was down there. Is there—there *is* something down there, isn't there?"

She was embarrassed at betraying her ignorance.

"Yes," the old man answered gravely. "Yes, indeed there is."

Vaughn could have hugged him.

That was it—she'd missed the whole point. No wonder she hadn't been able to write the layout! But now, this afternoon, Philip Ludlow was going to take her out there again. As soon as the next session was over, she'd see at last——

"Thank you for telling me," she cried gratefully. And then she asked, fearful this slippery thing would elude her a second time, "Do you think I'll see it today? It'll be late, you know, dark——"

The old man looked at her. He was a very placid old man. "I think thee will," he said. "We usually see what we look for. Might be thee wasn't quite ready the other time."

"What do you mean?" Vaughn asked, startled, but the old man

hadn't heard. "What do you mean?" she repeated, as loud as she could, so that the question echoed against her own eardrums.

"Way will open," he assured her.

Those same words—Greek, to Vaughn.

"Young people trust too much to the evidence of their senses," Edmund Mansfield mused. "They forget some things are only to be seen with the inward eyes, just as some things are only to be heard with the ears of the soul."

"The inward *eyes?*" Vaughn cried. This mystical talk was getting on her nerves.

Edmund Mansfield looked at her searchingly, and suddenly he seemed struck by a different thought.

"Did thee mean some object?" he exclaimed, his placid voice taking the quavery tone of a worried old man. "Some tangible object?"

Vaughn held her breath a second and nodded violently. At last she'd got through to him! "A skeleton?" she whispered. Suspense had drained her voice of strength.

"I'm sorry," the old man said, seeing her agitation. "I didn't understand thee at first." He shook his head. "My hearing isn't what it was, thee sees. When one's eighty-five——"

"Is it a skeleton?" Vaughn broke in.

He shook his head again. "I thought thee meant the testimony left in that hole, the testimony to the way of love."

The testimony——

Vaughn didn't listen any longer. "Oh!" she groaned, too disappointed to care whether the old man noticed or not.

The *testimony——* And she'd thought—he'd led her to think—there really was something, that she had only to look once more. That hole, with its damp, nauseating smell, was just as empty as the sheet on which she'd planned to write the layout.

Edmund Mansfield looked at Vaughn sorrowfully, obviously in a fog, yet aware he'd caused her disappointment. Then his face brightened with forced hopefulness, as a grownup's does when he tries to make up to a child for taking away his treasure by promising some treat.

"This afternoon," he confided to her, "when thee comes to the homestead, I'll show thee the diary."

Vaughn bit her lip. What did she care about a diary?

Something else was flashing through her mind. When she told Philip Ludlow the first night that it hadn't really been necessary for her to come and see the hiding place, he'd answered that he was doubtful whether anyone, even seeing it, could imagine——

So he knew all along, she thought, suddenly angry at him. He knew then that I wouldn't be able to write it. Why didn't he tell me?

Was that what he'd meant yesterday when he'd said she could always come back if way didn't open this time?

Good Lord, how could this layout be such an impossible thing to do? Merely historical material slanted toward the public, applying sales pressure—she'd been trained for this, hadn't she? How had it turned into a spiritual problem? Naturally she wasn't prepared to handle religious stuff.

Could anybody else write it? Katie Martin? Could Katie, seeing the hiding place, imagine——

A touch on the arm brought her back to the old man. He was trying to get her attention.

"They're waiting for us," he said, indicating the people at the tables. Vaughn had a feeling he'd spoken before. She'd been too distraught to notice. "Isn't thee hungry?" he asked. Without waiting for an answer, he took Vaughn's arm and led her slowly across the grass to the place that had been saved for her between Philip Ludlow and Bart Brown. Then he went and sat down beside his wife.

As Philip Ludlow jumped up to push in her chair, the uncon- cealed pleasure in his face at her coming reminded Vaughn again of that first night, when he'd exclaimed, "So you're going to interpret the Underground Railroad . . . What a help!" That was the way he'd looked—so pleased that she'd thought for a moment he expected to get something out of her project himself. A rake-off was what she'd thought then, fool that she was in those days.

But now she knew what it was he expected. Smiling up at him as he was about to bend his head in the sudden hush, she knew: he expected way to open.

6.
Like a primitive, Vaughn said to herself as she peeked up through her lashes: the old people with a special character deeply marked in their faces, the forthright younger ones, the unsophisticated children, all reverently still before the meal, bowing their heads in the shade of the big trees.

Peeking at them, Vaughn wondered what, if anything, these people were saying to themselves.

All at once, unintentionally, she dropped her eyes, caught in their act of devotion. Her mind turned in, away from the world for a moment, at the same time looking farther out than usual, remembering the millions of people who weren't sitting down this noon to a square meal.

As suddenly as it had ceased, conversation broke out again, rippling up and down the tables. People beamed on one another with naïve pleasure, as if they hadn't met in years.

Bet a cookie it wasn't more than a few weeks ago, Vaughn said to herself, amused. If this is Sixth Month and they meet quarterly——

She would have been content to sit back quietly and take it all in, moved by the enchanting little picture. "Gentle" was the word she thought of. It suited both the mood of the assembly and the scene. But everyone had to speak a friendly word to her, even people she didn't know.

There was something about the way the women dressed that puzzled her. Homemade or mail-order clothes she would have understood here in the country. But they wore good things, and yet they had absolutely no style.

It's how they feel, she decided. They only want to be clean and neat and don't give a hang about looking smooth.

Philip Ludlow had piled food on her plate—cold meat and salad and homemade rolls. And on her other side Bart Brown was filling a paper cup with lemonade for her.

Of all the people in the whole crowd, why was she sitting next to him, the one person she disliked? Had Philip Ludlow engineered this? Yet, really, she thought, glancing sideways for a quick instant, he wasn't so bad. Quite a nice face, now that he'd shaved, with that purposeful expression and eyes that looked right at you.

"How old is your son?" he asked.

Vaughn was taken aback. Why should he be interested in Neil?

"Fourteen. Had his birthday last week."

"Philip Ludlow says he's a good kid," Bart went on. He had a very slow way of speaking.

"But he doesn't know him!" Vaughn exclaimed, swallowing the whole cupful of lemonade. Such a hot day——

Suddenly Vaughn was aware that Alice, the eldest Lancashire, had come over and was standing behind her chair, waiting, hoping no doubt to be noticed, yet doing nothing to gain attention. Her pigtails were wound around her head now, probably with the idea that this would make her look more grown up, but actually it only gave her eager face a more childish roundness. It was touching the way she seemed attracted to Vaughn, as if she were faint for a breath of the city.

Two bits she wants to be a copy writer, Vaughn said to herself, turning in her chair to greet Alice, or maybe a fashion designer, and nobody here understands her.

"I was looking for you," Vaughn lied, in her desire to show interest in the kid. "How're things?"

Alice dropped her eyes.

It might have been simply shyness on Alice's part, or that she was too overcome by Vaughn's glamour to speak, but to Vaughn that mute answer was like a cry out of her own adolescence. Things were terrible, it seemed to say, nothing but homework and housework, be-a-good-girl, go-to-meeting, thee-and-thy . . . High school stinks. Mother won't let me have dates . . .

Vaughn saw it all the way she'd known it in East Bolton, now modeled on Kendal lines. Her heart went out to the child.

"How would you like to come down to New York someday?" she asked. Someday——

The girl's eyes flew open in an ecstasy of unbelief and gratitude.

"In the fall," Vaughn promised lightly. Then, as the girl walked away, she regretted the words.

How soon one forgets that it's impossible to wait at that age, Vaughn said to herself. To her, fall seems years away. Turning back to the table, she thought, it isn't fair. I understand this kid, who's nothing to me. While Susan——

Both her neighbors were engaged in conversation, leaving Vaughn to her lunch. She noticed that while she'd been talking to Alice, Bart Brown had refilled her cup with lemonade.

As Philip Ludlow had predicted, there was nothing spiritual about the way Friends enjoyed their food. They were right, too, Vaughn decided, as she began eating. Everything was wonderful.

She was having a good time, but she felt vaguely uneasy. Something seemed about to happen—she didn't know what.

The sun shining through the trees made a shifting pattern of light and shade on the paper tablecloth. It fell softly on the people opposite. Everyone was bareheaded.

There's something about these people—an inner vitality, Vaughn thought, trying to analyze it.

She looked at Bart as he sat talking earnestly to Sally Ludlow. What was it he had, what was it they all had that she didn't have, so that she couldn't grasp the simple essence of her layout? "Inward eyes," as the old man had said?

Fat lot of good inward eyes would do me at the agency, Vaughn thought, smiling to herself as she took a drink.

Tepid lemonade in a paper cup. The sour-sweet mixture, faintly tinged with waxed cardboard, brought back to Vaughn in one sudden flash the whole sequence of her childhood summers—lazy afternoons on the porch in East Bolton with a couple of other kids, or alone out in the hammock under the trees, reading, a pitcher handy on the grass . . .

She let the cooling, carefree liquid dribble slowly over her tongue, remembering those happy days before she went to boarding school, not separately, but in a haze of sunlit memories, till she felt drunk on lemonade. Not all the drinks she'd ever sipped had made her feel so high.

The jug was within reach, and Vaughn helped herself to more.

Sundays they went to the lake. She would lie in the bottom of the boat, looking up at the sky, making animals out of the clouds. Her father rowed. He had very strong arms. No matter how sunburned and freckled they became, the inner sides remained white. Her mother always had some surprise for dessert. An easy, uncomplicated life. Vaughn went docilely to church. Boys hadn't yet appeared on her horizon.

Cupful after cupful she let the lemonade trickle down her throat, remembering those happy days.

But then—then they'd sent her away, out of this Eden, into a world of nasty little brats, where she'd had to claw and bite a path for herself till she got to college.

They'd sent her too young, not too young to close her buttons and comb her hair, but too young to understand her parents, to have known them as fellow adults.

I don't even know now, she thought sadly, what they really believed behind that East Bolton stuffiness.

She held the empty cup in her hand, trying to remember her father and mother—not their faces, but the people they were—but she couldn't even remember clearly how they looked.

When she'd left, she was still an adolescent in revolt. Everything about her parents was wrong. If she'd seen them later, with grown-up eyes, would she still be carrying around this bitterness?

But she'd never gone back. She'd only tried to show them: she was better than they thought her; she could get on in the world, be important, make money. She had more in her than they gave her credit for—they'd see.

Sitting here in Kendal, in this little Meetinghouse Yard among strangers who, for some reason, were feeding her and admitting her to their fellowship, though she wasn't one with them at all—here, in this unlikely place, Vaughn looked at her parents for the first time as a grown woman. Certainly they'd made mistakes, but she hadn't trusted to the goodness of their intentions. She'd only judged their clumsy deeds.

Never, till this moment, had she wanted to make up for the past, go back, discuss things.

Now, suddenly, she felt homesick, desperately, sickeningly home-sick—now, when there was no one left to go home to. She sat squeezing the paper cup, twisting it between her fingers. Homesick here, because perfect strangers were being kind to her. Why hadn't this happened while there was still time?

She stared down at the paper cup, afraid she couldn't hold back the tears. Then she was startled by what she heard.

"We're not strangers any more."

She turned quickly to look at Philip Ludlow, but he was eating thoughtfully, and she saw he hadn't spoken. It was only the echo in her mind of what he'd said last night when he cut her the rose.

She could never go home. Still, here, where she had such a sense of well-being—she could be here.

But you can't, something said in her, you can't! This isn't where you belong. You've simply crashed it by the merest fluke.

She'd slipped out of place—like a portrait loose from its mat. What was she doing here, anyway?

New York was her world—the apartment, the office, their circle of friends—with all the values and goals she'd set for herself in it. Not this.

She felt a little frightened, not by the thought that she'd slipped out of place, for, after all, that was merely momentary—of the day—but by something in the atmosphere, a sense of impending doom. Instinctively she found herself moving a fraction of an inch closer

145

to Philip Ludlow. But he didn't notice. He was talking to the Brown girl about shipping clothing to relief centers overseas.

Bart turned, and, without speaking, offered Vaughn a plate of ice cream, glancing at her with a hesitant grin, so that she wondered whether her unhappiness showed. He seemed eager to say something, but he was evidently not a conversationalist.

Vaughn realized that she ought to be a little civil after he'd manifested such an interest in Neil, but all she could think of was that she was dying for a smoke, and it was clear to her, looking up and down the tables, that smoking wasn't done around here. Even Luke and Sally were restraining themselves. How did they stand it?

"I hear you're doing a wonderful job with those boys," she managed to say finally, though she didn't feel much sympathy for the whole business.

Instantly Bart's bony face, homely in repose, lit up with an enthusiasm that seemed to glow in him, radiating outward so warmly that Vaughn couldn't ignore it.

This means everything to him, she thought, like my job to me.

Yet not like it. There was something in him—— "Vision" was the only word Vaughn could think of. He saw something with those clear eyes of his—inward eyes, maybe—that gave a fiery importance to his little project. That was what moved the Ludlows so. She understood now.

"They need a lot, those kids," he said gravely. "If we just had a place—— They get something out of being together. And they're doing more than just tinkering when they help me with the boats. Some of them would make handy craftsmen, if they only had a chance to work with tools. A beach isn't the place."

"Couldn't you find some little loft?" Vaughn asked practically. It didn't seem so impossible. "Is it a question of money?"

"Partly," he answered. "It would have to be given to us. But, you see, that wouldn't help. They'd think of it as a handout. What they need is something they can feel they have achieved for themselves. A handout implies pity. And what they crave is friendship—personal recognition of the good in them. Their faults have been pointed out so long."

"But if anyone were to give them the means of securing a place, wouldn't that imply friendship, a kind of friendship, even if it isn't exactly personal?" Vaughn reasoned.

Bart looked at the tablecloth thoughtfully.

Yes, Vaughn said to herself, watching him, I know now what the old man meant by "inward eyes." There's a force here I've missed.

"It's easy to give some *thing*," Bart was saying, still looking down, "but it's hard to give your self. And that's the most valuable article you have to give."

As he spoke, so slowly and quietly, yet with an earnestness that seemed to Vaughn to imply his whole aspiration, she was suddenly struck by the most surprising idea: this queer man could write her layout.

Hands tied behind him, Vaughn thought.

"Exciting, isn't it?" he'd asked that day, when she returned from the homestead and saw him working on his boats.

No, she cried to herself, it's impossible! Why should he, of all people, when I don't even like him?

But the longer he spoke, the more certain she was. He could do it easily. She would only have to ask him, she thought, and he would tell her, in his shy, almost monotonous voice, what there was about the hiding place. And she could go right home and make that layout, infusing it with the same excitement.

It's his vision, she thought. I don't have it.

When the uncanny feeling in the atmosphere, which had made Vaughn tense throughout the meal, finally broke, she wasn't expecting it.

Listening to Bart, trying to catch the shape of that vision, she hadn't noticed the cloud which slid across the sun till the rain suddenly hit her arms. Without warning the world had grown dark. She was shivering, not just with cold; she felt vaguely frightened.

Large drops were falling on the table and into the pitchers of milk. Then water began pouring out of the sky.

Everyone jumped up.

"Only a minute ago," Bart was murmuring with a sadness that puzzled Vaughn, "the sun was so good." He looked up unbelievingly as rain hit his forehead.

If he really was a man with such courage as Luke had said, why should he mind a little water?

Food and chairs were scooped up and carried away. People rushed madly for the Meetinghouse.

Vaughn felt a hand on her arm, and then she was whisked away over the grass by Philip Ludlow. But in her inappropriate shoes she couldn't run fast, and by this time it was raining so hard, it was impossible to make the Meetinghouse. Dripping and panting, they took refuge in the carriage shed.

"Oh," Philip Ludlow wailed, looking down at Vaughn, where they stood in the lee of the storm. "Oh."

She gave him a questioning glance.

"Your hat!" he cried, like a child with a damaged toy. "It's all droopy." He put out both hands and lifted the soggy organdy that was flopping down over Vaughn's ears. "And it was so pretty."

So he liked it, she thought, taking off the hat. Yes, it was ruined. But good. If she'd only thought of it when the shower began. She'd forgotten she was wearing anything.

As Philip Ludlow hovered over the hat, trying vainly to perk up its limpness, she remembered how deeply she'd hoped on Thursday, sitting in the millinery shop, that he would like her in it.

"I haven't forgotten about taking you to the hiding place," he was saying. "As soon as Meeting for Business breaks——"

Vaughn sighed. "Don't bother," she said. "I don't think it would make any difference."

He nodded. This was obviously what he'd thought all along. Then, turning his attention to the hat again, he looked crushed. "Can it be revived?" he asked anxiously.

Vaughn smiled up at him. "It doesn't matter," she said softly, both to console the child with the damaged toy and because that was what she really meant. "It doesn't matter any more," she repeated, "if I can just answer——"

She looked quickly at the floor of the shed. How could she tell him she no longer cared about answering that of man in him so much as that of God? She couldn't say anything.

She could only look up again at him happily, thankfully, as, without noticing what she was doing, she crumpled the hat in her hands.

7. "This is more in my line—business," Vaughn said to Sally as they took their seats in the Meetinghouse before the next session.

Luke had gone up to a little writing desk on the high bench, facing the Meeting, and one of the women Vaughn had met at lunch was beside him, taking notes. Philip Ludlow was with the Mansfields near the front of the room, where the old gentleman could hear.

It would hardly be like business conducted at Hamiltons', Vaughn realized, smiling at the ludicrous comparison, but at least there wouldn't be that silence in which one's soul was so terribly exposed. Actually, though, she was glad she'd been here this morning. Once in a lifetime it might be a good thing——

Just before the Meeting began, the Browns settled down with their child on the other side of Sally.

Yes, Vaughn admitted to herself, there was more to that fellow than she'd first thought. He had vision. His whole bearing showed it. And such a gentle way with the little girl.

Luke stood up and announced in his nice, easygoing voice, "At the Quarterly Meeting of Friends held at Kendal, Rhode Island, in Sixth Month." Then he sat down.

Was that all? They were plumb in one of those silences again. These people couldn't seem to transact an item of business without submitting it first to that. At this rate, if they had an agenda, how would they ever get through?

Just when Vaughn was becoming reconciled to the stillness, someone got up and gave a report about relief work which was being carried on in various parts of the world, and involved, apparently, the expenditure of a good deal of money. This provoked a little discussion and, sure enough, just as Vaughn bet herself it would do—another silence. Finally a decision was arrived at, though just how, Vaughn couldn't imagine. A vote was never taken.

After that Edmund Mansfield rose slowly to his feet. Reporting for the committee on the care of the Meetinghouse and grounds, he said, it was necessary to advise the Meeting that the old carriage shed could no longer be considered safe. He submitted a carpenter's estimate for its repair.

Another discussion. Some people thought the whole shed had better be taken down. The estimate was very high, and the shed was no longer in use. Others said the shed had been built along with the Meetinghouse and should be preserved.

At the end of another silence Philip Ludlow got up.

"I've been wondering," he said, "whether we might not restore the shed to usefulness. Bart Brown works down at the beach. The boats he's putting into condition aren't, as most of you know, his main interest. Any boy in town who's in trouble has a friend in Bart. A whole crowd has gathered on that beach. If those boys had a place of their own to meet in, a place to work, they could be helped a lot more. Couldn't they have the shed to fix, shore up the beams, close in the open side, make themselves a workshop? They'd be proud of it. They'd take care of it."

"There's the old potbellied stove down cellar we used to have in here before the furnace was installed," someone put in. "They could use that. Build a little chimney——"

"Yes," Philip Ludlow said, "there are many ways the Meeting could give them support. Friends know that if Bart were to take over this construction, things would be done properly."

But there was opposition. An old-timer got up and said if the shed was going to be closed in, it would lose its character anyway, so they might as well tear it down.

"Why doesn't Luke say something?" Vaughn whispered to Sally. "He believes in Bart."

"Luke can't. He's the Clerk. He just gathers the sense of the Meeting."

The sense of the Meeting. It was the strangest thing Vaughn had ever seen gathered, for there was no ballot, no show of hands, only expressions of approval.

Sally explained in a whisper that those who disapproved worded their view cautiously, so that if the Meeting as a whole wished to adopt this measure, there would be no dissenting voice.

"There has to be unity," she explained.

"But the majority are obviously in favor," Vaughn argued.

"We don't go by majority," Sally whispered back. "The Meeting has to be in unity."

The way they seemed to think they could arrive at that was by not discussing the subject at all. During the drawn-out silence Vaughn wanted to scream. Why, for the love of Pete, couldn't they just let the kids have the shed? Why go bothering God with a piddling question like that? If even she could see it was the right thing, surely He must.

Someone at the back of the room stood up and suggested that Philip Ludlow be appointed to form a committee for considering what Bart could do with the shed.

Hurray!

Vaughn didn't have to have this explained to her. Seeing the happy glow on Bart's face as murmurs of, "I approve," rippled over the Meetinghouse, she knew that the shed was his.

I hadn't realized, she said to herself, as she sank back and took a deep breath, how I was rooting for that man. If they hadn't let him have his shed——

She didn't have a chance to decide what she would have done, in that case, for Luke had stood up and was announcing that he would read the Queries.

151

"What are they?" Vaughn asked in a whisper.

Before Sally could answer, Luke had begun to read, very slowly and distinctly.

"Do you maintain strict integrity in all your relations with others?" he asked. Then he sat down.

Silence. Perhaps people answered the question privately.

But I don't have to, Vaughn thought with relief. It's nothing to me. I don't belong.

Yet it echoed in the boredom of her mind: Do you maintain strict integrity——

Well, I should think so! Do they suspect me of being dishonest?

It was a little insulting, come to think of it, to ask that of any decent person.

Vaughn shifted impatiently on the bench. A command she wouldn't have minded—she'd have rebelled. But this was no command, only a question about simple honesty, and nobody seemed to expect an answer.

Still, she didn't like it.

Once, long ago, on a Fifth Avenue bus, the conductor hadn't noticed her get on. Vaughn was already seated, looking out of the window, when he came by, half extending his little coin meter, but her innocent expression must have convinced him that she'd already paid. Anyhow, he passed her, so she slipped the dime back into her purse.

Such a petty thing—childish, rather than dishonest, she'd always thought.

I *was* grown up, though, she thought now.

Why had this one trip stuck in her memory, instead of those hundreds when she'd paid her fare?

Maybe, she admitted to herself with surprise, it's good to be reminded.

The Clerk rose again. "Are you careful," he asked, "to keep to moderation in the pursuit of business, that it may not absorb your time and energy to the hindrance of your service to God?"

Moderation in business—really! Vaughn almost laughed out loud.

Did that, she wondered, mean you only tried to make a little money and then quit? This was the first time she'd ever heard of anything like *that*.

Queries is a good name for those questions, she thought, amused. They're queer all right.

But to the others in the Meetinghouse they seemed to be an earnest matter. No one spoke, yet the intense hush indicated contemplation.

When Luke rose to read a third time, Vaughn did hope she wouldn't giggle.

"Are you endeavoring," he asked, "to make your home a place of friendliness, refreshment, and peace, where God becomes more real to those who dwell therein and to all who visit there?"

This wasn't funny. Vaughn opened the snap of her handbag and shut it again.

Frankly, no. God wasn't real to anyone in the apartment. As far as the Hills were concerned, He didn't exist, unless for Susan, who was always making things up. Their friends knew they weren't religious. Yet plenty of people seemed to like coming.

It *is* a place of friendliness, Vaughn insisted to herself, and refreshment.

Then she did almost laugh again, because the Quaker Query obviously didn't mean that kind of refreshment—liquid, mostly. When a woman works all day and has very little help, cocktail parties are the only ones she can swing, though Vaughn was always wanting to have people in to dinner.

No, our home isn't the place of refreshment and friendliness and peace that Philip Ludlow's is, she admitted to herself sadly. Or the Mansfields', even Mary Lancashire's, where the bed had lumps. Those homes have something——

Why, she asked herself wistfully, couldn't theirs be like that?

She fiddled with her bag and flicked a speck of lint off her skirt.

Maybe it could. Maybe she could make it over. Why not? One didn't have to be churchy to have a nice feeling in one's home, did one? One didn't have to say grace and read the Bible. Just the atmosphere——

By golly, she said to herself, suddenly sitting up straighter and grabbing the hat tightly, that's what I'm going out for.

Where did one begin? It would involve some fundamental change. She saw that instantly. It wouldn't be easy. Such transformations weren't simply a matter of redecorating, furnishing the place in some other style. They had to come from inside. She knew that. But she was willing to try. Since such a long time, things hadn't been really right. Come to think of it, had they ever? Neil and Susan—— Children deserved to have that feeling in their home.

Oh, Vaughn thought, suddenly anguished, we've cheated them. It's the most precious thing a child could have—that kind of a home. And they never did.

From now on, though, things would be different. If she could take back some of the Kendal atmosphere—— Why couldn't she and Denny start all over again, trying to do better, get along without those little spats, "answering that of God in each other," as Philip Ludlow would put it? Was it so impossible?

She'd have to sell the idea to Denny, of course, and he'd laugh at her. But once she'd made him see, everything would be wonderful.

There'd be no difficulty persuading the children.

Vaughn remembered Susan's face; the way she'd looked that day after she'd been to church with Angela; how she'd hesitated to tell her mother, almost as if she were confessing.

"Wasn't it beautiful?" she'd asked, when Vaughn told her that she herself had been to Quaker Meeting.

That's why she'd gone—not for an adventure. She was trying to find "that of God" to "answer" to.

Poor kid, Vaughn thought, poor little kid. I hadn't dreamed she might be troubled, searching perhaps desperately. If she is, oughtn't I to be helping her?

But how? What does one tell a child when one has no belief oneself?

Maybe even Neil, though he'd never mentioned anything——
I wonder, Vaughn said to herself.

And Denny, behind all his unhappiness since he returned from
overseas—could God possibly have anything to do with that? It
had never occurred to Vaughn before. She'd always been so certain
that Denny was the last person to take anything of that sort seriously. But maybe——

Suddenly the terrible, sickening feeling came over her again the
way it had during lunch, when she was so surprisingly homesick
for her parents. Only now it was Denny and the children she
longed for, not the sight and the touch of them—she would have
these tomorrow evening—but this kindly new relationship. And
something else was tightening her throat, so that she felt choked,
as she'd been in the window, another kind of homesickness.

For God?

The question entered her mind with the shock of a needle jab
in the skin. *Homesickness for God?*

Not she—Vaughn Hill. It was unbelievable.

She'd suspected Susan of being that way and Neil might be.
Children were strange. Maybe even Denny, though she didn't
believe that. But that she—she should be homesick for God——

Never, never would such a thing have seemed possible. Not till
this minute.

Oh, but it's true, she thought miserably. How is it I never knew
till now?

So that's what Philip Ludlow meant, when he spoke in Meeting
of feeling forlorn. So sometimes he too—— And for him it was
eased in this place.

I must try to think, she said to herself desperately. I must just try
to think it all out while I'm here.

Tomorrow she'd go back to New York. Monday she'd be in the
office. She'd have to think fast. Her whole past life, the values she'd
accepted without question, the things she'd worked for, her ambition—nothing seemed of much use to her now. She had to begin all
over again.

Was it possible?

Why not? she asked herself. Thirty-eight isn't too old to make a new beginning.

She felt excited, tingling with the possibilities that suddenly opened. She and Denny would grow wiser, they'd all be so much happier. All this future wonder, the enlargement of their whole horizon . . .

Just this one experience, this one mysterious thing happening to her here, and their lives were changed, or would be, as soon as she got home and told Denny. Why in the world hadn't she seen it all sooner?

They'd start over again. It wouldn't be easy, but they could do it. Now she suddenly knew where she had to begin—in herself.

That part's a cinch, though, she thought, feeling new strength. It's working on Denny's going to be the job.

In the wonder and excitement that had suddenly broken over her Vaughn had forgotten about the Meeting, forgotten everything but the beautiful future she had.

Now Luke, standing up again, brought her back to the present. "If there's no further business," he said, looking from face to face around the room, "we adjourn, purposing to meet again in Ninth Month."

There was a ripple of movement in the room. People shook hands and got up. Quarterly Meeting appeared to be over.

As Vaughn turned, smiling, to Sally, she caught sight of Philip Ludlow, still sitting in the front of the room with Edmund Mansfield, and for a second all her new excitement stopped in its tracks, as if a detaining hand had been placed on her arm.

It was something about the way Philip Ludlow looked in that second. Though he was returning the old man's handshake, the movement was mechanical, as if his spirit were lagging in the silence, still worshiping, not ready to go back to its outward routine. Looking like that, removed from actuality, he seemed to Vaughn pathetically defenseless, like a sleeping child.

It was only a second before this expression changed, and Philip

Ludlow appeared to be once more conscious of his outward existence. But in that second Vaughn felt the invisible hand on her arm.

Would it be as simple as all that, making over their lives?

Then Philip Ludlow came to take her home and, as he looked down on her with his usual smile, all Vaughn's doubts vanished. She felt elated again by her wonderful discovery.

8. After supper Philip Ludlow lit a fire. Vaughn took the rush-seated chair and watched the flames brighten the room against the rain outside.

Sally and Luke were on the sofa. Though they sat no closer than strangers, though they hardly looked at each other, some unseen communication between these two made Vaughn think of that identical inner rhythm.

Denny and I'll be that way again, she said to herself ecstatically. The discovery she'd made in Meeting would change their whole lives. As soon as she told him——

Suddenly she caught her breath, dumfounded.

What am I waiting for? she asked herself. This is the most important thing that ever happened. Why am I sitting here, staring stupidly into the fire, when I ought to be with Denny, telling him——

If he'd only understand, if he wouldn't make fun of her——

It's so important, she insisted to herself.

She had to tell him. And here she was, marooned in the country. Twenty-four hours till she'd reach home. She couldn't bear it, she simply couldn't. She had to go now, this minute, tell Denny, start immediately rebuilding their life. . . .

Oh, she cried to herself in sudden terror, *will he understand?* Will he listen even?

Half the time when she spoke to him he didn't hear her. He never noticed what she had on. He was always off in a world of his own, though he might be right beside her. Now, when she had something so terribly pressing to tell him, how would she put it across?

Never mind, she told herself, the main thing is to get out of here, to get hold of Denny——

Philip Ludlow was talking about Bart. He was so pleased that the boys were going to get the shed. What did Vaughn Hill and his cousins think of that plan of his for starting a worker-owned business with those boys, not right away, but in a year or so, when the boys were ready to assume responsibility?

"How about distribution?" Sally asked. "They'll have to find a market."

"With a little capital they could advertise," Luke said.

Advertise! All the way up in the train Vaughn had planned speaking to Philip Ludlow about Kendal Radio. She'd wanted to urge him to put the account in the hands of a competent agency. But there was no time to speak of that now. If only she'd thought of it sooner.

"Yes," Philip Ludlow was saying, "if they advertise carefully——"

Vaughn stood up, clutching her handbag, as if she needed to make no further preparation, only to step out of the house, start——

"I—— Please excuse me," she broke in, opening and closing her handbag. "I have to go home. Could you call a taxi?"

Philip Ludlow looked at her with evident concern.

Vaughn instantly realized she was being rude. Hadn't she told him, only last night, that she was staying till tomorrow? One didn't rush away like this. Besides, come to think of it, she'd have to pack. "It's just something I want to tell my husband," she explained. "Something terribly urgent. It—it really can't wait."

Philip Ludlow nodded, accepting this. In a way he didn't seem surprised. But, looking at his watch, he was grave. "The train's left," he told Vaughn.

The train! Vaughn had forgotten this complication. She wasn't used to being in the sticks.

"We'll drive you," Sally offered.

"Oh no, thank you," Vaughn answered, sitting down. "It's not that serious. Just——"

"There's the ten-forty," Philip Ludlow murmured, "but that doesn't get to New York until three-thirty in the morning."

"And what's more," Luke put in, "it's generally late."

Vaughn looked from one to the other, considering. "I'll take it," she announced, getting up again.

"And arrive at that hour?" Philip Ludlow asked, aghast.

Sally and Luke both argued with Vaughn. They insisted on driving her home.

"Once we get onto the Merritt Parkway," Luke said, "we'll make good time. It's only a little after eight now. We could be in New York by one and back here in time for breakfast with Cousin Philip."

"In this rain?" Sally asked doubtfully.

Vaughn wouldn't hear of it. "That train's perfectly all right," she told them. "It'll be fun traveling at night," she added, knowing this was an absolute lie.

Philip Ludlow looked a little worried, but he didn't try to dissuade Vaughn. "Can you reach your husband?" he asked. "He doesn't know you're coming, does he?"

"Of course not. I only just decided."

"Then hadn't you better telephone? He won't want you arriving in the middle of the night without coming to meet you."

Vaughn looked at Philip Ludlow, wondering. Would Denny come to the station? How did he feel about her now? Oh, if she could only make him understand! Denny, Denny!

The circuits were busy when Vaughn put in the call. She stayed by the telephone, too eager to move far. What would she say, if Denny asked why she was leaving sooner?

I'll tell you when I get there, she said to herself, in imagination already connected with Denny. I'll tell you all about it. Denny—— She waited for him to ask, "Yes?" But he didn't. Denny, do you love me?

When the bell rang right next to her, Vaughn jumped. It seemed seconds before she managed to get the receiver off the hook.

That number, she was told, didn't answer.

"I'll try it again in twenty minutes," the operator promised.

"Please do," Vaughn begged.

Going back into the living room, she found that the Ludlows were speaking of Bart again. But Vaughn's mind was rushing ahead, through the night, racing along the tracks, beating her home. She was already confronting Denny with her great discovery, explaining . . .

"Well," Luke was saying, "if Bart believes it can be done, I'm behind it, though I don't see how he's going to manage. But, then, I never thought he'd be able to do anything with those boys, either, in the beginning. You know, it's remarkable."

Philip Ludlow shot him a look of assent.

"Not only has it made the boys into useful, self-respecting citizens," he said, "it's done a lot for the townspeople, seeing them change like that."

Vaughn glanced at her watch. Twenty-eight minutes. The operator hadn't called back. Maybe they were still out. No need to get excited, she told herself. There were nearly two hours till the train left. Two hours—— She had time——

"Philip Ludlow," she began eagerly. Then she hestitated. Never before had Vaughn been shy about suggesting to an executive that his firm advertise. Yet dared she stick her neck out here? She didn't care if he didn't give the account to Hamiltons', though they could do a good job on it, but he ought to let some agency handle it.

He was looking at her inquiringly.

"Why doesn't your firm advertise?" she asked bluntly.

"We do," he insisted.

"I mean," she explained, "why don't you do it right, through some agency? It's a skilled trade, like any other, you know."

He nodded. "Yes," he agreed, "I know." He was thoughtful a minute. "It's not that we don't want professional service," he explained at last, "but anyone who isn't associated with us right here can't quite evaluate our products. An outsider might tend to give the impression that we have more to offer than we actually do. As long as we write the copy ourselves, we feel sure of not overstating."

"But when you just list the bare facts about a product," Vaughn argued, "the ad doesn't have any emotional appeal. And the primary function of advertising is to stimulate desire through emotional——"

"No!" Philip Ludlow cried. "The primary function is to acquaint the public with our ability to satisfy a need."

Vaughn sighed. It was no use arguing with this man. Anyone else would have made her fighting mad. Where, she asked herself, would Hamilton Company be if every potential client reasoned that way?

But Sally and Luke seemed to agree with him, though Luke's face showed some inner struggle.

"Thee has to think of thy employees, I mean thy fellow workers, too, Cousin Philip, doesn't thee?" he asked. "Suppose thy firm goes on the rocks—an awful lot of people will be thrown out of work."

Philip Ludlow winced as if he'd been struck.

On the rocks! So things were even worse at Kendal Radio than Vaughn had been told.

Philip Ludlow turned his face away, staring into the fire.

"I shouldn't like thee to think," Luke was saying anxiously, "that I don't believe in following the leadings of the inner light in business as in everything else, but isn't it sometimes necessary to make a compromise?"

Vaughn looked quickly to Philip Ludlow for his answer. He said nothing. Except for his hands, which spread and contracted themselves on the arms of his chair, he didn't even move.

Sally and Luke were quiet. They looked troubled, as if they feared Luke had said too much.

Luke's right, Vaughn said to herself fiercely. Why can't the poor dear see it?

Sitting so still, fumbling occasionally, the eagerness gone from him, Philip Ludlow seemed old. And yet, as he stared into the fire, Vaughn noticed that childlike look emerge, the questioning, trustful glance a small child gives a parent, when he is uncertain of the way.

Seeing that look, Vaughn felt a sudden pity for this man, such as she'd hardly ever known for anyone. If he'd been sure of himself, clinging stubbornly to some jelled conviction, she wouldn't have been so moved. But, watching him struggle to integrate his ideals with reality, she was wrenched with pity. She was young enough to be his daughter, probably, yet she felt go out from her that same protective, comforting love she used to give to Neil and Susan, when they came to her with bumps.

She could help him; she knew exactly what his business needed. If only he'd let her. If only he'd find it possible to compromise— just a little. Luke was a Friend, too, and if he thought Philip Ludlow ought to be more realistic——

But, watching Philip Ludlow's expression as he hunted for some direct answer to give Luke, Vaughn saw the underlying toughness of his belief stamped in his face, so that, even before he spoke, she guessed what he would say.

She never heard it, because just then the telephone rang once more. Though she jumped up automatically, Vaughn felt less eager now to rush away.

I wish I didn't have to leave him, she thought, looking over her shoulder at the still figure before the fire. He—needs me.

"On your call to New York," the operator began.

The number still didn't answer.

I wonder where they are, Vaughn said to herself, glancing at the grandfather clock by the dining-room door.

It was nine-thirty. Where could they have gone?

Philip Ludlow seemed his usual cheerful self again when Vaughn returned. He was putting another log on the fire, skillfully setting it down on the embers. Although his hands were displaying strength now, Vaughn was reminded of how tender they could be when they held the picture of his wife for her under the lamp.

She was still sorry for him. What was this inner light, anyway, that demanded such sacrifices from a believer?

"Do you mind if I ask you a question?"

He turned to her encouragingly.

"What's 'inner light'?"

Vaughn was surprised to hear Luke burst out laughing.

"That's a tough one for you, Cousin Philip," he said.

Sally laughed too.

Vaughn had noticed before that all these people had a tendency to stand off and look at themselves with detachment, often with humor. That, she supposed, was why they didn't seem stuffy about their religion.

Philip Ludlow looked amused too. "It is tough," he admitted, rubbing his forehead. "I don't know that I can define it. Friends aren't much good at framing their belief in words. They rely on the experience——"

"Experience!" Vaughn broke in impatiently. "It's like when you're starting out hunting a job," she told him, laughing, though she was really serious. "You can't get one if you haven't had experience and you can't get experience unless you have a job."

"Yes," Philip Ludlow agreed, serious too. "But, one way or another, those who try do get a job. They may have to serve a longer apprenticeship than they consider necessary, but in the end they get the experience. I think the phrase 'inner light' goes back to this thought: that God has given us, every one of us in particular, a light from Himself, shining in our hearts and——"

The telephone rang.

"That'll be for me," Vaughn exclaimed, jumping up and rushing into the hall. "Yes," she cried, though she barely had the receiver in her hand.

"On your call to New York——" the operator began.

"Yes!"

"You the party who called?"

"Yes. Yes, I am."

"On your call—that number still doesn't answer."

"Oh!"

"I'll try it again in twenty minutes."

"Yes, do. Please do."

Vaughn hung up. Had Denny taken the children to the movies? She felt a little hurt that he should have put himself beyond her reach, so that now when she needed him——

"Time to leave," Philip Ludlow told her when she returned to the parlor. "Did you speak to your husband?"

Vaughn shook her head. "It doesn't matter," she assured him. "I don't mind going home alone. There'll be plenty of taxis that time of night."

She rushed upstairs and threw everything into the overnight case, including her hat. She couldn't wear it. Maybe it could be steamed, she thought, as she tossed it in, but she didn't care.

Philip Ludlow came to get the bag. He was taking Vaughn to the train.

As she stood in the parlor, bareheaded, saying good-by to Sally and Luke, Vaughn thought, I'll remember this. Her eyes pricked. Even when I'm an old lady, she said to herself, I'll remember the friendliness of these people.

"It's going to be a long ride," Philip Ludlow was saying, as he went to the bookshelf. "Let me give you something to read." He took down a little volume and placed it in Vaughn's hand.

The Cloud of Unknowing, she read, as she opened the overnight case again and shoved it in on top of the hat. Never heard of it.

She started into the hall. But, going out, she glanced back once more, briefly, triumphantly, at the photograph of Philip Ludlow's wife.

Soon now, very soon, Vaughn, too, would be getting that deep, undying love.

9. The ticket office was closed. There wasn't another soul in the station. Vaughn was the only one leaving Kendal at this time of night.

It was still raining. Philip Ludlow took her to a protected spot on the side of the building and there they stood waiting, saying very little. He expressed no disappointment at her leaving early, and yet, Vaughn thought as she glanced at him in the hard light of the station lamp, he looked sad.

She herself couldn't forget how pitiful he'd appeared to her when he was considering the possible fate of his business, and she ached for him anew.

"If you're ever in New York," she said eagerly, "do come up and meet Denny. And drop in at the office. Let me show you the kind of work we do. You'll——" She started to say, "like it." But would he? That Redbrook Furnace job, which had been such an exaggeration——

"Thank you," he answered, looking down on her almost tenderly. "I'd simply love to know your family." He didn't refer to Hamiltons'.

When they heard the train whistling in the distance he took off his hat and held out his hand. "I do hope way will open for you," he said.

Vaughn's heart sank. The layout. Till that moment she hadn't remembered that she was going back no wiser about it than when she came. And this trip had been her one hope. "I just can't understand," she confided to him quickly, though he knew nothing about advertising, "how a simple thing like that could turn out to be such a hard job."

He looked at her keenly for a long second. Then, bending to pick up the overnight case, he made the queerest of all the queer remarks he'd ever made to her: "Yes, it seems love is a thing one sometimes has to work at."

The train came in just then with so much clatter Vaughn wasn't sure she'd heard right.

"Work at?" she repeated incredulously, at the top of her voice. "I always thought love was a feeling you either had or didn't——"

"Work at quite hard," he added, as they hurried to the nearest car.

Those were his last words to her. She'd hardly got on, turning to say good-by, when the train began moving. It didn't waste much time on Kendal. Vaughn remained in the vestibule, looking back as long as she could see Philip Ludlow.

One man against the world, she thought sadly, as the solitary figure standing under the lamp vanished from view.

Then she entered the coach.

I mustn't think of him any more, she told herself. I'm going back to Denny now.

But still, choosing one of the many empty seats, she wondered: what did love have to do with her layout? Or had she misunderstood? Was he referring, instead, to her and Denny? Then he'd guessed—— Even if he did, what could he mean?

It was stuffy inside. The green plush seats in the cars they put on at night didn't lean back like the new ones. The few tired passengers weren't like people who travel in the daytime, either. Most of them had their feet up.

Vaughn took out her handkerchief and mopped her hair. Wouldn't you know, the one time she didn't have a hat, it'd rain?

Looking up, she noticed that there was a check stuck in the seat before her. It might be good to New York. The conductor, coming through and seeing it, might not ask her for a ticket.

Opening the overnight case, she took out the book Philip Ludlow had given her and, putting her feet up, too, settled down comfortably. It was a very small book. *The Cloud of Unknowing.* What an odd title, and yet mysterious, beautiful. *A Version in Modern English of a Fourteenth-century Classic,* the subtitle explained.

Whoever you are who possess this book in any way, it began, *whether you own it, or have borrowed it, or simply carry it for another, I charge you by a vow of love, that you will not wilfully read it, nor even permit it to be read except by one whose purpose, in your judgment, is to become . . .*

She didn't have anything smaller than a ten-dollar bill and conductors were always very unpleasant about making change.

. . . a perfect follower of Christ. By that I do not mean a person

*who is devoted only to deeds of mercy, but one whose purpose is
to come to the pure contemplation of God, or to the most sovereign
point that it is possible for him to come in this temporal life.*

Vaughn shut the book swiftly, banging the cover down on the
first page, as if, she thought wryly, there were something inside that
would bite her. Was she one whose purpose, in her judgment, was
to become a perfect——?

If she happened to be asleep when the conductor came through,
she couldn't feel guilty about his passing her by.

She folded her coat and laid it under her head, but, though she
shut her eyes, she didn't want to sleep.

This morning, when she'd prayed not to be led into temptation,
didn't it mean just some little thing like this?

She took the coat out from under her head and laid it on the
seat, afraid now that she might really be asleep when the conductor came through, and so, if he should pass her by, she wouldn't be
able to stop him.

She sat up straight, reopened the book, and read the first words
over.

*. . . whether you own it, or have borrowed it, or simply carry
it for another, I charge you by a vow of love . . .*

She closed it again.

By a vow of love . . . No, she couldn't read it, though she was
curious to know what was inside—why Philip Ludlow had given it
to her. He must have hoped that in her judgment she could read it.
But, no. *By a vow of love . . .*

This book wasn't her dish. Monday morning she'd mail it back.
She lifted the lid of the overnight case to put it in, but the lifetime
habit of looking at the last page of every story checked her.

For in God's merciful eyes, the book concluded, *it is not what
you are or have been, but what you would be.*

Putting the book in the overnight case, Vaughn stared at the
dripping black windowpane. She couldn't get those words out of
her head: *not what you are or have been . . .*

What was she? What had she been? She knew what she "would

be." The vision had come to her this afternoon in the Meeting-house, and it had been so overwhelming that it was sending her home now, in the middle of the night, to tell Denny——

But what was she? How did her soul look without its make-up? Did it, like her face, show her at this particular moment a woman of thirty-eight (well-preserved), or was one's soul composed of every stage of one's life, a permanent record, like a photograph album kept up faithfully, from the baby book to the present?

She would have to look back, she saw, start at the end, and turn the pages left-handed one after the other: Vaughn the career woman, pressing ahead at the agency; Vaughn the army wife with two babies—with only one; the young-married Vaughn, engaged, coming to New York looking for a job (and a husband); Vaughn on campus at State, editing the paper; in high school; singing in the church choir; in primary, counting on her fingers. She could hardly see further.

She was getting very sleepy, and if the conductor didn't come soon——

It would take so long to study each pose, to analyze what determined her choices, why she'd been unable suddenly to go to church, for instance, and why she felt bound to drive forward at the agency with such ambition.

Now that she thought of it, she saw with surprise that that wasn't only fear of Denny's losing his job. It wasn't only for him and the children that she pressed so hard. There was something else, some need in her to show what she could do, as if she were still that little girl way back in one of the first pages of the album, who had to climb every wall in East Bolton, just to show that, even if she was small for her age, she could do it and not fall off.

She'd never seen that till this moment. Yet it was true. But surely she couldn't care more for showing what she could do than for Denny? Still, he'd never liked her being at Hamiltons'.

It wasn't, he used to point out, though he hadn't mentioned it for months now, that he objected to her having a job; he didn't think Hamiltons' the place for her.

"You're not that kind," he used to say, and in the beginning she'd understood what he meant, but there was no chance of getting into a better firm. And now she didn't even see anything wrong with Hamiltons'.

I guess I've grown like them myself, she thought grimly.

Sighing, she shifted on the seat, uncrossing her legs and crossing them the other way. It was hard sitting so still and looking at herself this way, very hard. She felt tired, not only sleepy, but weary clear through to the core of her being.

Was it necessary to do this to herself? Why couldn't she doze off for a moment?

It would be horrible arriving at Grand Central in the middle of the night alone, no matter what she'd told Philip Ludlow. Why had Denny gone out, where she couldn't reach him? She'd have to get herself a taxi. At the house the elevator boy would be dozing in one of those Napoleonic chairs in the foyer.

Should she ask him to wait while she let herself into the apartment?

Turning the key in the lock there she'd be—home again. She could see herself looking into each room as she went down the hall: Neil, lying in that burrow he always scooped out for himself in the bedclothes, his back and arms bare, that babyish curve to his mouth, which still showed when he was asleep; Susan, unconsciously composing her limbs into a beautiful mass, even in bed. Her bright hair would be lying softly over the pillow and her neat little features would be calm under the lovely skin. Her eyes were always so wide open in the daytime you couldn't see the fine, blue squiggles on her lids. Now——

My chicks, Vaughn thought fondly.

The coach door slammed, and there he was at last, the conductor. Even before he reached her Vaughn opened her purse and fished out the ten-dollar bill. He was quite decent about making the change. When he'd gone Vaughn tucked her coat under her head again. Now she could sleep!

Only, her eyes wouldn't shut. She was still getting home, going down the hall. At the door of her own room she felt constrained, fearful lest the welcome she craved——

But Denny's asleep, she reminded herself.

How could he give her any kind of a welcome when he was asleep?

I'll wake him, she decided. How can I wait till morning to tell him?

And if he was too sleepy to take it all in, the wonder and freshness of it, if his mind was still cuddled up, though his arms might mechanically embrace her, she'd shout at him, she'd beat her fists softly against his chest to make him hear.

Denny! she'd cry. Denny, we'll start all over again! Don't you hear me, Denny?

She tried to imagine his expression, tried to see the joy gradually dawn on his face as he grasped her meaning, but she couldn't. She could only see him lying sprawled all over her side of the bed, with one arm over his eyes, which was the way he'd been sleeping ever since he came back from overseas.

And then she thought with an awful start: even if he's awake, he'll be just like he was when I left.

She sighed and sat up, sticking her forehead against the cool glass to see whether she could glimpse a name as the train whizzed through some station. No, it was too dark. It had stopped raining, but the country looked terribly lonely. Only a few lights here and there. A long way from New York.

If only she'd get there soon; if only she hadn't started. To be with Denny, or Philip Ludlow, not just alone like this, in the middle of nowhere, with all those horrible ideas about her soul.

Leaning back once more with the coat beneath her cheek, she shut her eyes against the glaring lights of the coach. It was better that way—with her eyes shut.

Suddenly she was on an escalator, going upstairs in a large department store, moving between two floors. She kept looking eagerly at the merchandise below and at the people, but all the time terror was mounting in her. She wouldn't know when to jump off, her foot wouldn't move fast enough. She tried to scream to the people to stop the escalator, but no sound came out of her frightened throat. The step was about to slide away beneath her, she'd be carried off on those cogs, sucked through the grating, down, down. She could never get off.

The lurch of the train woke Vaughn.

Opening her eyes, she couldn't believe she was already in the caverns of Grand Central. But she gave a deep sigh of relief, remembering the escalator. She was almost home now, almost with Denny.

Everyone had left the car. She was alone. As Vaughn pulled herself together, a brakeman came through and grinned at her.

"Top of the morning," he shouted playfully.

She smiled back at him sleepily. But where on earth was her hat? Climbing on the green plush, she was able to see the top of the rack. Then she remembered.

Bareheaded, she got out, squeezing the handle of the overnight case, preparing herself as she started up the ramp to meet that feeling that always lay in wait for her in the vaulted station—the horror of being inside a perfectly enormous whale.

She pushed on, holding her elbows against her ribs, to the top of the ramp, pushed on through the gate, smack into the arms of Denny.

Part 4

1. "Honey," he cried, holding her tightly. "Honey, I was so worried about you." Denny laid his cheek against her head, kissing her hair.

Safe, Vaughn said to herself, I'm safe again. And he loves me. He's forgotten the awful things he said before I went away.

They stood there, clinging to each other, alone, it seemed, in the vast station.

After a minute Denny tipped up Vaughn's face and scanned it anxiously. "You all right?"

"I'm fine," she said.

"Guy treat you all right?"

Vaughn could only answer with her eyes. She swallowed, choked up. How could she describe, in this first hurried moment, how Philip Ludlow had treated her?

Oh, she thought, the rose——

It was still in the toothbrush glass on the candlestand. She wished she'd remembered, in her haste, to take it with her. But it would have been ridiculously sentimental. At her age, a faded rose——

"Where's your hat?" Denny was asking. And when Vaughn told him what had happened to it, he remarked, studying her curiously, "Never saw you downtown without one." Then she thought he sniffed her.

"*Huh?*" she inquired, puzzled. After you've been married to a man fifteen years, you don't use words about things like that.

But Denny didn't answer.

Vaughn decided she'd been mistaken, imagining—— "Darling," she said, "how did you know?"

"Ludlow called me up."

"He called you up!" Vaughn cried. "Well!"

Denny glanced at her searchingly. "I couldn't see why he would, how he got the number, unless you told him to. I was worried."

"When *I* called up," Vaughn said, "you were out."

"Movies," Denny explained, as they started together toward the staircase. "Kids get restless when you're not home. Anyway," he concluded cheerfully, "you're back, and will they be glad!" He squeezed her arm.

"It was sweet of him," Vaughn mused, "to think of letting you know I was coming sooner."

All at once Denny stood still. "Why did you?"

"Tell you in the taxi," Vaughn promised, moving on.

"What's the hurry? Let's celebrate. Aren't you hungry?"

Vaughn couldn't decide.

"How about the Oyster Bar?"

"No," Vaughn answered, tugging at his arm. She was suddenly impatient. "Let's go home. I want to see the children."

"They're asleep."

"I know, but I can look at them, can't I?"

They reached the taxi stand, and Vaughn filled her lungs with New York air.

"Beautiful night," Denny observed as they got into a cab. He gave the address to the driver.

"But you can't see the stars very well," Vaughn answered. "In Kendal——"

"Tell you what," Denny said, "let's drive home through the Park. By the time we're uptown, it'll be about light. Remember how we used to drive through the Park?"

Vaughn snuggled close to him and nodded her head against his shoulder, remembering, before they were married . . .

"It's going to cost you a lot more, mister," the driver warned, when Denny gave the order. "We're headed straight up Madison now."

"He thinks we're hicks," Vaughn whispered.

This struck them both as funny.

"Never mind what it costs!" Denny shouted. "Take us through the Park."

"I feel like a hick," Vaughn whispered. "Haven't I just come from the country? Denny, it's nice there. It's so nice I simply had to come home."

176

He turned to look at her. "That doesn't make sense," he declared.

"Doesn't it?" she asked, glancing up at him lovingly. She dropped her head contentedly against his shoulder, wondering how to begin telling him all that was in her mind. "It was so nice," she whispered finally, "I couldn't stand it without you any more."

Though he kissed her tenderly then, he was obviously puzzled.

If Vaughn could just explain how she'd felt in Kendal, that there was something, if you could just understand it, something—that maybe Denny and she——

"Philip Ludlow's a darling," she began.

"You said you went on business," Denny broke in, his voice harsh. "That doesn't sound like business to me."

"Well, it isn't easy to see the connection," Vaughn admitted, rubbing her forehead, "but I think I know now what was wrong— why I couldn't write that layout. I didn't have the—well, vision."

He relaxed a little as he asked, "Hiding place look different to you this time?"

"Oh," Vaughn said negligently, "we didn't go there."

"You didn't——"

Though he moved away from her she could feel his body stiffening again.

"Say, what is this, anyway?" he asked. Then he muttered bitterly, "I thought all the time you were pulling the wool over my eyes when you said you were going for another look at the hole."

Oh, Lord, Vaughn thought, now we're back at that again.

"Denny," she pleaded, "please, Denny, try to understand, won't you? It's important."

He moved closer again, but said nothing.

"You're crazy to be jealous of a sweet old man," she said quickly. "He's nothing to me but a—a——"

"A what?"

Vaughn couldn't say. There was no word in the English language for what Philip Ludlow was to her. It was a special thing. Maybe no one had ever been loved impersonally before, the way he had seemed to love her, even before she arrived, so that everything had begun to change for her when she got to Kendal that first time. Probably no one had ever been loved this way, and that's why there was no word for the relationship.

And then Vaughn laughed at herself, inside her head, because, of course, Philip Ludlow loved everybody that way and she knew it. She just liked to imagine that she . . .

"I don't understand how he got this hold on you," Denny was repeating over and over.

"If you knew him," Vaughn answered, "it wouldn't seem strange. I wish you'd been there. He did too."

"He *did?*"

Vaughn ran her fingers shyly up and down his sleeve. "Denny," she whispered, "have you ever thought there might be something in us—some inner illumination that would make our marriage and everything about us better if we only stopped to let it?"

The words Denny and she were accustomed to using with each other didn't express what Vaughn wanted to say, and yet she had a driving urge to share her Kendal discovery. She glanced up to see whether he was taking her seriously. If he made fun of her now, when she was talking in a way she'd always made fun of herself——

But he looked at her very gravely. "Sometimes," he answered.

"Really?" she asked. "You really think that way sometimes?"

He nodded.

"Why I had to come home," Vaughn rushed on, "was—I went to his church with him and there—it's a queer place, just bare, with no minister or music or prayers, but nice, real nice—there I got to wishing we could begin our life over again." She tugged at his sleeve. "We could, couldn't we, Denny?"

"How?"

"I don't know exactly. But we're not too old to change things. If we could talk them over together, decide why we get on so badly sometimes—you know——"

"Yes?"

"Well, couldn't we go back and act like we were starting out again, just married, and not make the same mistakes?"

"Can one ever?" he asked.

She thought this over. "I guess it would take a lot of faith," she declared at length. "Before I went to Kendal, I wouldn't have dreamed one could. But now—— I don't know how to explain. I really believe it."

He turned to her and, though the day was still dim, she thought she saw a light in his face that hadn't been there in years.

"Would you want to change things?" he asked. His voice was shaky.

"Yes," she answered eagerly, taking his hand.

"Gee," he whispered. "Gee, I never heard you talk like this before. You come running home in the middle of the night without your hat and you talk like this——" He was breathless. His face looked the way it used to, years ago, before he enlisted.

The cab jolted and then stood still.

Vaughn turned quickly to the window. "Look," she cried, "we're home!"

As they got out and Denny paid the driver, they grinned at each other because they'd been so wrapped up in themselves they hadn't even seen the Park, they didn't even know they were in it.

The cab drove away.

Denny took Vaughn's arm and kept her standing there, on the sidewalk in front of the house, looking across the East Side, to where day was beginning to break.

"Haven't seen the sunrise in ages," he murmured, "except New Year's, and then it's too cold to watch. Don't you wish it would stay like this all day? It was terribly hot while you were gone."

Vaughn nodded. She was thinking that it was like poetry: the beginning of a new day, of a new life.

She looked higher at the sky. "Is that the morning star?" she asked. It reminded her of the stars in Kendal. Without waiting for Denny to answer, she asked, "What did he say when he phoned?" phoned?"

"Who? The old guy?"

Vaughn looked down and turned to Denny. "What made you so worried?" she asked suddenly.

"He said you were on the train, and it would be at Grand Central at three-twenty. It wasn't, though. I waited forty minutes."

"What did you say to him?" Vaughn asked, searching Denny's face.

"Well," Denny answered slowly, "I asked him were you sick that you were coming home sooner. He said, no. So then I naturally thought he mustn't have treated you right, and I saw red. Because, if he hadn't, Vaughn," Denny said fiercely, "I'd have rushed right up there and busted him one."

So he cares, she said to herself blissfully. He really cares.

"I would," he assured her, taking her in his arms right there on the sidewalk. (But there was no one around.) "I mean it."

She laughed. "Oh, Denny," she whispered, clutching him. But she still felt worried. "What did you say?"

"'Well,' I said, 'if she isn't sick, why is she coming home?'"

"He doesn't know why," Vaughn said quickly. "At least I don't think he guessed——"

"He said he didn't know, but——"

"What?"

"He said you were lit."

"That's a lie!" she exclaimed, backing away. "I never had one drink the whole time."

"It's true," Denny insisted. "He said it was inner light."

"Denny!" She laughed. She laughed and laughed.

"What's so funny?" he asked, holding her at arm's length so he could study her face. He looked a little sheepish. "Did I get the guy wrong?" he asked. "It sounded queer, not only the way he put it—I mean, you said he's such a gentleman, and a gentleman wouldn't say that about a girl, no matter how stinking she was. Just before he hung up he said another thing made me wonder if I'd got him wrong."

"What?"

He shook his head.

"Denny, tell me."

He smiled, remembering, but he wouldn't tell her. She coaxed and insisted, but he wouldn't tell her. He took her arm and marched her into the house.

The elevator boy was sleeping in the Napoleonic chair, just as Vaughn had imagined he'd be when she was riding home. Denny woke him.

"Glad we don't have to go to work today," Vaughn said, yawning as they rode up in the stale air.

That reminded Denny of something. He looked suddenly grave. "By the way, Vaughn," he said, as they were getting out. "I have some news." He hesitated. "About the vacation. I'm afraid we'll have to change things."

"*Change things?*"

"Yes. Boss says I can't go in August. Have to take the first two weeks in July."

"Denny!" She stared at him, horrified, but he didn't face her. He was fumbling with the key. "How can we?" she said. "We promised the Hamiltons. You *have* to have August. Didn't you explain that to your boss?"

"Sure. He said it's out." He stood aside to let her walk into the apartment. "What do you do when your boss says a thing is out?" he asked.

Vaughn threw her handbag on the hall table. She didn't go in to see the children. She just went to the living room and flopped into a chair.

"Want a drink?" Denny asked, looking down at her. He had a helpless expression.

"No," she answered, and suddenly she felt her temper rise. "What good is a drink?" she asked bitterly. "Is that all you can do for me, make me a drink? Why can't you stand up to your boss? Where does he come in to shove you around like that?"

Oh, she cried to herself, as the tears sprang into her eyes, it's too much. It's just too much.

She rushed into the bedroom and got herself out of her clothes, letting them drop on the floor where she stood. This wasn't the way she'd imagined her beautiful home-coming.

She didn't even put up her hair or cream her face. She just crawled into bed, the messy bed out of which Denny had gone to meet her. Daylight was beginning to shine into the room. It bothered her, even when she closed her eyes, but she was too tired to get up and pull down the shade and too mad at Denny to call him.

She just lay there, furious.

It didn't feel nice in the rumpled sheets. She couldn't get to sleep.

After a while Denny came in, carrying a cup of fresh coffee. Vaughn hadn't realized he was making it for her. He carried it carefully, never taking his eyes off the cup till Vaughn had it in her hands. The steam and smell were reviving.

Denny sat down on the edge of the bed and watched Vaughn drink. He looked tired and troubled, with that deadbeat, dogged patience in his eyes that, for some reason, made her even angrier.

"We couldn't change things, Vaughn," he said, looking down at the bedclothes and smoothing them nervously as he talked. "I mean, our life. When people once set a pattern for themselves it seems to be for good and all. I know what you mean you were thinking in church. But things look different in church. In reality they don't work out."

She was even more furious with him now. Here she'd ridden all night on a local with horrible plush seats, just to tell him, and he didn't believe her. She was so mad she wouldn't answer.

"Don't think I'm angry, Vaughn," Denny pleaded. "It's a fact. That's the trouble with religion. It means fine, but it doesn't square with life. Millions of people go to church and look at the mess the world's in."

She had finished her coffee and handed him back the cup without a word. Lying down again, she felt better.

He stood up and started toward the door.

"Denny," Vaughn called, when he was almost there.

He turned back and looked at her with an eagerness which she was too wrapped up in misery to appreciate at the time.

Later, tossing in the dark, she suddenly guessed he must have hoped, when she called him, that she was going to ask for a kiss, a sign that she didn't hold it against him about the vacation. It would have been so easy then to reach out her arms to him. He would have come. She knew he would have come.

But in that moment, when she called him and he stood at the foot of the bed, waiting for what she was going to say, she didn't see that. She simply shut her eyes, absorbed in disappointment.

"Yes?" he asked hopefully.

"Pull the shade down, will you?"

2. It was early when Vaughn reached the office. Hardly anyone was in yet. She'd wanted to get out of the apartment, to be alone. She was so upset——

That terrible comedown Saturday night—it wasn't like the other times, not really a spat at all—much worse than a spat. Hopeless finality. Denny's and her life could never be changed. He should have been man enough to get the vacation.

I can't go into staff conference feeling like this, she thought, putting her hat away. I must look a wreck.

She took out her compact. Then, without even lifting the little mirror in the lid, she put it back into her handbag. The trouble was inside her. She knew it.

I have to *do* something, she thought miserably, sitting down and bending a paper clip.

She still had twenty minutes. Was it possible, she wondered, for a person to "center down"—as Philip Ludlow called it—alone? There was time.

She leaned back in the swivel chair to get herself in the mood.

Then she remembered that Brockridge layout. Ham had said Friday to rush it.

Not now, she told herself, just making a little memo and sticking it in her blotter for later.

If she could only begin. But how? For her, of all people, to repeat the Lord's Prayer, here, in the office, first thing Monday morning, seemed downright affected. After all, it wasn't as if she'd really got religion. She just wanted to think.

There must be some way people get going, she said to herself.

Did one have to be in a meetinghouse, perhaps, to center down? But, no. Philip Ludlow had told her expressly that Friends didn't consider the place sacred, that they could meet anywhere.

When she was trying so hard, for once, to be reverent, how could her mind start playing tricks now, making up gags for an advertisement: *Travel by Railroad, A Testimony to the Way of Love.* Wouldn't that look cute, posted in all the stations?

Shut up! Vaughn said to her mind. Don't you see I'm trying to center down? Oh, she thought suddenly, Philip Ludlow's book.

She'd forgotten to take it.

It was silly, the way she'd held the little volume a minute when she unpacked the overnight case and then laid it lovingly on her bureau. Just because it was his, a link with Kendal. Waking up this morning, she'd looked immediately toward the bureau. But she'd meant to wrap the book up after breakfast and mail it in the noon hour. Then it had slipped her mind.

There was a lot of noise outside the office door. People were coming to work. How could it be so hard to concentrate when you wanted to? Vaughn closed her eyes, trying with all her might to find the way back to that wonderful place she'd discovered during Meeting in Kendal. But it was no use.

Was it impossible for one person, alone? Did two or three have to be gathered together?

A scraping sound, close by—— Vaughn's eyes flew open.

Ham stood in the doorway, looking at her. "What's the matter?" he asked. "You sick?"

184

He had his Monday-morning look. The skin around his eyes was like a pricked balloon.

Vaughn greeted him with forced gaiety.

"Thought you were having a dizzy spell," he explained, coming over and standing beside her desk, "the way you were sitting there with your eyes closed. Just your yoga?"

Vaughn laughed. If he knew——

"Say," he said eagerly, "got something for you." He held a sheaf of papers before him, but he sounded like a person holding a surprise behind his back.

"Which hand?" Vaughn asked.

"Yes," he said. "It's wonderful." He began spreading the papers on her desk. "You see," he explained, the eagerness leaving his face for a moment, "I know you're in a spot over the railroad layout." He fiddled with his tie. "Why, you're making such a fuss over it is beyond me."

"It's——" How explain to Ham?

"Never mind," he said, waving his hand, eager again. "This just came in." He rearranged the papers. "Thought I'd show it to you instead of letting Katie Martin go to work on it, because if you could do a bang-up job with this, there'd be something to show Dad and my uncles."

The bosses!

Ham looked Vaughn in the eye and said significantly, with unmistakable feeling, "I want you in Katie's place."

She gave him a grateful glance, too happy to speak.

But then, it seemed to her, the look he returned was a pleading look, as if he hoped he could *will* her to succeed, and she suddenly saw that he wanted her to have Katie's job more because he liked her than because of faith in her ability.

"Now, see here, Vaughn," he said, turning fatherly. "Just put your mind on this, will you?"

"Yes, Ham."

He sat down on the edge of her desk and explained. "It's for Royce and Hodgkin over in Jersey," he said. "They're marketing a new kitchen gadget. Just at present they haven't got a lot of capital, so this gadget has to have a big market right away."

Vaughn raised her eyebrows. It sounded a little fishy.

"Here's the picture," Ham went on. "An electric can opener attached to a mixer. That's the novelty part—the attachment. Every housewife wants a new gadget every few months."

"Yes," Vaughn agreed, nodding earnestly.

"Trouble is," Ham observed, "they don't wear out fast enough. Well, see what you can do with it, Vaughn." He gathered the papers together and left them in a pile on her desk. "This is big-time stuff. I want you to write something terrific that's going to bring in a huge volume of sales right away."

Vaughn took up the picture and studied it. "Is it any good?" she asked.

"Is what any good?"

"The gadget," Vaughn said. "The thing they want us to write this high-powered copy for. Is it any good?"

Ham looked at her incredulously. "What do you mean, is it any good? How should I know?"

"Don't get excited, Ham," Vaughn begged. "All I want to know is, does it work?"

"How should I know does it work?" he asked, grabbing a bunch of rubber bands off Vaughn's desk and rotating them between his palms. "I'm no engineer. That's not my busines, and I mind my business. You just mind yours. Hear?

"But, Ham," Vaughn exclaimed, trying to get through to him, "how can I write convincing copy if I don't know whether the thing works?"

"For heaven's sake, Vaughn," Ham shouted, jumping up and striding toward the window, then turning to her again, "what's the matter with you? Since when does it make any difference how a product works, just so it sells? That's our job, to make it sell. That's what we get paid for."

"Maybe," Vaughn conceded. "I'm not working that way any more, though."

He stood staring down at her, speechless for a moment. "What's got into you?" he asked finally. "You want Hamiltons' should go broke? Like that Kendal Radio you're always asking me about? Here we are, still not back where we were when the recession hit us, radio this morning says there's some trouble over in Asia and the market's breaking, and what does little Vaughn Hill come up with? 'Is it any good?' Nuts!"

He turned away from her in disgust, flinging the rubber bands across the room.

Vaughn squeezed the paper clip till it made a deep dent in her finger.

She didn't know what to say.

But Ham was waiting.

"It's a—a testimony," she said softly.

"What do you mean?"

"Strict integrity——" Then she couldn't go on. What was she doing anyhow, for heaven's sake, talking this way to *Ham*? Did she think he was Philip Ludlow? "Forget it," she said finally. "I'll do my best."

"I knew you would," he answered, sounding greatly relieved. He made for the door.

"Oh, Ham," Vaughn said, and he stood still. "Come back a minute. I have something to tell you."

He moved closer and looked at her.

"Denny's boss won't let him have the first two weeks in August."

"That's too bad," Ham said politely. "We'll sure miss Denny. But Marilyn and I'll take care of you, see you don't get lonesome."

"Me? I'm not going."

"But it's all settled. You can't go back on that now."

"But, Ham," Vaughn argued, lowering her voice in an effort to appear reasonable. "I can't go the first two weeks in August. Don't you understand? Denny's firm won't let him. He has to take next week and the one after."

"Denny's firm," Ham repeated, disposing of it with one sweeping gesture. What do I care how they arrange their vacations? Let him take next week if they want him to. I know it won't be as much fun for you without him, but you have to think of your firm, too, Vaughn."

"Oh, Ham——"

"We were going to plan the fall campaign," he reminded her, facing her sternly. "You can't just walk out on that."

"No," Vaughn admitted slowly, lowering her head to examine the mangled paper clip. "That's true. But Denny and I couldn't take our vacations separately like that. We've never——"

"You won't be alone," Ham said patiently, as if he were a little tired of going over the same ground. "Marilyn and I'll give you a good time, and Denny'll have the kids, won't he? You know," he added, "they say couples get along better if they take their vacations by themselves sometimes."

Vaughn glanced up swiftly and stared at Ham. Did he guess that she and Denny——

Quick, she thought, put up a bluff——

"That's crazy," she said.

"'Strue."

Denny hadn't really wanted to go with the Hamiltons. Maybe he'd be glad if he didn't have to. It really would be more fun for him just being home and fooling around, going out to Jones Beach. They always used to do that.

"Then it's settled?" Ham asked.

If Denny didn't go, they'd save a lot of money. It would take care of what to do with Susan too.

"I'll speak to Denny," Vaughn said finally.

Ham leaned forward and patted her arm. "That's the kid," he said affectionately. "Now then"—he straightened up—"time for staff conference. Let's get down to business."

He walked toward the door a second time and stood there, waiting for Vaughn. "Coming?"

"In a minute," she said. She needed time to think.

Am I being unreasonable about this? she asked herself, as Ham went out. After all, I did agree to it, didn't I? He went ahead and made arrangements.

It wasn't being quite fair to him. That question about maintaining strict integrity in all one's relations with others—didn't strict integrity demand this sacrifice?

It was a temptation to begin one of those imaginary conversations with Philip Ludlow again. If he thought it was all right to leave Denny—— But Vaughn didn't dare. She knew in advance what Philip Ludlow would say.

"Yes," he'd murmured as the train came in, "it seems love is a thing one sometimes has to work at—work at quite hard."

The book—she might keep it awhile.

A sort of talisman, she said to herself.

Time enough to send it back in a week or two. He couldn't have expected her to finish it on the train. Come to think of it, he'd never mentioned sending it back. She couldn't read it, of course, because of that "vow of love," but it would be nice to have around.

Looking down at the papers Ham had left on her desk, Vaughn wondered how she could ever have lost control of herself like that with him. She'd only just managed to get away with it—just.

I bet nobody in this agency ever did before, she said to herself, remembering stories she'd heard. If Ham didn't happen to be a little sentimental about me——

It was all Philip Ludlow's fault that Vaughn had talked to Ham that way. That sweet, innocent old man was turning out to be the most dangerous person she'd ever come up against. If she let herself be influenced by him now, she was done for. But good. He was willfully ruining his own future. Was she going to let him ruin hers too?

She must never, never let herself go like that again, she thought, squeezing her hands together. Denny, the children—what would happen to them if she took one more false step? Things were bad enough at home already. If she lost her job——

Philip Ludlow was just a menace. Really, when you stopped to think of it this way, that's what he was—one dangerous menace.

189

I guess I was a little romantic about him, Vaughn said to herself. Not in the way Denny suspected—the nut. But attracted to his standards and his way of life. That's why I wanted to make Denny's and mine over, only——

After all, wasn't that a romantic notion, too, that they could begin again? They weren't kids. As Denny himself pointed out when he brought her the coffee that night—she was furious with him at the time for thinking it, but she saw now he was perfectly right—people can't change just like that. She'd come home with this beautiful idea and then, just because something hadn't panned out the way she'd expected, it was spoiled.

No, Vaughn thought, opening her compact, Philip Ludlow's way wasn't for Denny and her. Maybe if Denny were different——

And if they couldn't have the future she'd dreamed of in the Meetinghouse at Kendal, wasn't it better to go out frankly for the other thing, get as far as she could in her career, make money, take the cash, and let the credit go? If she started wobbling, making testimonies, when she didn't have what it takes to back them up, she'd have nothing—just nothing. She'd be out on the street, like Katie Martin, too old for another job.

What good would that do anyone?

Maybe, she said to herself, as she touched up her mouth, I'd better send the book back. That's just romantic, too, keeping it when I can't even read it. At my age——

Yes, it was better to cut the whole thing off clean. Kendal and Philip Ludlow had been a charming little episode in her life. She'd always cherish it. Maybe, if she'd landed there when she was younger——

I'll have to break it to Denny, she decided, as she glanced from the mirror to her watch. Five past ten! Five minutes late for staff conference—*five minutes!* We'll just have to be sensible, Vaughn concluded, hurrying toward Ham's office. Maybe next year——

3. When Vaughn got home the book wasn't there. Everything on the bureau was the same as usual, only Philip Ludlow's book was missing. Maybe Anna moved it, dusting. But this wasn't Anna's day.

Vaughn hurried into the living room to ask Denny if he'd seen it. He was lying on the sofa, reading a magazine. Watching him a second, Vaughn held the question back. She'd have to explain how she'd got the book, what it was about, and he'd laugh at her. Besides, she had more important things to say.

He looked so tired and thin. If only that wonderful light that had transformed his face the other night, when they were riding home in the taxi and talking about starting life over again, could have stayed.

She squeezed herself onto the leftover edge of the sofa and rested her back against his knees.

Denny put down the magazine and looked at her attentively but with hardly any life in his eyes.

"Have we made up?" Vaughn asked hopefully, putting out her hand to him. "I know I was crazy that night, saying all those things. You were right about us not being able to begin again."

He nodded and took her hand, but said nothing.

"I guess I was a little high when I came back from Kendal," Vaughn added. "Know what I was drunk on? Lemonade!"

"Rats!"

"No, really, I mean it. I drank about a gallon for lunch that day. It was so hot just before the storm broke, and the lemonade reminded me of when I was a kid. You know, Denny, I should have gone home before the folks died."

"You didn't want to."

"I know. But I got to thinking as I was sitting there—— Well, anyway, what I want to say is: I talked to Ham about the vacation."

"Yes?"

Vaughn sighed and looked away. "I couldn't get anywhere with him," she said. "Don't get mad at me, Denny. Honestly, I tried.

But he said I owed it to the firm to go to Maine and work on that campaign, even if you couldn't go. Do you mind terribly?" Before he could answer she said quickly, "You didn't really like the idea in the first place, and Susan'll keep house for you."

Oh, she thought, watching disappointment bring life into his eyes, he minds——

She was in such a spot, with Ham pulling her that way. It was terrible—to be tied hand and foot to one's job.

"Well," she said, getting up and moving toward the bedroom to change into her housecoat. "Have to get dinner. And I must sew on Neil's name tapes tonight. His camp uniform——"

But she stood there uncertainly. Everything was so muddled up—— "Got a new piece of work today," she said, just so she could stand there a little longer. "For Royce and Hodgkin, a Jersey firm. Ever heard of it?"

Denny shook his head.

"Ham snitched it from Katie Martin for me so's I could show the bosses what I can do. It doesn't matter about Katie. She's on the way out, anyhow. It's a wonderful opportunity. Only——"

Denny looked at her quickly. Her voice must have given her away.

"Well, I don't know anything about the gadget. And how can I write enthusiastic copy if I don't even know whether I ought to urge people to believe in it? This might be like that Redbrook Furnace thing."

"Mm," was all Denny said, but he looked worried.

"Ham doesn't know a thing about it," Vaughn added. Then an idea struck her. "At least, that's what he tells me." Maybe Ham was holding out on her.

"Well," Denny said with a sigh, " 'wear it as long as thou canst.' "

Vaughn screwed up her face. "What are you talking about?"

" 'Wear it as long as thou canst,' " he repeated. "That's what George Fox said to William Penn when Penn asked if he should go on wearing his sword, after he'd become convinced of this light in men's souls. Don't *you* know?"

"Never heard of it," Vaughn answered indifferently. "I don't see what it has to do with me, anyhow."

"Skip it," Denny said, smiling at her for the first time. "Just a piece of information I picked up in the library today. Went over in lunch hour to look up something. Say, how about food?"

He never mentioned the vacation. Just that look—— But he was smiling now.

While she was cooking supper, Vaughn wondered what Denny'd meant, saying that.

The archaic speech he'd used made her think of Kendal.

Yes, she thought, a charming little episode. . . .

"Denny," she called out, "what was that you said? William Penn?"

"You know who I mean, don't you?" he asked, coming into the kitchen. "Not the guy on the whisky bottle." He smiled again, and gave her a kiss.

Vaughn dropped the spoon she'd been stirring the soup with and thought a second. "How long did he wear the sword then?" she asked.

"Not long."

Why had she asked? Vaughn couldn't imagine. She wasn't interested. Just that speech—— It reminded her of Kendal.

Philip Ludlow's book—it was on the bureau only this morning. Somehow she didn't want to ask Denny.

"Darling," she said, putting her arms around him, "I'm so glad you don't mind about the vacation."

He didn't answer that. But the look returned.

Anyhow, I don't have to leave yet, Vaughn thought, taking a can of beef stew from the shelf.

The children came in, crowding the kitchen.

"We'll have the Fourth of July together," Vaughn said, suddenly finding one thing to be happy about. "Next week—Tuesday."

"Won't be able to go anywhere," Denny muttered. "Crowds at the beach, no seats in the trains——"

"Well, we'll just stay home," Vaughn decided practically. And then she saw Neil.

"I won't be able to stay home," his eyes were saying to her, though his lips said nothing.

He was leaving for camp on the third.

Vaughn quickly turned her attention to the can opener, but at that moment it broke.

"Damn it!"

"Moth-er!" Susan admonished. "You're always scolding me for swearing. Now you did it."

"Couldn't help it," Vaughn muttered. "This is the third can opener that's broken on me since Christmas. Why can't they make these gadgets right?"

"Here," Neil said, coming to the rescue. "Let me have it. I can fix it."

"I'm glad you're not twins," Vaughn said to him later, when they were all in the living room and she was working on his uniform. "I don't think I could manage sewing two orders of name tapes."

"I wish I was going to camp," Susan said.

"Maybe next year," Vaughn murmured. "You're needed here this summer to keep house for your daddy during his vacation and when I'm away."

Vaughn bit off a length of thread and would have liked to bite her tongue along with it. Why did she have to harp on going away? It would be so much better to drop the matter for now.

"You're always going away," Susan wailed.

"That's not so," Vaughn answered crossly. Instantly she regretted her tone. There'd been no reproach in the child's voice, only sadness. "I never go anywhere except on business," she added more reasonably. "Even when I go to Maine it'll just be to work with Mr. Hamilton."

Denny looked suddenly at Vaughn, then turned away.

Susan said nothing. She was subdued. After a while she murmured, her little face screwed up in self-pity, "It's awful being a latchkey child, underprivileged——"

"Susan!" Vaughn cried. "Haven't you got a grain of sense in that head of yours? Why, you're the most privileged child in the world— a lovely home, the best of care, dancing lessons——"

There was no use going on. Studying her, Vaughn saw that Susan believed in her preposterous fantasy.

She did have a latchkey, naturally, because she usually got home before anyone else. But that didn't make her a——

Does it? Vaughn asked herself, taken aback.

Had she in some way been neglecting Susan? But what else could she do, working all day?

Looking at her again, Vaughn thought, there really is something pathetic about her.

A few months ago there had seemed to be a hidden unfolding— what Vaughn had thought of then as a seedling in the child's soul. It had seemed very charming. But now there was only wistfulness, as if the seedling were undernourished.

It made Vaughn's heart ache.

The name tapes were finally finished. Though Vaughn was dying to go to bed, she went in and packed Neil's trunk. It was going in the morning. Neil and Susan were playing Canasta, and Vaughn was grateful that he wasn't around when she finally pushed down the lid. She couldn't have faced that expression in his eyes again, especially now, when she was so tired.

At last the trunk was closed. The children trailed off to bed. Denny went out to put the chain on the hall door, and Vaughn emptied the ash trays.

As she was plumping up the sofa cushions, she thought, I was deadbeat that night, after traveling till four in the morning. Maybe if I hadn't been so worn out——

She picked up the last cushion. There, in a corner of the sofa, was Philip Ludlow's book.

"How in the world?" Vaughn cried aloud. But when Denny asked on his way to the bedroom what she was talking about, caution held her back. "Nothing," she said.

After Denny had passed, she held the little volume close to her a minute. It had come to mean that whole other way of life.

Then, slowly, she went to the highboy and took out a piece of brown paper and some string. Lovingly, gently, she wrapped up the book, handling it with what she knew to be idiotic tenderness.

I can't help it, she sobbed inside herself, though her eyes were dry. I'm giving all that up now, forever. . . .

Taking out her pen, she wrote, shaking a little:

Philip Ludlow,
Kendal, R.I.

It's better this way, she assured herself as she put the parcel on the hall table, where she'd be sure to remember it in the morning, but she still felt as if she were sobbing.

In bed she didn't trust herself to speak for fear of breaking down. Denny would wonder.

When he heaved a sudden sigh, Vaughn knew he was feeling troubled too.

"It's the vacation," she said, turning to him. "You do mind about the vacation, don't you?"

"Yes," he said. "I mind. I'd rather have you with me than send you to Maine with that Ham. But that isn't really it. I mean, if everything else was all right, I'd make the best of it."

"Everything else?"

"If you were making all these sacrifices for a decent outfit. But that Hamilton crowd——"

"That's how it is in the advertising business," she said, shrugging.

"No!" he whispered so vehemently that Vaughn thought the children would hear at the other end of the house. "That's not true. Advertising's all right, if it's done carefully, honestly. But those Hamiltons—— It kills me seeing you stoop to their level."

Was he just saying that because he was disappointed, bitter, maybe even a little jealous?

"Look, Denny," Vaughn said. "Grant you that they sometimes

stretch a point, exaggerate a little. Where would you find a firm that would push me along the way they're doing? It's phenomenal, when I've only been there——"

"That doesn't make them honest, just because they're giving you a break. Other firms would take you, too, though they might not push you so fast, because they wouldn't need a person who'd be willing to play that sort of a game for them."

"What do you mean?" Vaughn asked furiously. "Are you implying——"

Denny wouldn't answer.

Vaughn didn't press him, but turned away in anger, while admitting to herself that there was something in what he said. He wasn't being jealous now.

But not realistic either. The way he talked about the advertising business reminded her of Philip Ludlow. And only today, after staff conference, Ham had told her that, according to the very latest report, Kendal Radio was ready to fold up.

I'm glad I have the guts to send the book back, Vaughn thought.

Then why did the sobbing inside her begin again? It was a break she'd had to make, and now that she'd done it, she ought to feel better.

Suddenly she wondered whether Denny'd been the one to move the book. Could he have been reading it? *Denny*?

But no—that "vow of love." Denny would be just as decent about that as she'd been. Still——

"Denny, did you——"

But Denny was fast asleep.

4. The escalator—Vaughn was on it again, only it was at Hamiltons' this time. For some reason which wasn't clear she was being hoisted to a floor high above the agency. The desks and files and drafting tables below kept growing smaller and smaller and all the office workers bent over their layouts were getting farther and farther away.

Vaughn didn't know how she'd got on this terrible machine again or where she was heading, only that she was being carried up and she couldn't stop herself. She couldn't jump off. When she came to that last sliding-under step, her foot wouldn't move fast enough, she'd never make it.

In panic she turned wildly everywhere for some escape.

Then it was that she saw Denny and the children standing at the top, waiting for her, Denny in his mustard-colored tweed. Susan was wearing her little bolero suit with the new Mary Janes on her bare feet. Neil was in camp uniform. Rows of name tapes were sewed across the chest. Neil Hill, Neil Hill, Neil Hill . . .

The three of them stood there, looking down at Vaughn, anxious for her, eagerly waiting, but though Vaughn strained forward with all her strength, she couldn't reach them.

She must get there, she must! The escalator—— Putting out her foot as the top step began to slide under, she tried to jump off, but missed. She was carried down, down . . .

"Denny!" she shrieked. His name sounded clearly in her head, yet she knew it hadn't come out of her mouth. "Denny——"

She screamed and screamed, but she couldn't cry his name. And all the time she was falling, she was falling . . .

"Honey," Denny whispered, "wake up."

She was lying in his arms.

"Oh, Denny——" The relief. "Hold me tight," she begged.

"I am," he said, squeezing her. "It was just a nightmare."

"Un-n," she muttered, opening her eyes to the darkness. "Oh, Denny, it was ghastly!"

"Everything's all right now," he said, and his voice poured comfort over her. "Everything's all right."

"You and the children were waiting and I couldn't get off——"

"Off what?"

"Off——" The dream was no longer clear enough to describe, but the fear was still pounding in Vaughn's heart. "Oh, Denny," was all she could say.

He held her tightly.

She took a deep breath and shut her eyes again, turning her head and snuggling into the curve of Denny's shoulder. The wonderful safeness was wrapped all around her, the sureness of his love. She'd been falling through space, but Denny'd caught her.

Vaughn lay still and, after a while, her heart grew quiet. Then she remembered.

"Were you reading that book?" she asked.

"What book?"

"On my bureau. Somebody——"

"Oh," he said, "that one. Sure. It's nice."

"You mean you read it?" she asked, appalled. *"You?"*

"Was it something private?" Denny inquired. "I didn't think you'd mind."

"Not private," Vaughn explained, "but it says in the beginning that you mustn't read it unless your purpose is——" She couldn't remember the words. "Unless you really want to be——"

"Doesn't everybody want to?" he asked in surprise. "People don't know how—except Gandhi, one or two like that. But everybody wants to."

"You mean," Vaughn exclaimed, "everybody wants to be a do-gooder and think all the time about God? You couldn't have read it right."

"Not think all the time," Denny said slowly, "but act the way one would if——" He stretched out in the darkness for Vaughn's hand. "I guess it is above my head," he admitted, "but part of it—— The Quakers have something with that idea of God in everybody."

Vaughn was lost. "Quakers?" she repeated. "That isn't a Quaker book. Or is it? I didn't read it. But I thought it was Middle Ages, and Quakers didn't start till—I don't know when, but much later."

"Seventeenth century."

"How do you know?"

"Looked it up. Noon hour went to the library."

"You mean—you mean——" Vaughn couldn't put it all together. "You've been looking up about Quakers?"

"Vaughn, honey," he said, squeezing her hand, "anything that means so much to you I just had to know about. First, I thought it was the man you were falling for up there in the country, but then Saturday night, when you came home, I saw it was something else—spiritual. I'm sorry I was jealous in the beginning. He must be a wonderful person. If this thing means so much to you, honey——"

"But it doesn't," Vaughn broke in and, to her surprise, she began to cry. She'd just parted with all that forever. "It doesn't," she sobbed. "Oh, Denny——"

He lifted himself on his elbow and bent over her, patting away the tears that streamed down her cheek.

"Never mind, then," he said gently. "Never mind. I just had the idea that it did, so I read up a little. That's nothing to get upset over, me reading a couple of books. Forget it."

"Don't you see," Vaughn asked, wiping her eyes, "it isn't just ideas in books, or words or prayers. It's a way of life. One has to *be* that way, and in practice it doesn't work out. We have to have security. I thought for a while, that night I came home, when I was feeling high, that we—— But we couldn't. Then today, in the office, I realized that Philip Ludlow is really nothing but a dangerous character."

"*Dangerous?*"

"Yes. Oh, not a bad man. I've never known anyone really good like that. But dangerous—— If I try to do what he believes in, I'm through. I tried it today, and came within a hairbreadth of landing on my ear. It doesn't work."

First Denny said nothing, then he whispered, "So that's what gave you the nightmare—what you were trying to get off from—the agency, for my vacation."

"It was just a dream." Vaughn couldn't see any connection.

"Seems Ham and the old Quaker are fighting for your soul,"

Denny said, adding, with a catch in his voice, "If I could just throw in my weight—— But you wouldn't listen to me."

Ham and Philip Ludlow fighting for her soul—what a strange picture, Vaughn thought. How could they, hundreds of miles apart?

"Thing is," Denny whispered brokenly, "I love you so, Vaughn."

If it had been like this, she said to herself, the night I came home, if it had only been like this——

They lay quietly, without speaking.

And now, when she no longer had any conscious wish to do so, Vaughn felt herself moving through this silence into the sense of understanding she'd known in Kendal. The furious drive in her to grasp and overreach, to get on against all odds, fell away.

Inward eyes, ears of the soul. She wouldn't have put it in those words, but what she saw and heard in this distant place to which she felt herself carried now was like nothing in her whole experience. The certainty of some power beyond her, more competent than herself, relieved her of the necessity she always felt to run everything and everybody. For the first time in her life she knew a small willingness to surrender management, to listen humbly.

But wasn't she through with all that sort of thing? Through forever? Hadn't she decided, only this evening, when she wrapped the book?

All at once she knew that she was not through, that she would never be. The determination to resist being carried away broke in her, cracked and split open, widened by the pressure of a whole flood of new feeling, a longing for something beyond her even more intense than any she'd known in Kendal.

It had been formless in the beginning, this longing. Each time it returned, though, it became more distinct and intense, as an object would be more discernible the closer one came. And now it was clear to Vaughn that this wasn't so much a matter of Ham against Philip Ludlow, the way Denny'd put it, as of her will against God's.

The thought was terrifying—as frightening as the escalator—worse. There'd be no waking this time to find it was only a dream.

She would yield her will. A little—not all at once. But she would try a little. Enough, maybe, to read the book. If Denny could——

I'll try a little, she promised herself.

Wasn't that as much as a person her type could be expected to do?

Thinking this, taking a faint comfort in it, she nestled more closely against Denny. Though she'd been off for a second in that distant place and he hadn't spoken a word, she seemed nearer to him now than before, nearer than they'd ever been together, even years ago, when they'd been so much in love. It was surprising, since she hadn't been thinking of him, off in that distant place. She'd thought she'd left him behind.

Suddenly she wondered whether he too—— Could Denny have been there? Was that why they seemed so close? Had they been together in that place? Never! Not Denny.

Still, she wasn't so sure. She'd have liked to ask, but it would have meant explaining, and no words could explain this.

"Know what I've been thinking," Denny said, and though he whispered, the sound of his hushed voice breaking across Vaughn's distant mood startled her for a second. "I was thinking, maybe you were right after all that night and I didn't have enough faith in us —well, maybe in God—to believe we could start all over. But——"

He took her hand again and held it tightly, breathing hard, as if he didn't trust himself to go on with what he had to say. "Don't you think we could?" he asked finally in a choked whisper. "Don't you, Vaughn?" he pleaded.

She didn't try to answer. She knew no words would do, no promise would be effective, only a remaking of herself, not her whole self, not a drastic change, but a little——

Just that little would take so much strength. Where would she ever find it? Nestling closer against Denny's shoulder, begging in her heart for fresh insight, she turned again to the silence.

It gave her a feeling of restedness, of being cared for to surrender so, and now she awaited eagerly some flash, some revelation of a new way to arrange their life, to start all over.

That didn't come. She wasn't full of ideas; she hadn't any. But she could feel the stillness in her. It covered the burning trouble of her mind with healing, cool and soft, like clean sheets after a weary day.

5. In the morning Vaughn didn't stop to cook breakfast, only coffee. School was over, so Susan could give Denny and Neil their orange juice and eggs. Vaughn wasn't hungry.

She had to have it out with Ham. Not that he'd be in the agency this early—nobody of importance would—but Vaughn hurried down nevertheless, so as to catch him the minute he arrived.

He wouldn't fire her for this, would he? She'd always been so loyal——

It's just nervousness, really, Vaughn told herself in the subway, makes me go at this hour. I must pull myself together. Like this, I won't be in control of the situation.

And she would have to be in control—to play her cards very carefully. The thing to do, she decided, was to keep the whole question on a personal level. It was impossible for Vaughn to take her vacation any time except the next two weeks. True, she'd agreed to, but a woman had to consider her husband first.

Still, the work—— What was going to happen to the work? This Royce and Hodgkin layout and the new job, Katie Martin's, that Ham was grooming Vaughn for?

What about it? she asked herself uneasily.

To Vaughn's surprise she found when she reached the agency that Katie was in ahead of her. Was Katie nervous too? She looked the same as ever, greeting Vaughn with that wide-mouthed smile of hers that was rather attractive, in a homespun sort of way.

Wonder why nobody married her after her husband died, Vaughn said to herself, stopping for a moment at Katie's door. She's not so bad-looking.

"Cleaning up," Katie explained to Vaughn, seeing her surprise at finding Katie in this early. "When you've been in a place years and years, you accumulate an awful lot of junk."

Vaughn nodded. It was pathetic.

"I always knew I'd have to go some time," Katie went on, turning away to gaze out of the window, "but deep down I didn't believe it. Somebody else—sure. But not me. Like dying. That's strictly for other people. I can't believe I'll ever die, can you?" She turned back and faced Vaughn.

"Never thought about it."

"I mean," Katie went on, "with my intelligence, yes. But deep down I'm sure I'll live forever. Can't even believe I'm old, no matter what Hamiltons' say——"

If she just knew how to make up, Vaughn thought, sorry as anything for Katie. She could fool them. She could take ten years off her age just with a little tinting alone. And mascara would do wonders.

Considering Katie's eyes critically, Vaughn's attention was suddenly diverted from the pouches and shadows beneath them to the inner feeling they revealed. What she saw then shocked Vaughn in a way she never remembered being shocked: the hurt unbelief of a person who was unwanted, who no longer counted——

The Underground Railroad flashed through Vaughn's mind. She didn't know why, at this moment, she remembered wondering whether Katie Martin would be capable of writing that layout. Catching Philip Ludlow staring at her with pleading and compassion, Vaughn had realized for the first time that perhaps one had to care, that she herself didn't.

It made Vaughn feel mean and guilty, looking at Katie, though, goodness knows, it wasn't her fault that Hamiltons' was hard-boiled. There was nothing she could do about it. And yet she felt mean.

She would have liked to stop longer and be sweet to Katie, but suddenly she remembered her own problem. Where did she come in to offer sympathy? She herself was in a spot. If Ham wasn't reasonable now——

"Excuse me," she said to Katie, breaking in on some story that didn't seem very important, "I have to run. Something I must see Ham about, soon as he comes in."

She hurried off, relieved to get away from Katie's eyes. That hurt look——

In the outer office Vaughn bumped into Ham. He was earlier than usual.

Not because he's nervous, Vaughn thought, smiling wryly to herself. It must be wonderful to be at the top, where you can do what you like without fear of losing your job.

"Have you got a minute?" she asked him. "I want to speak to you."

Ham seemed eager to hear what she had to say, but he was also fidgety, grabbing at his shirt front, pulling his ear.

He's nervous, too, Vaughn thought.

It struck her as funny, but she was too upset to consider that side just now.

"Ham," she began, when they were both in her office and she'd closed the door carefully, "I spoke to Denny. He was so disappointed, I just can't go with you and leave him home."

First Ham stared at her as if he simply couldn't believe what she was saying. Then she thought he'd blow a gasket.

"Don't be mad at me, Ham," she begged. "It isn't my fault the way the thing turned out."

"But Marilyn and I count on you," Ham exclaimed. "We absolutely count on you."

Vaughn looked straight at him.

That Marilyn, she said to herself. He can't bear thinking of spending two weeks alone with her.

"You're letting me down," Ham said, half in a whisper, and his whole face seemed to crumple.

He was scared. There was a hollow shadow in his pupils, and he fiddled with his tie, pulling on it till Vaughn thought, he'll choke.

So he was just using her, he just wanted Vaughn along so he wouldn't have to take what for from his wife the whole time——

Suddenly he turned angry again, wild. "What about the Royce and Hodgkin layout?" he asked. "You can't just go on your vacation next week with that to do. You know how important——"

"Katie can do it," Vaughn broke in.

And then, suddenly, she saw the whole thing—what it would really feel like to be Katie, what she, Vaughn, would have to do. It wasn't enough to fix things so she could spend Denny's vacation with him, she wouldn't have a moment's peace unless——

"Katie can do it," she repeated, with rising conviction. "You never should have taken it away from her in the first place. You know that."

"It was only for you, Vaughn," Ham said, in an injured tone. "I was only trying to help you produce something that would rate with the bosses, so they'd give you Katie's job."

"I wouldn't take it," Vaughn cried. "I wouldn't take another woman's job away from her, just because she's past forty——"

"Forty-five."

"Okay, forty-five. That's no reason to let her go. She's good, and she has to work. I wouldn't——"

"You wouldn't?" Ham shouted. "You were waitng for it with your mouth wide open day or two ago. What's got into you?" He looked at her incredulously a second. "Pointing your little pop-gun at me," he asked with a forced smile, "so you can have your way about the vacation? Go ahead and take next week," he conceded, "if that's what you want. No need to act up about Katie's job too."

"I'm not acting up," Vaughn said. She felt like stamping her foot, but she knew she'd make her point better by appearing quiet. "It's just that sometimes you have to do a thing simply because it's the right thing, even when you know it isn't to your advantage."

Ham looked at her in amazement. He scratched his head. "First time I've ever heard you say anything of this kind," he muttered. "It isn't like you."

"I've been doing some thinking," Vaughn said.

"If you ask me," Ham answered, "you're not yourself. I guess it'll do you good to get away. Yesterday, when I looked in, I thought the heat had gone to your head. Well," he concluded, sighing and turning toward the door, "toodloo. Have fun. I'm going to Buffalo tonight, so I won't see you till you get back—two weeks from Monday. Take it easy. Stay in bed late. It'll do you good." He smiled at her.

"Thanks, Ham," Vaughn said. "I guess we'll go to the beach some. It won't be like going to Maine, of course. Tell Marilyn I'm awfully sorry and that love is a thing you sometimes have to——" She started to say "work at," but, looking at Ham, decided not to. Marilyn wouldn't understand.

An affectionate tolerance replaced the anger in Ham's face. "Look, Vaughn," he said, in a tone of long-suffering, turning to her with his hand on the doorknob, "when you get back don't try to pull any more of that testimony stuff's got into you lately. I'm not running a Sunday school. We're in business to make money, and don't you forget it. I put up with a lot from you lately because I like you, but——" With a significant look he went out.

Vaughn was furious.

He thinks I'm Marilyn, she thought, feeling the temper rise in her throat as Ham shut the door. He thinks my wanting to be decent is just a whim that he has to put up with. He wants me to know he's overlooking it just because——

She grabbed up a whole handful of paper clips and threw them at the door.

6. The heat and the sudden attack in Korea had everybody edgy. Hamiltons' was in a state of tension.

It was getting on Vaughn's nerves.

Good thing I'm getting out of here, she thought, as she left for her vacation Friday afternoon. I could never have stuck it out till August.

There were still odds and ends left to be done for Neil. His trunk was gone, but Vaughn had a list of little things to get before he left on Monday—a tube of toothpaste and penny post cards which she'd self-address when she got home. She wanted to get him a present too —a book or something else he'd like, so as to—well, not exactly to make up for sending him to camp. That was a ridiculous idea, when it cost so much.

But Vaughn hated seeing how unhappy the kid looked. Now that it was too late, she began to wonder whether it had been right to insist. If he were only like other boys—— Any other boy would have been thrilled to go. And if Neil weren't going to camp, what would he do all summer? The city——

All week end Neil sat in his room, saying nothing, not really doing anything, just looking at his things. Once, when Vaughn came in, she caught him poring over that ad for the sailboat he'd wanted to buy in the spring.

She had to run out of the room.

Denny wasn't bright either. He seemed to be taking Neil's going very hard. And Susan went moping around because all her friends had left town for the summer. The house was like a doctor's waiting room, with everyone staring dumbly at everyone else out of his private suffering.

When Monday came it was almost a relief.

As soon as he's with the other boys, Vaughn assured herself, on the way to the station, as soon as he gets up there——

But now, in the taxi, Neil was silent, going to his execution like a man.

He and Susan sat on the little folding seats. Vaughn, in the rear with Denny, was almost glad she couldn't see the boy's expression.

Denny tried to cheer Neil. "You're lucky," he said, "going off for the summer. Gosh, I wish I were going some place where I could fool around all day in a boat——"

"Yes," Susan put in jealously, "and be a skunk and practice for the play and learn those songs for Parents' Day."

"Shut up."

It was the only thing Neil said the entire journey.

This is no time to tease him, Vaughn thought sadly, wishing she could catch Susan's eye.

"Have you got your trunk key, dear?" she asked aloud, and Neil grunted but didn't face her.

"Darn lucky," Denny was saying. "I wish I was on my way to camp, instead of having to spend my vacation in this stuffy old town. Going to the country—gosh, wouldn't I love it!"

"Me too," Susan put in.

"I wish we could go home," Denny murmured wistfully.

"Home?" Vaughn repeated. "New York's home for us. There's no other place."

"I know," Denny said with dreamy sadness. "I was only wishing."

As if I don't feel bad enough already, Vaughn thought, now Denny's like that.

The whole weight of everybody's misery was converging on her, bearing down on her chest, so that she felt suffocated. She tried to move closer to the window, but her hot clothes were sticking to the upholstery of the cab.

Oh, she cried out in her heart, I can't bear it another minute——

Wildly searching for some escape, she turned to Philip Ludlow, though only a week ago, when she wrapped the book, she'd given him up forever.

"Just remember," he said, seeing her distress, "you can always come back."

"Denny," she exclaimed. "Oh, Denny, you wouldn't—would you go to Kendal?"

Suddenly it seemed to Vaughn that all the desire she'd ever had to go anywhere—to parties when she was a child, to New York, when she was still in East Bolton—all the wish to feel herself absorbed against a background on which she felt content rushed over her till she thought it would shatter her completely if Denny didn't——

"Kendal?" he asked.

"Yes," Vaughn answered, hearing her anxious voice give her away. "We could stay with Mary Lancashire. She invited us. Oh, Denny, would you?"

He looked at her searchingly. "Kendal?" he repeated. "You mean me too?"

"You and Susan."

As if a shot had been fired, both children turned around in their seats.

"*Me?*"

"Certainly, Susan, you'd love it. All those little pigtails—they're like the quaint little girls you like to read about."

And then, Vaughn didn't know what made her do it, but instead of turning toward Susan to see how the child responded to the suggestion, she turned her head the other way. It was Neil whose eyes she met, though something in her must have warned her beforehand that she wouldn't be able to bear the anguish and reproach in them.

"Sure," Denny was saying, "I'm game, if that's what you'd like and it doesn't cost too much."

"Oh, boy!" Susan exclaimed.

"What would we do there all day?" Denny was asking. "There isn't anything, is there?"

He hadn't noticed Neil.

"There's the——" Vaughn choked. If she mentioned the river Neil would—— "Sally and Luke'll probably invite us over to their place sometime," she said instead, grabbing at safety.

"What would we do there?"

Vaughn squeezed the catch of her handbag, pretending she hadn't heard. Why were men always so dense?

"Neil," she asked shakily, leaning forward to look at the boy with tenderness, "have you got your money?"

Thank the Lord, here they were at last. A redcap was opening the door of the taxi. Maybe now, getting out with all Neil's luggage, passing through the station, meeting the camp group, they'd forget Kendal. After Neil left the three of them could discuss it.

Denny strode ahead nervously and Vaughn followed, the children trailing behind.

Why didn't I think of it sooner? Vaughn asked herself. That river—— Kendal's just the place for Neil. He's a natural for it. And Philip Ludlow was always putting out those little feelers, reaching toward the kid in that way he has of loving people he doesn't know.

Entering the station, Vaughn was caught again, caught in the stomach of that monster.

Oh, he feels like me, she cried to herself suddenly, and the thought was such a saddening surprise that she stood still a second. He feels like me when they sent me to boarding school. But that was so strict—I thought camp would be fun. *Like me——*

She looked up, and the vaulted dome overhead, the belly of the whale——

"Denny," she cried, hurrying after him again, almost in tears, "Denny, wait for me!"

He looked back, stopped by the tone of her voice, her breathless cry. "What's the matter?" he asked, coming to her.

"Oh," she said, "how could we ever have said we'd send him?"

"I don't know," Denny muttered. "I think we're the cruelest, rottenest parents."

"Why did we do it?"

"You told me he had to go. It was supposed to be good for him."

"Why didn't you say something, before it was too late? He's your child too."

"Vaughn, don't make a scene now," Denny begged. "It's bad enough——"

They pulled themselves together and shook hands with Pop Miller and his counsellors. Then they moved away a little from the camp crowd, a family again.

Vaughn looked over at the clock on top of the Information Desk. Why did Miller always tell the parents to come an hour before traintime? If only Kendal wasn't mentioned again.

"Fellows look nice," Denny observed, still trying to cheer Neil.

Yes, Vaughn thought, nice, but different. He's sweet.

He stood there, holding his bag and tennis racket and staring at his feet.

"Why don't you go over and speak to them?" Vaughn asked him. "Aren't there any you know from last year?"

"Sure," Neil answered, shrugging. "But I can see them all summer. You'll—— Is it settled," he asked urgently, looking up at her, "are you really going to Kendal?"

"We haven't had time to think it over," Vaughn murmured.

"How will I know where to write?" Neil cried. "The cards are all addressed to the apartment."

"*Are* we going?" Susan asked insistently, pulling on Vaughn's arm.

"I don't know. Let go. It's up to your father."

Denny's enthusiasm for the country was gone. He was just looking sadly at Neil.

"How can *I* decide?" he asked Vaughn. "We aren't even sure we could stay there."

"But I have to know," Neil said, and his voice almost broke. "The train's going soon——" He was just a scared little boy leaving home now, a lost little boy who didn't know where his parents——

Denny saw it. "Could you call the woman up?" he asked Vaughn. "Why don't you, right now? Then Neil'll know where we are."

Vaughn looked at Denny in amazement. "*Now?* You'd go?" she asked. "You'd really go? I don't want to ask Mary Lancashire unless you're serious."

"Go on and call her up," Denny urged. "Look, I'll come with you. Neil, take your sister over and introduce her to some of the fellows. We'll be back in a few minutes."

He looked so grim as they headed for the long-distance telephones that Vaughn kept still.

Only, when she'd given Mary Lancashire's name and address to the operator and she and Denny stood waiting, she said, "She probably isn't home. She's probably out. What'll we do if she isn't home?"

But Vaughn was ordered to a booth and hurried over. She spoke tensely into the instrument, while Denny stood outside, watching her through the glass door.

"We'd love having you," Mary Lancashire said, sounding genuinely pleased. "Any time. Why don't you come this afternoon? Yes, there's plenty of room. You and your husband can have the guest room, where you slept that time, we'll put Susan in with one of the girls, and your boy can have Alice's room. She's staying at the homestead. I suppose you know——"

"Neil isn't coming," Vaughn broke in, cutting Mary Lancashire off. It was a toll call, and local gossip could wait till they got to Kendal. "Neil's leaving for camp in ten minutes." She looked at her watch. "In fifteen minutes."

"I'm sorry about that," Mary Lancashire said with unmistakable disappointment.

"So am I," Vaughn answered. "But it'll be just the three of us. I'll speak to my husband and send you a telegram, soon as I know when we're coming. Well, good-by. Oh—how's Philip Ludlow?"

"Terribly upset. He's taking it very hard."

"Poor thing," Vaughn murmured. "I'm so sorry. I wish I'd been able to help."

But there was no use repeating on long distance that Kendal Radio should have advertised, so Vaughn said good-by again quickly.

She burst out of the booth, so excited that she almost threw herself against Denny, but there were people around.

"She says to come right away. This afternoon."

"This—— Gee——" He looked as happy as Vaughn felt. "How much does she want?"

"I didn't ask her."

"You didn't? Vaughn, for a businesswoman——"

"I know."

"Three of us can't just go and spend a vacation without knowing what it's going to cost. Suppose it comes to more than we can afford?"

"I don't think it'll cost anything. I mean, not more than we'd spend at home for food and whatever else we use."

"You're joking."

"No, I think it would hurt her feelings if we tried to pay her. She sounded so happy about our coming, I just got that impression —that it would spoil everything if we tried to make a business arrangement."

"But isn't she the one you said was a widow trying to raise five kids? Three people can't just go and park on a person like that without paying."

Vaughn shrugged impatiently. "Money!" she cried. "Is that all you can think of—money, Denis Hill? There are other things that count in life, things Mary Lancashire needs more than money."

"Like what, for instance?"

"Company. She's lonely."

"Oh," Denny said. "I didn't think of that. Still, she must be nice to ask us all. She must see what it will mean to us too."

They looked at each other happily and then started back through the station toward the children.

"Isn't it wonderful?" Vaughn cried. "I'll have nearly two whole weeks without cooking. That'll be a real vacation." Seeing Susan now down at the other end of the station, she added, "The Lancashire girls act like I'm something out of *Mademoiselle*. I wonder what they'll think of Susan."

"Too bad she isn't the one who's going to that camp," Denny remarked, smiling.

All the boys were standing around Susan. But Neil—Neil stood alone.

"Denny," Vaughn said suddenly. "Neil would simply love that place."

"But he's going to camp—he's nearly left."

"I know. But he'd love it. Couldn't he—couldn't we take him along?"

"To Kendal? You mean now, when he's faced all this, you want to take him to Kendal?"

"He'd be so glad—— Oh," she exclaimed, her voice flattening, "I forgot about his trunk. It's left!"

"Never mind the trunk. Neil's the one to consider. We've got to act fast if we——"

"I don't suppose that Miller man would give us our money back," Vaughn said.

"Money!" Denny cried. "Is that all you can think of—money, Vaughn Hill? There are other things that count in life—a kid's happiness."

They stood still, facing each other, and laughed, and it felt wonderful to laugh.

"We'll put that in the telegram," Vaughn said; *"bringing Neil."* Then she added sadly, "I don't see how I could have been blind to his real need when I love him so. Denny, did you ever think that one sometimes has to work at loving?"

He looked at her quickly.

"I mean," she went on, "I always thought it was just a feeling, but sometimes, it seems, one has to work quite hard——"

"Vaughn," Denny broke in, "if you don't stop talking now, Miller'll have Neil on that train and going to camp. Susan too."

They hurried on, laughing together, not touching, and yet——

We have that same inner rhythm, Vaughn thought happily.

"If we're going to catch the Kendal train, we'll have to hoof it," Denny said, turning serious. "Get home, have lunch, pack——"

"Oh!" Vaughn exclaimed suddenly. "I——" As Denny spoke a horrible thought struck her. "I don't have a thing to wear."

Denny looked at her anxiously.

"We can't go till tomorrow," she announced. "I can shop this afternoon. Have to get my nails done too."

"Tomorrow's the Fourth of July. That's no day to travel. Haven't you anything from last year?" He looked crestfallen.

"Last year?" Vaughn repeated.

How could she wear last year's? And her nails——

But she was dying to leave. It would be so lovely in Kendal, cool and cheerful. The river——

In a swift flash she reviewed her wardrobe. As if the hangers were suspended from a rod inside her mind, she pushed aside as unsuitable one number after another. If only there were something——

"It isn't such a dressy place, is it?" Denny was asking, begging her.

"Dressy?" The idea of Kendal being dressy made Vaughn laugh again. "Not the least bit," she told Denny. "They're all what they call 'plain.' It's just that I haven't a thing——"

They'd almost reached the children now, but Denny grabbed hold of Vaughn and made her stand still. Then he took her in his arms, right in the middle of Grand Central.

"Vaughn," he whispered lovingly, "Vaughn darling, you're not going to Maine with the Hamiltons any more. Remember? We're going to Kendal."

Part 5

1. By the time the train left for Kendal, they were all four in a daze. There'd been so much to do between the moment when they'd rushed out of Grand Central, to the stupefaction of Pop Miller, and the moment when they came hurrying back—— They'd had to defrost the refrigerator, put a note for the milkman in a bottle by the door, tell the elevator boy not to deliver the papers . . .

And getting everybody's things together—Vaughn didn't see now how she'd done it, couldn't remember what she'd packed. Poor Neil had only the underwear he was standing in. The rest was in his trunk, neatly marked, at camp. Denny's shirts hadn't come back from the laundry, and all his socks were dirty. Susan kept running in to ask Vaughn what she should take, when there were so many other things on Vaughn's mind—rubbers and bathing suits and Denny's hair tonic.

But Vaughn understood. The child wanted to wow the little Lancashires and yet to dress simply in order to be like them.

I know how she feels, Vaughn thought, remembering her own preparations for Quarterly Meeting. What an idiot I was——

In the end they just threw things in, finished up the leftovers, hastily washed the dishes, locked the windows, and rushed out to a taxi.

When they'd gone a couple of blocks, Susan suddenly let out a gasp and rolled her eyes. "Ooh!" she wailed, putting both hands to her mouth in horror, "we forgot the Canasta set!"

Thank the Lord, Vaughn exclaimed to herself. *Canasta—in Kendal!*

They found two seats together on the train. Denny and Neil turned the forward one around. Susan got carsick when she rode backward, at least she used to, and Vaughn didn't want to take any chances, especially with all the excitement. So both children sat by the window.

Neil's the one to worry about really, Vaughn thought, glancing at him. What he's been through——

He showed it.

As long as she lived, Vaughn would never forget the happiness in his face when he was told that he needn't go to camp, that he was bound for Kendal instead. Denny had even added in that historic moment that there was a river.

But it had been too sudden, a last-minute reprieve. Neil was as white as a sheet.

Come to think of it, Vaughn realized, leaning back and shutting her eyes a minute, I've been through something myself the last ten days. Ham was right—I need the rest.

And she thought again how wonderful it would be with no housekeeping.

Opening her eyes, she looked happily across at Denny, too exhausted to speak. But when the train crossed the Connecticut and she saw the little lighthouse standing out on a point in the river, sparkling with late-afternoon sunshine, she remembered the first time she herself had gone to Kendal and all the joy of her discovery there came over her with a rush.

"You'll love it," she told Denny eagerly and, hearing her, the children turned from the window. "The beautiful old houses and the trees—I never saw trees like those in Kendal. There's a huge maple in the Meetinghouse Yard. When Philip Ludlow was a little boy he used to cut a whistle from it every spring."

"I always thought you had to have willow for whistles," Denny said.

Vaughn shook her head. "Philip Ludlow's was cut from that maple," she said gravely. "You know," she added, picturing the place to herself, "the shrubs around the Meetinghouse don't look cultivated. They've been allowed to grow as they like. I don't mean the Yard's not nicely tended, but the personality of nature has been"—she hesitated—"respected. That sounds silly, doesn't it?"

"No," Denny answered thoughtfully, "I know what you mean. It shows the people who take care of it are nice."

"And that little old Meetinghouse," Vaughn went on, "so plain, it hardly seems like a church, but when you're in Meeting——" A sudden thought filled her with consternation. "We ought to go on Sunday," she told Denny. "Do you think you——" She almost held her breath, waiting for his answer.

Denny gave a satisfied nod. At any other time this would have astonished Vaughn, but things were so unusual now, as if they'd entered a world where the unexpected quite naturally happened—she wasn't even amazed.

"I'd better explain it to you," she told the children. "They believe in God, you know." She felt a little self-conscious, but she went on. "In something of God in every single person, whether he thinks about it or not, so they don't have a minister because people can make connection with Him by themselves."

Susan regarded Vaughn wide-eyed. "Even kids?" she asked in a little voice.

"Even kids," Vaughn assured her.

"Gee!" Susan murmured.

Neil said nothing, but he was so intent on Vaughn that she tried to go on.

"They don't have music or things to say out of a prayer book," she said. "They just sit still."

"Like a bump on a log?" Susan asked.

"Well, yes."

"What happens?"

"Two or three people talk a little sometimes, if they feel they have something to say. Sometimes nobody speaks at all. Nothing *happens*, exactly."

"Then what's the good of going, if nothing happens?"

One had to be grown up to understand the meaning of the silence, to love the plainness, Philip Ludlow had remarked once. How was Vaughn going to enlighten the child?

"Susan darling," she said slowly, "a lot happens, only it's inside people—in their soul." And then, though she'd never meant to say this to anybody, she blurted out, "Something terrific happened to me there. I think it's changing my whole life—a little. If it hadn't been for that, we wouldn't be on our way——"

It was an admission she instantly regretted making. She didn't dare meet Denny's eyes, but quickly tried to find something else to say.

"Where do you suppose they keep the key?" she asked, laughing. "On the outside wall!"

"What about burglars?"

"They don't seem to worry. Anyone may open the door."

"I like that," Denny put in.

Neil, Vaughn thought. What is there about the place that would appeal to a boy?

"There's an old carriage shed in back," she remembered. "Long ago horses used to stand there gnawing the beams while their masters were in Meeting. You can feel the worn ridges still." And then she added, more for herself, "I wonder whether Bart Brown and his gang have started fixing it up."

With that, panic suddenly seized Vaughn.

Neil— She glanced at the boy in fear. He mustn't be exposed to that crowd. Delinquents. I'll have to speak to Philip Ludlow about that right away.

"What beautiful names these places have," Denny remarked, looking out of the window at the passing shoreline. "Mystic, Stonington, Westerly . . ."

The train was still a long way from Kendal when Vaughn began getting ready.

"Can you manage the bags, do you think?" she asked Denny anxiously. "They'd hardly have a redcap, place like this."

He looked at her and laughed. "Relax," he said. "We'll make it." And then he whispered, "So happy to see you happy, honey."

"I am happy," she exclaimed. "Oh, Denny, I always wanted you to come here. So did Philip Ludlow, I think."

"Yes," Denny said, "I know he did."

Vaughn, adjusting her cartwheel, stopped suddenly and stared at him, her hand still reaching to the crown of her hat. "You *know*? How could you?"

"He told me that night. He said he hoped someday a way would open up for us both to come."

"That's what you wouldn't tell me——"

There was no time to reproach him now for holding out on her. The train was slowing down, coming into Kendal.

"Do you think Mary Lancashire will meet us?" Vaughn asked in the vestibule. As if Denny'd know——

Maybe she'd be too busy getting supper. Four extra——

The train hadn't quite stopped before Vaughn caught sight of Philip Ludlow.

"Look," she cried. "There he is! See him, Denny? He's meeting us."

He was standing just where she'd seen him last that night in the rain, on the side of the station. There was a young man with him.

Now Vaughn was going down the steps, she was on the platform, Denny was lifting out the bags, the children——

Her first thought, as Philip Ludlow came toward her, was: he looks older. Yet it's little more than a week——

A crease Vaughn didn't remember saddened his mouth. She'd expected him to look so gay when he found that she'd brought everyone—Denny and both children.

His business really has folded up, she concluded.

But as Philip Ludlow left the young man and moved toward Vaughn, his face came alive with happiness.

"What a wonderful surprise!" he exclaimed.

"Philip Ludlow," Vaughn cried, "I'm so happy to see you. This is Denis Hill," she announced, just, she thought, like a proper Quaker.

The way they looked at each other—not with the cautious sizing up Vaughn had expected, but almost as if there were a bond between them—made her faintly jealous of Denny. Wasn't Philip Ludlow *her* friend?

"And Susan," she said, pushing the child forward.

Philip Ludlow smiled down at Susan and took her hand with

the same grave courtesy which had once made Vaughn herself feel like a queen.

When he was introduced to Neil, his warmth and gentleness went out to the boy. But then a shadow crossed his face. He glanced back for a second at the young man standing by the station, and he looked old and sad.

Turning once more to Neil, Philip Ludlow showed his pleasure again. "I hope," he told him, "you'll want to use John's boat that's down in the boathouse. May need a bit of caulking in the seams. Hasn't been used for some time."

Poor Neil! Overcome with this crowning joy, the fulfillment of all his desires, he couldn't speak.

At that moment a stream of little girls on bicycles came riding around the station, pigtails flying. They surrounded Susan curiously, but with a touching welcome.

"They've come to get you," Philip Ludlow explained to her. Then he turned to Vaughn. "Mary asked me to tell you she's sorry she couldn't be here. Jeanie Brown wanted her."

Casual, Vaughn thought, when she's expecting a houseful of people. As if she couldn't visit the Brown girl any time——

"The girls will show you where everything is for supper," Philip Ludlow was saying. "I'll drive you there——"

Susan interrupted, coming over and pulling on Vaughn's arm. "They talk just like other kids," she whispered. "From what you said, I thought——"

Philip Ludlow noticed the child's disappointment. "Come and see my grandmother's dolls when you have time," he urged. "Your mother thinks you'd like them."

"Let's go," the biggest of the little Lancashires said impatiently, offering Susan a seat on her handle bars.

With an uncertain backward look at her family, Susan got on. But when she started moving, inelegantly dangling her legs, the delight of the situation clearly seized her.

"She'll be at home here in no time," Vaughn told Denny. Then, turning to Philip Ludlow, she added in a half-whisper, "I know

224

you'll want to take Neil to meet Bart Brown. But I don't think——"

"I'd like to meet him myself," Denny broke in, speaking shyly. "Sounds like a good guy. Overseas, a lot of men said if they ever got home, they'd spend the rest of their lives doing things for kids. After they got back I guess most of them forgot. I thought myself——"

Vaughn glanced at Denny quickly. What was he talking about? She'd never heard him say anything like that. But he had suddenly stopped in the middle of a sentence. A look passed between him and Philip Ludlow, a look Vaughn couldn't read.

"I wish you could have known Bart," Philip Ludlow said softly. "If only you'd come sooner——"

"What do you mean?" Vaughn cried, seeing anguish in the older man's face.

"Bart lost his life just a week ago. It was the Monday after you were here."

"Lost his life——"

"He saved Joe Jackson from drowning. One of those boys of his, you know. He was——" But Philip Ludlow could say no more.

Just for a second, the fraction of a second, Vaughn was angry with Bart. He was spoiling their arrival, casting a gloom over it. She'd expected Philip Ludlow to be so gay——

It was only the fraction of a second, and then Vaughn stepped forward and took Philip Ludlow's hand. "I'm sorry," she said sincerely, "so sorry. For you. I know what he meant to you."

"To the world," Philip Ludlow answered. "It's people like Bart who will keep it from destroying itself."

He turned away and blew his nose.

Neil stood staring down at his feet, embarrassed by grief, touched, Vaughn could see, as though it were his own. He could never bear to see anyone hurt.

When Philip Ludlow turned back to them again he seemed to have himself in hand. "That's why Bill Becker came down with me," he explained, nodding toward the side of the station. "Bart's boys are finishing work on his boats. I told them I knew someone

225

who could help, a younger man." He looked at Neil and smiled. "Bill's waiting," he said. "Okay?"

Neil didn't answer, but the look he gave Philip Ludlow——

Together they walked around to the side of the station, and Philip Ludlow made the introductions.

"Bart—a man with such vision," Vaughn exclaimed to Denny as she watched Neil and his new companion go off, "a man with such vision goes and gives his life to save someone who'll never amount to anything, just a good-for——"

Vaughn stopped, horrified, as if she were listening to some other person, appalled at the words which came out of her own mouth.

"There I go again," she cried, hardly able to keep from breaking down. "Oh, Denny, won't I ever learn to be a decent human being?"

2. She tried to see it now through Denny's eyes, the beautiful old town, cool and stately in the early evening light, wondering whether its special quality would get through to him. Eagerly, as they drove by with Philip Ludlow, she called attention to the fanlight above a doorway and the fluted columns which graced a neighboring house. But before Denny had time to turn and look Vaughn had something else to show him.

"That's where Roger Williams made friends with the Indians," she pointed out. "And over there," she continued breathlessly, indicating the spot across the street, "Quakers took refuge when they were whipped out of the other colonies."

She glanced toward Philip Ludlow, and he smiled assent, then quickly faced the road again.

"You're becoming quite an authority on Kendal," he observed.

There was no irony in his words; he certainly intended to compliment Vaughn. Yet, feeling the afterglow of his honest, uncritical smile, she herself saw the stupidity of this excessive eagerness.

Denny has eyes of his own, hasn't he? she thought, scornful of herself.

But Denny said nothing. And so anxious was Vaughn that he should notice each detail, see it exactly as she'd seen it the first time, that even while she recognized the folly of it, she had to go right on talking, on and on, till they arrived at Mary Lancashire's.

A series of explosions echoed in the distance.

"Seems some people can't wait till tomorrow," Philip Ludlow remarked. "But Bart's boys are going to work. It won't be much of a Fourth for them."

Neil! Vaughn cried to herself. Why had she let him go, when she knew——?

As the last suitcase was set down in the hall Philip Ludlow held out his hand. He had, he said, something to attend to at the homestead.

"Don't worry if Neil's late," he told Vaughn. "Those boys sometimes work till after dark."

"In the summer?" Denny asked.

"Just the next few weeks. You see, Bart's wife's taking the children back home to live with her folks. The boys feel if they can realize this money before she goes, it will help her."

He stood on the steps of the piazza, half turned, as if to leave, yet he lingered. "I was thinking," he said, "those boys, tomorrow—— Couldn't we take a picnic supper down there? They might invite their friends. Build a fire on the beach—you know?"

There was feeling in his voice, as if doing this would, for some reason, mean a lot to him, and that unusual vitality in his face.

"Do you think you could manage the sandwiches?" he asked Vaughn. "Mary has her hands full with Jeanie."

Vaughn never understood what possessed her then, but instead of promising sandwiches, she moved toward Philip Ludlow and, standing on tiptoe, lifted her face and kissed him.

Tears rushed into his eyes. "I always hoped you'd come back with the family," he said, looking down at her happily. Then he hurried away.

227

Vaughn and Denny stood alone, watching him go.

"What a swell guy," Denny whispered, reaching for Vaughn's hand.

She swallowed hard. "I'm glad you like him," she answered softly. "I wasn't altogether sure." They stood there another second, holding hands in the doorway. Then Vaughn said, "Come on up and see the room."

It was just as Vaughn had imagined it when, in the heat of her office, she'd sat dreaming of the cool white room. The counterpane welcomed her. Something from home.

Yes, she thought, it really is like coming home. Nice.

Through the open window she could see Susan chasing across the back yard with the little girls, yelling and laughing.

"Not a bad room," Denny was saying behind her. "Really very nice."

"I know. I guess the other time I wasn't——" Vaughn didn't finish. She was looking out at the trees. "Quite ready," was the way Edmund Mansfield had put it.

"Say, I'm starved. How about some food?"

"I'll see what there is," Vaughn answered, sighing.

Why couldn't Mary have stayed home, just tonight?

They went down to the vast kitchen. Vaughn found Mary's apron.

"That's going to go around you twice," Denny said, laughing as he watched Vaughn put it on. Then, glancing at the clock, he murmured, "I'm going to see if the radio works," and went into the parlor.

As Vaughn stood eying the kitchen, bits of the news came out to her, not enough to make sense. She stared at the old-fashioned cupboards. And then she saw it.

"Denny," she cried, suddenly horrified. "Denny——"

He came rushing back.

"Look at the stove," she exclaimed. "Coal——"

It was the last straw. Really——

"Oh," Denny breathed in relief. "Thought you'd hurt yourself."

After all she'd been through with Neil and packing everybody's things, hurrying to catch the train for Kendal, after all the worry of the past months, Vaughn was so tired, so in need of a vacation, and she'd thought, when Mary Lancashire invited them, that at last she'd get a rest.

What had she got? A coal stove. Four extra kids to feed. Dozens of sandwiches——

"I can't face it," she blurted out, crumpling.

Denny put his arm around her. "Don't worry, honey," he said. "I'm no good at managing a woman, but a coal stove——" He surveyed it calmly. "I was brought up on one like that."

Pushing her gently into a chair, he went over and lifted the black lid to examine the fire with a competent eye.

Vaughn stretched her arms on the kitchen table and dropped her head, sighing, but she turned so she could watch Denny.

"How's the news?"

"Bad."

"Oh, Denny! It means war, doesn't it?"

He didn't look at her. She could feel him not looking at her.

"Nice being part of the place right away, don't you think so?" As if he hadn't heard her question. "With us here, Mary can help Bart's wife more. Right away they counted on us."

Vaughn raised her head. "Then you like it?" she asked. "You're not sorry we came?"

"*Like it?*" he repeated, laughing.

He was going to say something else, but a sudden clatter silenced him. It was as if a truck were driving into the house.

"Oh," Vaughn exclaimed, jumping up and running to the window. "Look, Denny. It must be Sally and Luke. That's their jeep." She hurried out, and Denny followed.

"News travels fast over the Johnnycake Trail," Sally cried, as she came up the walk.

Luke lifted a basket out of the jeep. "Hope you haven't had supper yet," he said to Denny, as if they'd met before, as if they were old friends.

"You haven't, have you?" Sally asked Vaughn. "We brought some clams."

And now Mary's kitchen was a different place. Sally at the stove, preparing to steam the clams, Denny and Luke standing around talking, and the little girls all piling in because they'd just remembered that they were supposed to help.

"There's a platter of ham in the refrigerator," Pussy and Ruthie told Vaughn, "and salad. Johnnycake in the oven, hot rolls——"

"Don't talk about it," Luke begged. "I can't stand *hearing* about food. Bring it on."

Neil showed up in the kitchen doorway, but he didn't hang back long. Vaughn saw how Luke drew him into the conversation. "Ever sailed on Narragansett Bay?" he asked the boy seriously. One salt to another. "Well, you and your parents must come before you go home. I think you'd like it."

Think, Vaughn repeated to herself, watching Neil's face.

They were still at supper when Mary arrived, puffing, but she beamed as Vaughn introduced Denny and the children.

She really wants us, Vaughn thought. She's really glad to have us.

Sitting down at the table, Mary turned to Sally and Luke. "Philip told me he phoned to you soon as he heard the Hills were coming," she said. "He drove me down from Jeanie's just now, but he was too tired to drop in."

"No wonder," Luke observed. "The way he's been tending to that garden, after a day's work——"

Denny cut Luke short. "That's something I could do while I'm here," he said.

"But it's your vacation," Vaughn cried. And the moment she spoke she was ashamed. How could she——?

Denny has the right impulses for this place, she reflected, dropping her eyes. I'm a step behind.

"The children'll do the dishes," Mary announced, when they rose from the table. She led the way into her parlor.

It was a pretty room, in an old-fashioned way, Vaughn realized.

The other time she was here, she hadn't noticed the beautiful white woodwork around the fireplace and the portraits between the windows.

They talked of quiet, unimportant things.

No one wants to mention Korea, Vaughn thought. It's in everybody's mind, but no one wants to talk about it.

"Philip expects you later," Mary told Sally and Luke. "He's so pleased you're staying over tomorrow. We're having a picnic with Bart's boys, you know."

"Good," Sally said. "We ought to have a concern for those boys now. If only someone in Kendal had the time to do things with them——"

"Bart was just beginning to see results," Luke put in sadly. Then he exclaimed, getting up, "We'd better go. You folks must be tired."

When the Ludlows had left Vaughn and Denny went upstairs. Both children came to get their night clothes. For the moment they were just the four of them again, standing in the white room. The four of them——

Vaughn began to unpack.

"It's nifty here," Susan whispered, pulling at Vaughn's sleeve.

But Vaughn had just come upon a package she'd forgotten, lying at the bottom of the suitcase—Philip Ludlow's book—and she was thinking . . .

"The kids aren't quaint, like I thought," Susan chattered on, still pulling. "But Mrs. Lancashire says 'thee' to me. To Neil too. It makes a funny feeling up and down my arms." She stopped an instant, contemplating them. "But nice," she added.

Vaughn scarcely heard her. That book—she'd brought it to return—the very first thing. But maybe——

"Hurry to bed," she said, giving Susan a kiss. "It's late."

Neil stayed. "Could I have breakfast early, do you think, Mom?" he asked. "Eight o'clock's when we start work."

"Eight o'clock! This is supposed to be my——"

"Mrs. Lancashire said she'd make it."

"No. I'll do it." But how Vaughn ached, not alone with present fatigue, as already in anticipation of tomorrow's——

"Long hours," Denny observed.

"It's okay," Neil said, shrugging. "We take it easy around noontime."

"Fellows nice?"

"And how! I don't have to hold my own any. They don't speak good, but they don't push me around."

Vaughn stared at him. "You're speaking like them already." Instantly she regretted the criticism. Neil had looked so pleased till then. "We're taking a picnic down tomorrow night," she said quickly, to cover her remark. "Think the fellows'll like that? Make a fire on the beach, have their friends——"

"Gee!" Neil exclaimed, as he picked up his things and left the room. It was all he said, but it was all Vaughn needed.

She sat down on the bed, hardly able to undress. She wouldn't do her face tonight. It was too late. This was the first time she'd ever let herself go like that, but——

Sitting on the bed, taking off her stockings, she began to think about Philip Ludlow's book. Maybe, after all, she was a person who could——

I'll read it first, she decided, jumping up to get it.

As she tenderly undid the wrapping paper and laid the book on the table by the bed, it was as if a great weight had fallen off her heart.

"Denny," she cried suddenly. "Where have we been all these years?"

"I know," he answered. His voice was strained. "I know." He shook his head. "Us, living by and for ourselves in the apartment. What happens here is our business too—Bart and all. What happens to everybody everywhere. Nothing's separate."

Vaughn was the first in bed.

Pulling up the shade, Denny looked back at her over his shoulder. "How's the mattress?"

232

"Okay." Blissfully Vaughn stretched herself. "It's been some day," she muttered. The bed felt cool and soft.

"No lumps?" Denny inquired, turning off the light and getting in beside her. "Must be a different one."

The stars weren't visible now because of the leaves on the trees. But a heavenly freshness came up from the garden. Vaughn felt relaxed.

"I doubt it," she said absently. "It wasn't really bad enough to throw away. Just——"

All these years—— If she'd only been more aware of things, instead of trying so hard to get ahead—ahead of everybody else. She'd always had the idea that charity begins at home, and she'd worked for that. But it wasn't enough, not nearly.

Denny lay on his back, his arm stretched over his head. "It's not too late, is it?" he asked suddenly in the darkness.

It was a question, but his voice was so full of hope that it was almost as if he'd answered it.

Vaughn wanted to tell him no, it wasn't too late. She wanted to explain what she'd been thinking a moment ago. Only, she was so tired—— *Everybody, everywhere,* Denny'd said—such a lot to do. And she was so tired——

She lay there rhythmically smoothing the bottom sheet along her edge of the bed, dreamy.

All at once she discovered something surprising, so surprising that she had to turn over quickly and tell Denny. He was asleep, or almost, but she had to tell him.

"Denny," she whispered.

"Mm."

"You awake?"

"Mm."

"I just wanted to tell you—it's the same mattress. I remember the way it felt along the edge. It's just me—I'm different."

"Mm."

That was all he answered. He reached out, though, and laid his hand softly on Vaughn's cheek.

233

She smiled, barely able to make out his features in the darkness. But he couldn't have seen her smile, for he was already asleep.

3. "Those boys and their friends sure can eat," Vaughn exclaimed. "It took me all day, and in fifteen minutes——"

"Our own children didn't do badly," Denny reminded her, cleaning crumbs off the sandwich table. He moved cautiously, like a man with a sore back. "Have you noticed Luke, now he's through making cones?"

"No. I've been too busy."

"He's mixing the kids some pretty stiff drinks. 'Quaker Stingers,' he calls them. He begins with raspberry soda, orange pop, two scoops of chocolate ice cream, a dash of grape juice——"

"Stop!" Vaughn cried, laughing. "Never mind the rest."

The sun had almost set across the river, but what was left of the glow spilled over the horizon into the water. Down on the sand the boys had begun their fire. Neil was in the thick of things, piling on driftwood.

I can't understand it, Vaughn thought. He's a different child. Sure of himself, happy—— It must be all right, after all, but I can't understand——

A lot more people had turned out than Philip Ludlow had told Vaughn to expect. From the looks of it those boys must have invited about everyone they knew. But there'd been food enough, and certainly it was a most successful party.

"Look at Alberta Mansfield," Vaughn whispered to Denny, nudging him. "The way she's got those parents standing around her, lapping up every word she says, eating out of her hand. The girl friends too. She's a dear, you know it?"

"Do I know it?" Denny exclaimed. "She's the glamour girl of the picnic. Saying 'thee' and 'thy' to that crowd too—what do you bet?"

Vaughn laughed. "How did you guess?" she asked. "You've hardly had a chance to meet her yourself."

Denny looked thoughtfully at the river. Then he said, "Mary took me to their house this morning before we went to Jeanie's. The old man kept asking about you. Seems he's interested in the layout."

The layout— Here it was again.

"I know," Vaughn said in a dull voice.

All the rest of her life—was this thing going to nag at her, this wonderful idea, which had gone sour because of some insight she lacked?

She took up a paper plate and began nicking the rim with her thumbnail.

It doesn't matter any more what they think at Hamiltons', she told herself, tearing little sections out of the edge of the plate. Ham knows I can't do it. But why don't I have what it takes?

"What's the matter with me, Denny?" she blurted out, looking at him sadly.

"I don't blame you a bit," he said quickly, comfortingly, "not seeing anything in that hole."

"*Hole—* You mean you looked?"

"It's nothing but—"

"You looked into it? Denny, did you? Tell me."

"Yes," he admitted. "What's the matter? You mind?"

"No," she answered slowly, still tearing at the plate, "I don't mind. I just don't see why you did."

He shrugged. "No special reason. I was only trying to figure out why the job gave you so much trouble. It wasn't as if it had been some of that crooked stuff Hamiltons' want you to do. It was an honest job."

I know why, Vaughn said to herself miserably, I know why.

She squashed the paper plate as tightly as she could between her hands.

"It's because I didn't care," she told Denny in a whisper. "Don't you see? One has to care. Thing like that—it's not romantic or glam-

235

orous—the way I first thought. It's——" She hesitated. "Human. I mean——"

"I know."

"Well, that's why I couldn't write it. I didn't even understand why till now. It's just like what Bart——"

Vaughn looked off at the fire. The flames were beginning to leap, lighting the faces of the boys, lighting Philip Ludlow's, where he stood farther away, opening a box of fireworks. Quite harmless ones, he'd assured Vaughn this morning, when they talked over the picnic—rockets and Roman candles. Just a few, because, after all, it was the Fourth. His eagerness over everything they planned had been so touching——

Looking at his face with the glow of the fire on it, Vaughn remembered that time—Quarterly Meeting—when she sat down beside him at lunch, feeling just this way, despondent about the layout. He had looked at her then with such trust that she knew he believed way would open for her.

"Only a fool," she exclaimed, "would try to write about something like that, unless she'd experienced it."

"Or maybe had known someone," Denny added.

"Oh."

That was a new idea, and Vaughn started to think it over, but Mary was coming toward them. She had something to share.

"You know Tony?" she whispered. "The boy standing over there with his parents. I was passing by, and I overheard him talking to them, bragging a bit, I guess. But it made me very happy. 'See these people?' I heard him ask, nodding toward us. 'They're my friends.'" Mary smiled. "For years his parents have probably been telling him he's no good. In fact, one way and another, the world's been telling him that. And now he has all of us for his friends."

She looked so pleased.

"Yes," Denny said, nodding gravely, "to have people like you and the Ludlows and the Mansfields mixing with these guys and their folks, not just giving them a party, but having it with them—— I can see how they would feel."

The crowd was moving closer to the fire.

"I've been working on the railroad," someone began singing, and the others joined.

It was nice—the river in the twilight and the singing.

Some of the older people began a song of their own next—Italian, maybe, or Polish—Vaughn couldn't tell. But it was beautiful.

"They must have sung that in the old country," Mary murmured, "when they were children. Wistful. Yet lovely, don't you think?"

She looked as if she could do with a rest, but, noticing that Sally had her hands full cleaning up, Mary went over to help her.

"You know," Vaughn said, thinking aloud. "She's what Quakers would call a beautiful woman."

Denny looked after Mary appraisingly. "Too fat, if you ask me," he said frankly.

Vaughn burst out laughing. "Beautiful in spirit's what they mean."

"Oh." He turned serious. "She is. You sit here and rest awhile. I'm going to toast some marshmallows for the real little kids." He started toward the fire.

Left alone, Vaughn slumped onto a packing case. That layout—— Distress over her inadequacy was starting to seize her again when Denny returned.

"If you ask me," he said, looking down at Vaughn tenderly, "you're getting more and more beautiful that way yourself."

"Oh, Denny——"

But he had gone.

That's the nicest thing he ever said to me, Vaughn thought, feeling her eyes sting. The very nicest thing.

The crowd around the fire began singing spirituals, but slowly their supply of songs was giving out. At length there was a pause.

A quavery voice began a tune then. Very quavery it was, yet somehow, strong.

> "Go down, Moses,
> Way down in Egypt Land——"

Not many of the people standing around the fire knew this one. Only a few voices joined with the old man's—Philip Ludlow's and Luke's and some Vaughn didn't recognize. Only a few.

But to her it was like the opening measures of a great chorus, penetrating to her inward ear, stirring her imagination, rousing it, so that now, all at once, she wasn't staring into an empty hole, she was inside the feelings of those people who, long ago . . .

It wasn't just a song the old man had started. It was all the suffering of the world breaking out in a cry across time, uttered over and over, by different throats, in different captivities, different massacres, yet always the same anguish, the same cry.

And now Vaughn heard the answer to it, the quiet answer, made by the lonely man riding at night with a slave under the sacking in his wagon, made by the woman sitting in her rocking chair over the hole, with the baby in her lap, while the sheriff hunted a human being . . . The quiet answer——

She could hear it now, in her head and in her heart. She could retell it so the world would hear, would care——

Denny! He was squatting beside the fire, toasting a marshmallow, grinning at the little girls. Vaughn made her way swiftly through the crowd. *Denny*——

She had to tell him.

First Day in Kendal

Philip had gone to the homestead to get Jeanie Brown, but when he entered the Meetinghouse with the poor child at his side, it wasn't of her that he was thinking, only of his wife.

In this Meetinghouse they'd been married. It still seemed incredible that, of all the men in the world, he was the one she should have chosen. Here, taking each other's hand, they'd been joined, not by man, but by God. The moment was no longer a lively recollection for Philip, only faded and sweet, like a flower pressed nearly forty years ago between the leaves of a book.

Now, coming into the quiet company already there, he felt a present happiness, recognizing the bright-haired little Hill girl among the Lancashires. And, seeing her parents and the boy occupying the next bench, Philip thought, So they came——

Vaughn Hill was very quiet, yet her eyes, Philip noticed as he walked up the aisle, were straying around the Meetinghouse, seeking a way to begin.

She made him think of those lines, *Though ye have felt the light, yet afterwards ye may feel a winter storm, tempest and hail, frost and cold. Be patient and still, that ye may come to the summer* . . .

Jeanie had chosen the seat beside Denis Hill, and as Philip settled himself, he thought, There's something about this man——

With him a little of that goodness had come back to Kendal which had gone out of it with Bart, nothing like what had been lost, but a little something.

I wish they were staying, Philip thought.

Bowing his head and shading his eyes with his hand, he tried to clear these worldly thoughts from his mind. Remembering how, before the beginning of the century, his mother used to wrap herself in her shawl, so now, in the middle of it, Philip drew the silence about him, joining in the humble waiting for truth to be made clear.

"Whatsoever things are true, whatsoever things are honest, whatsoever things are just," he repeated to himself, "whatsoever things are lovely, whatsoever things are of good report, if there be any virtue and if there be any praise, think on these things."

How little his mind had been occupied lately with good and lovely things, Philip realized with a shock. Bart's tragedy, the fighting, business——

All week it was only in the garden that Philip had felt His closeness. Letting the seed slip through his fingers, handling the soil, holding the rounded fruit in his palm, he'd drifted serenely into the presence of God.

The Seed, early Friends called this awareness.

Philip thought, A gardener knows what they meant.

In the garden earth and the Kingdom of God seemed inextricably one. Hope lay in the seed and the soil. But everywhere else, wherever one turned now, one saw in people's eyes that new fear, greater than the wartime panic, the fear of a destruction from which none could escape.

Yet, Philip thought, shifting in his seat a little, is it any more to be feared than what will happen if we survive? If the earth isn't blown to pieces, will men go right on ill-treating their fellow men?

The low wail of a distant Diesel, the Boston train hurrying past Kendal, brought Philip's attention back to the Meeting. No one seemed moved to speak.

The Hill boy was looking at him. Was he pleading, as George and John used to do at his age, when they began to feel restless, pleading with Philip to close the Meeting?

No, he didn't think so. There was something else in the boy's appeal.

George and John—that look made Philip ache for a glimpse of them. He was glad they were being useful, but if he could just see them now and then . . .

With great effort Philip pushed back this yearning for his sons and let himself be enfolded again by the silence, that he might, as much as in him lay, accept the divine will. He knew that wasn't a matter of resigning himself to any bitterness which was destined for him or for the world, simply of assuming the obligation to bestow love freely "upon the just and the unjust, as His rain doth fall and His sun doth shine on all."

To Philip it was clear that only by accepting this fully did men have any call to survive.

And he prayed that when he went from here, not his words, but his "carriage and life might preach," repeating to himself the beautiful promise: "Then you will come to walk cheerfully over the world, answering that of God in every one."

The sun was making golden puddles in the Meetinghouse.

Susan had to keep telling her toes to lie down. They felt like dancing. Her toes never liked having nothing to do.

But the colors in this place were scrumptious, like looking through the glass counter in a bakery. The walls were iced with maple frosting, the benches were baked out of piecrust, and the blinds folded back against the tall windows made Susan's mouth water—they looked so much like brownies.

That was all wrong. She wasn't supposed to be thinking about food. She was supposed to be what the Lancashires called "centering down." They used a lot of queer words like that, and they wouldn't let Susan count out eeny, meeny, miney, mo, like the kids at home, because of the part about catching a nigger by the toe. What they said was crazy and hard, but Susan had practiced and she could do it now: Nonamesset, Naushon, Pasque, Uncatena, Cuttyhunk, you're out——

Yep, she thought, I got every one that time. Skip it, she added sternly. Think the things you're—I mean thee's supposed to.

Susan bowed her head. She really did mean to think about God, but she didn't know how. Nobody'd ever told her. In church, that time, she'd had goose-pimples. God was there, up at the top of the marble steps. But here——

Her eyes kept hopping across the floor with the little tan and brown design sprinkled over the carpet, and then they found a spot in the ceiling where the roof must have leaked. Outside, puffy clouds were lying on the sky.

Like meringue, Susan thought.

That big tree was the one Philip Ludlow climbed, long ago, when he was a little boy.

But he couldn't really have been a little boy, ever, Susan decided, turning from the window to look at him. He was so old. He had gray hair and his face was crinkly when he smiled, but not now, because he was thinking of God.

Everybody looked different thinking of God, even Betty and Kitty, Susan saw, squinting to one side of her, and Pussy and Ruthie and Alice, squinting the other way. Even her parents and Neil. They all had a shut-up, faraway look, not like real people.

Maybe they're not! What if I'm the only person here—the only person in the world? The only real, live person.

Thinking this, Susan felt so scared and lonely, she wanted to cry. All these people, quiet and solemn, not even moving—maybe they really weren't real.

Still, there was a sound—she could hear a sound, the way you always think you can hear birds when you see them fly by—an inside sound.

It must be their souls, Susan thought, and she felt shivery, terribly shivery.

Listening, she knew now—she wasn't the only person. There were all these others—her mother and father and Neil and the Lancashires, people in the Meetinghouse and millions outside, in Kendal and New York and across the ocean—even in those countries where they dressed and talked funny.

A great rush of things came over Susan. Her chest couldn't hold them. They were pushing her ribs out. Goose-pimples started crawling up and down her arms. In this kind of church there was no special place where God could be except, like her mother'd said, in people.

So that's why her ribs were pushed out like that—God was in her. In her! It was different, not at all the way she'd imagined Him other times, all dressed up like a king in a ballet, but so strangely wonderful that Susan knew: this was it.

244

Now Neil was in church for the first time in his life, he couldn't see it was so bad. This was okay if it didn't last too long.

John's boat still leaked, though Neil had patched it up the best he could noontimes. Yesterday, sailing down the river, he and his father and Philip Ludlow'd had to bail, but just the same, it was nifty. Such a surprise, tacking along that narrow little river to come suddenly to the ocean. Suddenly, there it was, with the sun shining on it, and Philip Ludlow pointed out the islands and an old fort and told them the names of the lighthouses. Seven, you could see from there.

It would have been nice to do nothing all day, just sail, but Neil had to work for Bart. The fellows talked and talked about him—how he'd looked up suddenly and seen Joe struggling in the water and how he'd jumped in so fast, he must have forgotten to let go the sander, because it was washed up later, at high tide. And how terrible Bart looked when they fished him out. But mostly they talked about what a wonderful guy he was. Over and over they tried explaining this to Neil.

"Seems like he was almost like Jesus," Tony had said once, and the others listened with scared sort of faces. "What I mean," Tony added quickly, "he was a carpenter, too, and gave his life. See what I mean?"

That made them all serious. They talked of something else.

But Neil couldn't see anything disrespectful about what Tony'd said. So a guy, just an ordinary guy, could be like Jesus——

Mr. Lacey was always gassing about Jesus in chapel. And God. He made God sound like another headmaster. It wasn't nice to speak about private matters like that, the way some grownups did.

Not Philip Ludlow, though. *He* didn't go gassing. Soon as he heard about Bart, the boys told Neil, he came right over. After the police and the reporters and all the other people went away he stayed with them. He asked, would they sit down together and be quiet a few minutes on account of how Bart was dead, and if anyone felt he had something special to say, shoot. But be quiet first.

So they sat down—him in his good pants on the bottom of a boat—and they'd said nothing for a while.

It was one of those days when the sun is bright but there's a lot of little clouds, and they sat there and watched the clouds looking like they were lying on the river. It was such a nice day you couldn't believe something so terrible had just happened.

Then Bill said there was something he wanted to say, and he did.

"Now I know," he'd said, "Bart was the bravest guy I ever knew. Punk over to Hannigan's mill told me one time Bart was yellow because he wouldn't go in the Army and went to work in a nuthouse instead. Cripes, a guy who jumps in to save some little shrimp isn't even related to him—guy like that isn't yellow. Wait till I catch that punk!"

After that nobody said nothing for a long time, and it was funny how saying nothing made them feel better.

Then Philip Ludlow said, " 'Greater love hath no man than this, that a man lay down his life for his friends,' " and also, " 'love one another as I have loved you.' "

He'd talked about Bart some, how all his life he'd tried to do things so people would get along better together and there wouldn't be no more wars, but not like a preacher, more like they was all buddies. Then they'd shook hands and the rest of the day they didn't talk much, but they didn't feel so bad.

And they worked long as there was light to see by, on account of Bart's job had to be finished. And Bill told Neil he didn't go back to Hannigan's mill and even up with that punk. He was through with evening up. That didn't get the world no place.

Tony mentioned something that still made Neil catch his breath. It was what Philip Ludlow'd said before Neil arrived. "I've got a hunch," he said, "this young guy's a bit like Bart."

Me, Neil thought for the hundredth time, me. Like Bart—gee!

Some of the fellows said, what about the shed now? Would the Friends let them have it? Where would they go later, when it got cold?

That worried Neil.

If Bart was around, he thought, he'd look out for those fellows. Now there's nobody.

In the boat yesterday he'd told this to Philip Ludlow, and Philip Ludlow had said yes, he'd been thinking about that too. Trouble was, they didn't have nobody now to take responsibility, some older man. It was tough, he admitted.

Now, in the Meetinghouse, Neil peeked sideways past his mother. He could see a little of Philip Ludlow's face, and he wondered, was the old gentleman saying prayers. Neil didn't know how. But Philip Ludlow could.

Please, he cried in his head, please ask God to send somebody quick. *Please—it's important.*

He wished so hard, he was so worried, the sweat started dripping inside his shirt. He looked at Philip Ludlow again to see if the message had got through, and Philip Ludlow caught Neil looking at him and looked back, but he didn't act like he'd got any message.

Then, Neil thought, give the guy a chance. No use to push him. So Neil just sat back and cooled off.

From what Vaughn had said and from what he himself had been able to make out of those books, Denny gathered that nothing was expected of him in this funny little old place—no singing or responses or getting up and sitting down. He could just rest his back.

If people wanted to think about God in Meeting that was all right. If, like Denny, they didn't go for that sort of thing, it was all right too.

It was nice just to sit here and think about the river, the way it looked yesterday, when he and Neil sailed down it with Philip Ludlow. What a keen interest the man took in the boy and in Denny. Not the curious kind of interest. He didn't ask questions and still he seemed to be inviting them to tell about themselves. Denny had caught himself talking in a way he hadn't done since years—about his work and the war and just stray thoughts.

He wanted to tell Philip Ludlow that he'd been jealous—they could laugh over it together. But of course that wouldn't do. And about Vaughn—how meeting him had made her—— But that wasn't right either.

"It's swell for us, being here," was all he could say.

Neil opened right up. The fellows at the beach were on his mind. What was going to become of them when winter set in?

Denny wondered about that too. The day after the picnic he went down to the beach to see if he could lend a hand, but there didn't seem to be any need for him, so he went away. He was disappointed. Maybe, if he went again . . .

Sailing down to the ocean in the clear afternoon, with a good breeze carrying them along, Philip Ludlow had talked a little about his own boys.

Something long suppressed stirred in Denny then, and he looked sadly at the other bank of the river. Things those men were doing— once he'd wanted—— When he came back from overseas making soap powder and cleaning fluid hadn't seemed very important. He wanted to give his life to something greater, but he didn't know what.

It had upset Vaughn. "We need security," she kept telling him.

And because he hadn't gone back to his old job fast enough, she'd got herself one with those crooks. That was the beginning of all their trouble.

Security, Denny thought now, where is there security?

The way people talked, the world was being directed by a sort of super madman who was steering it through space like a drunken driver with a truckload of atom bombs, throwing the clutch out as he rushed down grades, careening around curves, while people stood by, frozen with horror, staring popeyed, stretching their necks for the first glimpse of death.

It can't be like that, Denny thought miserably. There must be some plan. Maybe we don't see it.

He fidgeted and looked around the Meetinghouse, at the rows and rows of quiet people, all trying to understand the design of the world and the way they might shape their lives to fit it.

And suddenly he thought, If we could just stay here awhile—a year or so—long enough to get some of these things straight, for Vaughn and me to get a new start, the children to have what they've missed——

But, of course, Vaughn wouldn't. And how could Denny get a job in a place like this?

Wouldn't have to be such a good one, he thought wistfully. I'd take most anything, even farm work. Once my back got used to it——

Gee, he thought, what that would do for us, to live here without being pushed around, in the subway, at the plant, without having to push other people—— Just for a year——

But of course Vaughn had to return to Hamiltons'. Sadly Denny put the bright wish from him.

They had another week, anyhow. One week—not very long, hardly time to catch on to much. Still, in just these few days—— Once back home, surely something they'd felt here would stick to them, something——

Denny didn't go for that sort of thing. And yet, sitting here in the comfortable silence, very slowly, very unexpectedly, Denny began to grasp what that something might be.

Vaughn glanced uneasily at Denny, remembering how his foot that had been frostbitten in Belgium sometimes went to sleep at the movies, and then at Susan in the row of little girls. Would she get the giggles? Vaughn herself, coming here the first time——

Neil's nails were disgusting.

They'll get over it when he leaves here, Vaughn reassured herself. Then she thought, He ought to stay all summer. Susan too. It's the place for them. If only Denny and I could——

Looking down at her own nails, peeling and cracked from washing up, Vaughn said to herself, Good thing I didn't have them done.

Oh, the chicken—— Was it all right? She couldn't remember ever getting up so early Sunday morning, but that chicken had to be in the oven before Meeting. Suppose it needed basting——

It's years, she thought, since I bothered to stuff one. Now I know what he meant—that you have to work at loving!

Wasn't it time somebody got up and said something? If this turned out to be one of those Meetings where nobody spoke at all, Denny and the children wouldn't understand what it was about. Were they centering down? Were they?

I haven't even begun to myself, Vaughn realized then, moving a little so she could gaze out of the window.

The leaves of the maple were forming pools of shadow as they moved toward the glass. But what Vaughn really saw was the river, the way it looked to her yesterday through the little panes in Jeanie Brown's kitchen when she went up to tell the poor kid good-by.

Jeanie's little girl was trying to help Mary pack, while Bartholomew the Third, oblivious to tragedy, took his bottle from Alice. And Jeanie—poor Jeanie——

Vaughn wished she'd brought the girl something. Why hadn't she thought of that? But what? What did Vaughn have to give? Those new gloves, the nylon slip——

What Bart had said that day about it being easy to give some *thing*, but your self—— Overcome, because now Bart had given his self, Vaughn looked away, out of the window.

The river was higher than in March, but a boy like Neil would still be able to scramble over the steppingstones.

Jeanie must hate leaving, Vaughn had thought sadly.

Turning back into the room then, she saw that Alice was burping the baby. Just a child herself——

"Look," Vaughn had said impulsively to her, "when you grow up and take a job, make sure it's worth doing. Prestige and getting on don't count as much as you'd think. It's what you give your time to. I mean we only have one life——"

She didn't quite know what she did mean then.

Now, in the silence, the thought was clearer.

What I'd like to do, she told herself, is stay here. Not always. We belong in New York, I guess. But a year or two—long enough to get Kendal Radio back on its feet.

How Ham had lied about that—the firm wasn't folding up. Not yet, anyway. Business was very bad, but a bang-up campaign could rescue it.

Last night, when Denny and she called on Philip Ludlow, he said—it was rather sweet of him, Vaughn thought—that he'd been thinking over what she'd told him at Quarterly Meeting time and he saw she was right: a professional could do Kendal Radio's advertising with strict integrity. But, he insisted, it would have to be written on the spot by a member of the firm.

I know now how he wants it handled, Vaughn assured herself. I could do it that way. Get results too. With time people in the trade would understand that every word we publish is measured as carefully as the parts of a radio tube. Our spreads would be known as faultlessly accurate data, an exact, descriptive science.

She was intrigued with the possibilities of handling the merits of a product that way. It would take great skill, but she could do it. That sort of thing would catch on too. People were tired of being taken in by emotional blather.

She glanced sideways, past Denny and Jeanie, toward Philip Ludlow, wondering whether he'd give her a try. Then she turned away from him again.

No, she thought, her eyes resting for an instant on Denny. We have to go back. Denny's job——

She wondered again whether his foot was asleep. It didn't seem to be. He sat very still, looking almost as if he were centering down.

He's nice, Vaughn thought, bowing her head again, but moving a fraction of an inch closer to him. The way he is with those little girls and Mary—— He's nice. It's not just because he's my husband——

She thought again of Bart, of the simplicity of his goodness. Yet, when she first met him, she'd thought——

I didn't see, she said to herself miserably. I just didn't see. Where I come from——

She twisted her gloves between her hands.

251

Getting ahead, trying to make your way, like I've been doing the past years, there's no time for things like that. I didn't see——

Was she explaining to God?

All her uneasiness, the regret she was never willing to face, sprang up again, but she struggled to make her mind still, so she could expose this troubledness to the silence the way, she remembered, her father used to spread his mildewing sails to whiten in the sun.

I didn't see, she repeated to herself, thinking again of her first journey to the homestead.

She'd looked only for what was to her immediate advantage. With her head, not her heart. It was so plain to her now, the testimony of the hiding place, the compassion which had moved people there a hundred years ago. Like Bart's.

I could write it now, she thought, staring down at her hands. Ever since the picnic——

A pity she hadn't been able to grasp this testimony sooner, all those months she'd wanted to write the layout, a real pity. Because now she never would. Not for Hamiltons', anyway. Maybe for Kendal Radio. She'd never write another thing for Hamiltons'. She was through.

They'll just have to keep Katie, she thought.

Troubled though she was, thinking this made her grin.

And now, more and more, the silence closed in, flowing around Vaughn as if she were an island, as if she lay alone on the surface of this quiet sea.

Yet not alone. There was something in her—more than herself. Something very hardy. She'd never felt it before, though she'd recognized it in Philip Ludlow the first time she saw him. And, occasionally, she admitted with surprise, occasionally, a little—yes, in Denny.

Putting her hand over her eyes, Vaughn finally reached the moment when she could shut this reasoning and thinking and planning out, when she could close herself off for a little interval from all she'd ever felt or known. But this new resolve, this way, remained.

Seeing this more-than-self gleaming in her, Vaughn thought, suddenly very lighthearted, So that's what they mean by inner light! No wonder Philip Ludlow wasn't able to explain!

CHRISTIAN HERALD ASSOCIATION AND ITS MINISTRIES

CHRISTIAN HERALD ASSOCIATION, founded in 1878, publishes The Christian Herald Magazine, one of the leading interdenominational religious monthlies in America. Through its wide circulation, it brings inspiring articles and the latest news of religious developments to many families. From the magazine's pages came the initiative for CHRISTIAN HERALD CHILDREN and THE BOWERY MISSION, two individually supported not-for-profit corporations.

CHRISTIAN HERALD CHILDREN, established in 1894, is the name for a unique and dynamic ministry to disadvantaged children, offering hope and opportunities which would not otherwise be available for reasons of poverty and neglect. The goal is to develop each child's potential and to demonstrate Christian compassion and understanding to children in need.

Mont Lawn is a permanent camp located in Bushkill, Pennsylvania. It is the focal point of a ministry which provides a healthful "vacation with a purpose" to children who without it would be confined to the streets of the city. Up to 1000 children between the age of 7 and 11 come to Mont Lawn each year.

Christian Herald Children maintains year-round contact with children by means of a *City Youth Ministry*. Central to its philosophy is the belief that only through sustained relationships and demonstrated concern can individual lives be truly enriched. Special emphasis is on individual guidance, spiritual and family counseling and tutoring. This follow-up ministry to inner-city children culminates for many in financial assistance toward higher education and career counseling.

THE BOWERY MISSION, located at 227 Bowery, New York City, has since 1879 been reaching out to the lost men on the Bowery, offering them what could be their last chance to rebuild their lives. Every man is fed, clothed and ministered to. Countless numbers have entered the 90-day residential rehabilitation program at the Bowery Mission. A concentrated ministry of counseling, medical care, nutrition therapy, Bible study and Gospel services awakens a man to spiritual renewal within himself.

These ministries are supported solely by the voluntary contributions of individuals and by legacies and bequests. Contributions are tax deductible. Checks should be made out either to CHRISTIAN HERALD CHILDREN or to THE BOWERY MISSION.

Administrative Office: 40 Overlook Drive, Chappaqua, New York 10514
Telephone: (914) 769-9000